OK

Guilty Conscience

Guilty Conscience

Michael Underwood

St. Martin's Press
New York

Library of Congress Cataloging-in-Publication Data

Underwood, Michael.
    Guilty conscience / Michael Underwood.
        p.   cm.
    ISBN 0-312-09824-3
    1. Epton, Rosa (Fictitious character)—Fiction.
    2. Women lawyers-England—London—Fiction.
    3. London (England)—Fiction.
    I. Title.
    PR6055.V3G85   1993
    823'.914—dc20   93-26922
                                                        CIP

First published in Great Britain by Macmillan London Limited.

First U.S. Edition: November 1993
10 9 8 7 6 5 4 3 2 1

Guilty Conscience

Chapter One

'Snaith and Epton, can I help you?' The words tripped off Stephanie's tongue as they did several dozen times a day as she sat at the office switchboard.

'I'd like to make an appointment to see Miss Epton,' an educated female voice replied.

'May I have your name?'

'Henshaw. Mrs Evelyn Henshaw. My address is Riverview Court, Briar's End, though I'm spending this week at our flat in town, which is 38 Chiltley Mansions, Chiltley Street, W2.'

'Have you previously consulted the firm, Mrs Henshaw?'

'No, but does that matter?'

'I only wished to ascertain whether we have any record of an earlier visit,' Stephanie replied, undaunted by the caller's note of challenge.

'Well, you haven't.'

'When would you like to come?'

'As soon as possible.'

'What about three thirty tomorrow afternoon?'

'Yes, that'll suit me.' She paused. 'It is Miss Epton I'll see, isn't it? I don't want to find myself shuffled off on one of your clerks.'

Snaith and Epton's only clerk was a youthful and resilient Ben and Stephanie reflected that he would probably be more than willing to take on the staid Mrs Henshaw and hold his own.

'If I make an appointment for you to see Miss Epton,' she said with a touch of frost in her voice, 'then you'll see her.'

Half an hour later Rosa returned to the office from court and Stephanie informed her of the appointment that had been made.

'Did she give any indication, Steph, as to what she wanted to see me about?' Rosa asked.

'None.'

'Or how she got hold of my name?'

5

'No.'

It was apparent to Rosa that Mrs Henshaw had failed to win Stephanie's seal of approval, not that there was anything unusual in that. Snaith and Epton's telephonist-cum-receptionist was an efficient operator with a cool, dispassionate eye on the human condition. Rosa had a great respect for her judgment and a fondness for her as a person.

'Oh, well, we'll just have to wait and see what tomorrow afternoon brings,' she said. 'She doesn't sound like one of our regular clients.'

'More like one of Harrods' regulars,' Stephanie observed as she fielded an incoming call.

The first thing Rosa noticed about her visitor when she was shown into her office the next afternoon was her hat. It was not often that Snaith and Epton's office was graced by anyone wearing a hat and Mrs Henshaw's certainly enhanced the impression of somebody of both quality and substance. The hat, which was midnight-blue in colour, had an extravagantly wide brim to give it authority. In Rosa's view hats fell into two categories, the frivolous and the intimidating. There was nothing frivolous about Mrs Henshaw's.

'You probably want to know why I'm here,' Mrs Henshaw said in a voice that was at odds with her formidable hat. 'I saw you on television about a month ago. It was a programme about the difficulties wives have to cope with in marriage. You referred to the subterranean pressures to which they become subjected. If I may say so, you spoke with considerably more sense than the other members of the panel.'

Rosa smiled. 'Possibly because I wasn't an expert. I was only invited at the last minute when someone else fell out. The producer was determined to have a female lawyer taking part.'

As she spoke Rosa reflected that nobody could look less like a battered wife than Mrs Henshaw, though perhaps in her case the abuses were all subterranean. She remembered using the expression off the top of her head and hoped she wasn't now about to have to try and explain herself. She waited for Mrs Henshaw to go on, which she did after playing with her wedding ring for several seconds, turning it this way and that.

'Four years ago I married a man named Ralph Henshaw. We had both been previously married, his wife having died a year

6

previously, while I'd been a widow for over ten years. Edward Ashby, my first husband, had left me comfortably off and I had continued to live at Riverview Court. I . . . we still live there. We also have a flat off Bayswater Road overlooking the park where my husband spends the weekdays. I'm staying there this week as he's abroad on business.'

Rosa noted the conjunction of those two pieces of information, but refrained from comment. Instead she asked, 'What is his business?'

'He's in property.' She might have said in drains for all the enthusiasm she showed. 'His work takes him all over southern Europe and to other sunspots like Florida. That's where he is this week.' She paused and went on. 'He has two children by his first marriage, both now grown-up. Christopher is nearly thirty and is married with a child of his own. Anthea is a few years younger and works in an advertising agency.' Her voice became suddenly harsher. 'There's somebody else I ought to mention. A woman named Frances Gifford who is my husband's partner, having graduated to that position from being his secretary. She's a divorcée in her thirties. She's also an extremely determined woman.'

A familiar scenario seemed to be emerging. Unfaithful husband, wronged wife and predatory other woman, though Rosa still waited to hear what precisely had drawn Mrs Henshaw to Snaith and Epton's door. Though they did handle divorce cases, they were not, as one might say, a speciality of the house. Mrs Henshaw reached into her handbag for a tissue. Rosa watched her and decided to leave her to tell her story without prompting.

'Are you married, Miss Epton?' her visitor asked suddenly, then added quickly, 'I'm sorry if that's a rude question. I got the impression from the television programme that you might be; or, at any rate, have a satisfying relationship with someone.'

'I don't particularly wish to discuss my personal life,' Rosa said with a deprecating smile.

'No, of course not. It's just that you came across as an understanding person and I know that you're also a successful lawyer. It's why you've stayed in my mind and why I decided to bring my problem to you. My own solicitor is not somebody with whom I could possibly discuss personal things. I'm sure he's a dab hand at drafting a complicated will or unravelling a difficult conveyance, but he's not the sort of person to whom one turns in my particular circumstances.'

7

'What are your particular circumstances, Mrs Henshaw?' Rosa asked, when a prompt seemed necessary if the interview was not to end in silence.

'I believe my husband is planning to get rid of me.'

'Divorce you, do you mean?'

'No, kill me.'

She spoke in a matter-of-fact tone and Rosa could only stare at her. She might be suffering from some sort of psychosis, but there had been no such signs to date.

'You could be quite wrong,' Rosa said slowly. 'Obsessions operate in an insidious way.'

'It's not an obsession and I am not wrong.'

'What evidence do you have that he intends to kill you?'

'He needs my money. Also, his lady-friend would like to become Mrs Henshaw. She's avaricious and quite ruthless.'

'That's not evidence,' Rosa remarked. 'You may have suspicions, but that's not the same thing as proof.' Privately she suspected that her visitor was suffering from a form of paranoia. In Rosa's world almost everyone did. 'In any event,' she went on, 'I'm not clear how I can help you. If you really believe your life is in danger, you should go to the police.'

'A fat lot of notice they'd take. Moreover, I have no wish to involve them at the present time.'

'What exactly do you expect me to do?' Rosa asked with a note of exasperation.

'I'll pay you a retainer to accept me as a client and then should something happen to me, I'd like you to investigate. I don't want my husband to get away with it. By it, I mean my death.'

Though Mrs Henshaw looked sane enough, it was now clear that she had an outsize bee buzzing in her bonnet. A psychiatrist's couch would seem a more appropriate venue than a solicitor's office. So ran Rosa's thoughts as she said: 'Who are your closest family, apart from your husband?'

'I have a sister who lives in the south of France. We keep in touch at Christmas and on birthdays, but that's about all. My first husband was an only child, so there's no one on that side. As for my step-children, we get on all right now, but they have their own lives.'

'Did they resent your marrying their father?'

'Anthea did. Christopher was too busy chasing girls to mind.'

Rosa was silent for a moment, then taking a deep breath, she said, 'If something does happen to you, Mrs Henshaw, I still don't see what help I can be. It'll be a matter for the police if your husband attempts to kill you, though, as I've said, I suspect your fears are exaggerated. It can happen very easily once you begin to see something out of perspective.' She hesitated. 'Have you thought about talking things over with a psychiatrist?'

Mrs Henshaw gave her an impatient look. 'You say that if my husband does kill me, it'll be a case for the police, but what if I just disappear and am never seen again?'

Rosa frowned. 'Why should that happen?'

'If my husband provides a plausible explanation for my disappearance, the police aren't going to do anything.'

'Is there any reason at all for thinking such a thing?'

'It's what happened to his first wife,' Mrs Henshaw said with a touch of defiance. 'Now, I suppose you want to know what evidence I have of it? Well, I'll tell you. I first met Ralph and Jean – that was his first wife's name – on a cruise about six years ago. We became friendly and they were very attentive to me, which I appreciated, seeing that I was travelling on my own. We kept in touch afterwards and they came and spent a number of weekends at Riverview Court. It was on one of these weekends that Jean disappeared. She had got up and gone out early, about six o'clock on a Sunday morning.' She gave Rosa a bleak stare. 'She was never seen again. Ralph was distraught, though, with hindsight, that was obviously a well-rehearsed reaction. He said he had been vaguely aware of her getting out of bed and it was shortly afterwards he had heard the church clock chime six. Then he'd fallen asleep again.'

'Were the police notified?'

'Later, yes. First we made our own search. We have about eight acres of land, which includes a wood and a lake, so it took some time. But there was no sign of Jean anywhere. Later still we made some enquiries in the village, but nobody had seen her and she'd not caught the one and only bus to go through the village on a Sunday morning. That had been our first thought. It was only after we'd exhausted our own resources that we reported her as a missing person. It was all very horrible, with endless questions and a more thorough search of the grounds. Eventually the police said there was nothing they could do. There was no evidence against Ralph or against anybody else and Jean just joined the ranks of missing persons and that was that.'

'Who else was in the house at the time?' Rosa asked.

'Nobody. I've never had live-in staff. I prefer to make do with daily help.'

'And you didn't hear anything yourself?'

'No. My bedroom was on the opposite side of the house to the guest rooms. It was reckoned she had slipped out of a side door into the stable yard.'

'Did they have a car?'

'Yes, but she didn't take it. I'm telling you, Miss Epton, she just vanished into thin air.'

Whatever else Rosa might believe, it was not that. Fixing her visitor with a hard stare, she said, 'When did you reach the conclusion that her husband had done away with her? Presumably, it wasn't until some time later. How much later?'

Mrs Henshaw lowered her head so that her face was completely hidden by the brim of her hat. After several seconds she looked up and said, 'I suppose it must have been when he produced evidence to prove she was dead . . .'

'Otherwise, of course, you couldn't have got married,' Rosa interjected. 'You have to wait seven years before a court will presume death and you've already told me you married Ralph Henshaw a mere year after his wife's death. I'm afraid I've missed something.'

Mrs Henshaw blinked. 'I'm sorry, I'm not being very coherent. I should have mentioned that her body was found some four months after she disappeared. It had been washed up on a lonely stretch of beach in Dorset, but not immediately discovered. It was lodged between some rocks so that it was submerged at high tide and only exposed when the tide went out. Due to its decomposition the pathologist was unable to give a cause of death and an open verdict was returned.'

'Was your husband questioned again?'

'Yes, but he was unable to tell the police any more than he had when they first investigated her disappearance.'

'And nobody knows how she got to the place where her body was found?'

'No.'

'Presumably you have a theory. You must have one, seeing that you believe she was murdered. Murdered by the man who is now your husband.' Mrs Henshaw nodded as though mesmerised by

10

the inexorability of Rosa's reasoning. 'Did you have any suspicions when you married him?'

'Of course not,' Mrs Henshaw said apparently jolted into reaction. 'It was only a few months ago that I forced myself to face reality and accepted that my husband must have killed Jean and that my own life could be in danger. He had borrowed money at a high interest rate and was in a precarious financial state. He had suggested I should sell Riverview Court, which had been valued at over a million pounds, but I'd refused.'

'Did he benefit financially from Jean's death?'

'No, she didn't have any money of her own.'

'Then why did he bother to kill her?' Rosa asked brutally.

'Because he had already made up his mind to court me. I was a rich widow, waiting to be plucked.'

'Were you fond of him?'

'Yes.'

'Was Jean aware of your feelings towards her husband?'

There was a note of hostility in her voice when she replied, 'When I made an appointment to see you, Miss Epton, I wasn't expecting to be subjected to an interrogation.'

Rosa shrugged. 'You've told me an extraordinary story, questions are inevitable.'

'I've told you the truth.'

'Now tell me again exactly what you want me to do,' Rosa said, meeting the eyes that stared at her from beneath the brim of her visitor's hat.

'Is this some sort of test?' Mrs Henshaw asked indignantly. 'I hoped I had made myself clear.'

'Look, Mrs Henshaw, I'm a solicitor. My job is to offer legal advice to clients who seek it and, where required, to defend them in court. I'm still not clear what I can do for you.'

Evelyn Henshaw withdrew beneath her hat like a tortoise into its shell. After a while she said, 'I am ready to pay you a retainer to keep an eye on my safety. It may not be a legal matter as yet, but it could become one.' She bit her lip. 'I don't know who else I can turn to.'

'What about a private detective?'

'I don't wish to embroil myself in anything so unsavoury. A middle-aged man in a grubby raincoat is not the sort of person to whom I could unburden myself.'

'They don't all fit that description,' Rosa said with a faint smile.

11

'I know one who has been to Eton.' She didn't add that he had been expelled for running a gambling school.

'I dare say,' Mrs Henshaw remarked, in a tone that disposed of the suggestion. Leaning forward, she went on, 'I implore you, Miss Epton, to accept me as a client. I'm sure I didn't misjudge you the time I saw you on television. If I didn't fear for my life, I wouldn't be bothering you. Equally, should anything happen to me, I'd like to know that my death won't go uninvestigated.'

She reached into her handbag and fetched out a folded piece of paper which she handed over to Rosa. 'I've written down my addresses and telephone numbers, which you may find useful,' she said, as if she didn't doubt that Rosa would accept her as a client.

Rosa glanced at it and noted the flamboyance of her hand. She wondered if it mirrored her real personality.

Chapter Two

'So what are you going to do?' Peter Chen asked after Rosa had told him about her visitor when he came round that evening to take her out to dinner. They were on their way to a new Thai restaurant he had discovered and about which he had been enthusiastic on the telephone. He was always finding new places to eat, leaving Rosa to hanker, for the most part silently, after well-tried haunts, where the menus neither stretched the imagination nor required lengthy interpretation. 'If you take my advice,' he went on, 'you'll treat her as if she's radioactive. She sounds extremely dangerous.'

'Could be she is, but I'm intrigued.'

'As long as you don't accept her at face value.'

'That'll be the day,' Rosa observed sardonically. 'Snaith and Epton's clients are a crafty, guileful lot and often charming with it, but never, I repeat never, are they taken at face value.'

'So what are you proposing to do about Mrs Henshaw?'

'Before I make up my mind, I thought we might drive down to Briar's End on Sunday. I'd like to have a look at Riverview Court. It'll help me decide. Don't ask me how, Peter, but it will. I've met the lady, now I should like to take a peek at the house where she lives and from which Ralph Henshaw's first wife mysteriously disappeared.'

'Fine,' Peter said. 'We'll make a day of it. It'll set me up for three days in Geneva next week closeted with Swiss bankers. Can you think of anything less thrilling than that?'

'I really ought to charge you for all the vicarious pleasure you get out of my cases,' Rosa said with a laugh. 'While you buzz round the world serving the interests of your millionaire clients, I visit mine in Her Majesty's prisons in order to regale you with the gritty details.'

They arrived at the restaurant and were bowed into a corner

13

of the dimly lit bar. Peter ordered a Campari and orange juice for Rosa and a Scotch and water for himself.

'You've not told me what this woman looked like,' he said, 'apart from her hat, that is. What age was she?'

'Early to mid-fifties,' Rosa replied. 'Though she might have been anything between forty and sixty beneath that hat.'

'Hair?'

'From what I saw of it, mouse with touches of grey.'

'Sounds very sexy,' Peter remarked. 'So you wouldn't judge her to be a woman of passion?'

'Passion comes in all guises,' Rosa said. 'She certainly didn't exude it, but that doesn't mean it wasn't lurking beneath the surface. Anyway, why this interest in her emotional armoury?'

'Because she may have begun an affair with Ralph Henshaw while he was still married to Jean and helped to get rid of her. You've only heard her version of events.'

'Don't think I'm not aware of that! It's what intrigues me about the case.' She paused. 'I just hope, Peter, that I shan't suddenly find myself with a dead client and nothing else to go on.'

'That would indeed be frustrating.'

'It would be like reaching the end of a detective story and finding the final chapter had been torn out.'

'Relax, little Rosa, that won't happen.'

'Why do you say that? How do you know it won't happen?'

'Trust my oriental instinct. It's never let us down.'

Rosa gave him an affectionate smile. 'I suppose I must also trust it to order for me.' She picked up a menu and glanced down a list of elaborately described dishes.

'Just leave it to me.'

'If possible, something that's not garnished with chillis, peppers and garlic,' she said.

He sighed. 'Perhaps we should have gone to McDonalds.'

It was three hours later as she lay in his arms, being unromantically reminded of their dinner, that she said quite suddenly, 'I wonder if Mrs Henshaw has a guilty conscience about something?'

Sunday was a typical April day; or typical of any other English day, for that matter. The sun was mildly warm, there was a light wind with a cutting edge, and, depending on which direction you looked, the threat of rain.

Peter picked Rosa up at her flat around ten thirty, having

14

returned to his own home only a few hours earlier. He was wearing a pair of pale green slacks and a high-necked sweater the blurred colour of a Scottish moor. He smelt of a different after-shave from the previous evening.

Rosa had decided that the weather and the occasion called for her French mustard trouser suit with a display of deep red silk blouse beneath the jacket. She could never make up her mind whether the colour of the outfit suited her, but it was time to give it another airing and it allowed the weather to change without her feeling the need to do the same. Also, she knew that Peter liked it.

He had recently acquired a new Japanese car which he enjoyed driving. Rosa, for her part, was always content to sit and be driven. The physical manipulation of a car's controls gave her no sense of power or pleasure. For a few months she had taken to cycling to and from the office, before deciding that the cons outweighed the pros. The main cons were other people's car exhausts and what all the exercise was doing to her calf and thigh muscles. Stephanie had confirmed that she might be physically fitter, but that the price would be a lack of femininity in certain important areas. Though a working professional woman, Rosa had always set great store on her female attributes.

By the time Peter had pressed various buttons, soft music filled the car and the temperature was exactly right. Rosa doubted whether Concorde had a more impressive display of dials and coloured lights. The steering-wheel seemed a positive anachronism.

It took them seventy-five minutes to reach Briar's End, which was one of those straggling villages without an apparent centre. There was a small Norman church and next to it a community centre which looked as if it had been built out of left-over material. Beyond was a housing estate whose needs it presumably served.

'I don't see any sign of a river,' Peter remarked.

'I don't think there is one,' Rosa said.

'So how come Riverview Court?'

'There's a tributary of the Thames about a mile away. I suppose it's visible from the Henshaws' house.'

'There were a number of big houses on either side of the road as we came into the village.'

'But none of them were Riverview Court. I looked.'

'Then it must be on the farther side of the village.'

They passed an old-fashioned telephone kiosk standing on a verge beside a bus stop. There followed a butcher's shop and a bit further on a small general store. It was as if they had been dumped haphazardly by a giant who couldn't be bothered to carry them any further.

'I think I see a pub ahead,' Peter said. 'Let's stop and have a drink and ask the way.'

Rosa nodded. 'I'd sooner we weren't too obvious about asking the way.'

'Let's have a drink and not ask the way,' Peter said, as he pulled into the carpark of the Red Squirrel.

The saloon bar appeared to be deserted, but a woman with a thin face and a lot of honey-coloured hair like a large puff-ball appeared. She was wearing a salmon-pink dress and, Rosa couldn't help reflecting, would have looked more at home in a Soho club. She served the drinks that Peter ordered, but made no attempt to enter into conversation.

'Pauline,' a male voice suddenly called out and she turned and disappeared through a door at the back of the bar. About five minutes later a man appeared. He looked as if he hadn't long been out of bed. His hair was sticking up at the back and he was straightening the knot of his tie. He gave Rosa and Peter a long-suffering smile.

'I'm afraid I overslept this morning and Pauline's furious with me. She hates it here, anyway. Luckily we're not busy. You're our first customers of the day. Are you going to have lunch?' He spoke breathlessly in short bursts.

'We haven't decided,' Peter said.

'I'll fetch you a menu. I'm sure you won't regret it if you do. Pauline's a superb cook, even when she's angry. Anyway, she has every right to be, I shouldn't have overslept. I love it down here, I just wish she did.' He came round the end of the bar and handed them each a menu. 'The roasts won't be ready for another half-hour, but they're really worth waiting for.'

'Do you get many people in for lunch on a Sunday?' Rosa enquired.

'One or two locals come in regularly, but we don't get a lot of passing trade. Briar's End is a bit of a backwater.'

'I noticed a number of big houses as we came into the village,' Rosa remarked.

16

'There's no shortage of them. Trouble is their owners mostly eat at home. They have foreign couples to cook and bottle-wash.'

'Are there more big houses going out of the village toward the river?'

'There's Pond Mead and Riverview Court and one or two modern upstarts in bogus styles and with the sort of gardens you see on the front of seed catalogues. That's about the lot.'

'How long have you been here?' Peter asked.

'Only a couple of years, but long enough to know who's who.'

'You'd have to be interested in people in order to run a successful pub,' Rosa remarked.

'Too true,' the landlord said with a nod. 'That's partly Pauline's trouble,' he added in a lowered voice, 'she doesn't get on with people easily. She's dutiful, but that's not enough when you're serving behind a bar.'

'Do you have other help?'

'I couldn't manage on my own, not with Pauline spending so much time in the kitchen.' He counted on his fingers. 'I've got about six helpers in all. Part-timers from the village who are glad to earn a bit of extra. A couple of them should be in any moment.' He paused. 'I'm lucky, they're a good bunch. All ages and sexes.' He smiled reflectively. 'And there's also the Professor. We call him that, but he's not really a professor. I'm told he's a research student, but don't ask me what he researches. His name's Stefan. He lives up at Riverview Court.'

'Son of the house, is he?' Rosa asked in a guileless tone.

The landlord shook his head. 'I imagine he's a lodger, though the Henshaws aren't the sort of people to take in lodgers. Anyway, it's none of my business, but Stefan's a nice lad and he's good behind the bar. His parents are foreign and he has an unpronounceable surname, but he speaks English as well as you and me.'

Rosa wondered if Evelyn Henshaw had had any reason for not mentioning their research student lodger. There was no particular reason why she should have done so, on the other hand the omission surprised her.

After a brief consultation, she and Peter decided they would stay and have lunch. The landlord had been welcoming and they had learnt more than he might have expected from his innocent words.

Three young men from the nearby housing estate came in and

17

ordered drinks. They greeted the man behind the bar as Bob and Rosa made a mental note to look at the licensee's surname above the entrance when they left.

The roast lamb which they both ordered was certainly excellent, as were the vegetables. It was clear that Pauline's cooking had been worth waiting for, as her husband had promised. Rosa forwent a dessert, but Peter decided that home-made treacle tart was not to be missed.

'It's all right for you,' Rosa remarked wistfully as she watched him eating it, 'you never put on any weight.'

'A good thing too, a rotund Chinaman resembles a ball of marzipan.'

By the time they left, there were between thirty and forty people in the pub, including half a dozen lunching at the tables set out at one end.

'R. and P. King, licensees' Rosa read on the panel above the entrance as she and Peter left. Obviously Robert and Pauline King. She wondered how long their idyll would last, though it seemed to have already reached an end as far as the wife was concerned. Fortunately, it didn't seem to have affected her cooking.

'Pity we couldn't ask any questions about the Henshaws,' Peter said when they were back in the car, 'but with Stefan in both camps, the word would soon have got back.'

'I know,' Rosa said with a nod. 'I'd love to meet him and sound him out, but I don't see how I can without ringing alarm bells.'

'The odds are that he's a relative or the son of an old friend who's staying at the house as a matter of convenience,' Peter remarked.

'Maybe, but I'd like to know more about him.'

About half a mile along the road an unmade-up track branched off at right angles on the left-hand side. A rough wooden sign at the entrance said, 'Private road. Spangler's Farm and Riverview Court only'. Peter turned on to it.

'We may regret this,' he said, 'but I don't see any alternative.' His expression brightened. 'Anyway if Mrs Henshaw was baiting a trap, she'll be expecting you,' he added cheerfully.

After fifty yards, the track forked with a sign indicating Spangler's Farm to the left and Riverview Court to the right. Two brick gate-posts supporting an iron gate lay a short distance ahead. The track was bordered by bushes and a fringe of trees. The house

18

could be seen some thirty yards beyond the gates. It was large and unmistakably Victorian with a turret at one corner. In front of it was a sweep of lawn.

'Don't go any further,' Rosa said. 'I'd sooner we weren't seen.'

Peter began to reverse in order to turn round. As he did so, a young man steering a motor mower appeared from behind a clump of rhododendrons and manoeuvred the machine round a flowering cherry tree. He didn't look in their direction.

A woman came out of the house and walked toward him.

'That's her,' Rosa exclaimed.

'I don't know why you have to sound surprised. After all, she lives there,' Peter said.

'It's the effect of seeing her without her hat. She looks quite different . . .' Rosa's voice trailed off.

The woman they were looking at had very short hair, giving the impression at that distance that she was wearing a close-fitting cap on her head.

'I thought you told me her hair was mouse with touches of grey,' Peter remarked.

'It *was* when she came to the office,' Rosa said, frowning hard as she stared at the tableau taking place on the lawn.

After talking for a few moments, the young man glanced at his wristwatch, then switched off the lawn mower's motor. The two of them walked hand in hand toward the house and disappeared through the front door.

'Even though it's a bit early for tea and cucumber sandwiches, I can think of a dozen innocent explanations of that little scene,' Peter said quickly before Rosa could speak.

'He's obviously her toy boy, it stands out a mile,' she said, thoughtfully. 'But why did she tell me that spiel in the office? *And*, why's she now an ash blonde?'

Chapter Three

In the two weeks that followed Rosa heard nothing further from Mrs Henshaw, though that was not to say she didn't give her any thought. There were moments when she looked back on her visit to the office as part of a strange dream, with her own and Peter's trip to Briar's End as a second instalment which didn't fit the first.

Long days in the court, followed by a backlog of work which had to be tackled at home each evening, left her little time to brood on anything as improbable as Evelyn Henshaw's strange tale. Busy as she was, however, she was unable to banish it completely from her mind. As the days passed without further news, she found herself filled with a mixture of relief and curiosity.

Whenever she saw Peter, he regularly enquired whether she had further news from Briar's End.

'It's probably died a death,' he remarked one evening during the second week of silence.

'As long as *it* isn't Mrs Henshaw,' Rosa replied bleakly.

'You'd know if it was,' he said.

'Would I?'

'There'd be something in the papers.'

'Would there?' Her tone called for reassurance.

'If anything had happened to her I'm quite certain that word would have reached you one way or another. Incidentally, have you told Robin about her?'

Robin Snaith was not only Rosa's senior partner in the firm, but the person to whom she owed her professional start.

She nodded. 'I think he sometimes wonders what sort of an office we're running. He said Mrs Henshaw sounded like a femme fatale who was likely to bring us more aggro than profit, but it wasn't for him to tell me how to run my end of the practice.'

'Which was exactly what he was doing.'

Rosa sighed. 'Dear Robin, he's immensely patient with me. His advice invariably comes wrapped in tissue. I may have taken on some odd clients in my time, but everything's always worked out all right in the end.' She gave a small laugh. 'After all, I've not yet been struck off and I more than earn my share of the emoluments. Moreover Robin knows I'd never let the firm down.'

A further week passed before Evelyn Henshaw stepped out of the wings and took centre stage again.

As Rosa returned to the office late one afternoon, Stephanie said, 'Mr Henshaw's been on the phone. He wants to come and see you.'

'Did you say mister, Steph?'

'Yes, Mrs Henshaw's husband. He wanted to make an appointment, but I wasn't sure if you'd wish to see him.'

'And?'

'I told him you'd be in later today and he should call again. When he does, do you want me to put him through, make an appointment for him to see you or tell him you're too busy to see anyone for the next six months?'

Rosa was thoughtful for a moment. 'I think I'd like to have a word with him,' she said slowly. 'That is, if he does call back.'

'Oh, he'll call back all right,' Stephanie observed. 'I can tell the goats from the sheep, the ones who are genuine and the ones who are only playing games. And then of course,' she added, 'there are the deep breathers.'

'We don't get any of those, do we?' Rosa asked in surprise.

'Not many. I soon see them off. I tell them to hang on as the police'll be round in a couple of minutes. They usually drop the receiver as if it's caught fire.' She paused to take an incoming call. 'It's Mr Henshaw,' she mouthed at Rosa, who nodded and hastened along to her office to receive the call.

'Miss Epton?' a bullish voice said. 'My name's Ralph Henshaw. I'd like to make an appointment to come and see you. Would tomorrow be convenient?'

'What do you wish to see me about, Mr Henshaw?'

'I believe my wife's consulted you.'

'Even if she has, I couldn't discuss her visit. It'd be a breach of confidence.'

Rosa had quickly decided that there was no point in denying the visit when he plainly knew it had taken place.

'Miss Epton, I need to see you as a matter of urgency,' he said with a touch of impatience. 'My wife has disappeared.'

It was the next afternoon that he arrived to keep his appointment. Rosa noted that he was ten minutes late.

'Got stuck in a traffic jam and the driver couldn't find the street,' he said when shown into Rosa's office. She reckoned this was as near as he would get to an apology.

He was a tall, well-built man, with a head of wiry black hair, greying at the sides. He had a chin as aggressive as a mechanical shovel – and was every inch what Rosa's mother would have called a handsome beast.

'As I mentioned on the phone,' he said as soon as he had sat down, 'Evelyn's disappeared. In the course of looking for clues, I came across your name and address on a piece of paper in a handbag. I ascertained that you were a solicitor and guessed she had been to see you. Hence my visit.' He fixed Rosa with a speculative look. 'I know all about professional confidence, but I've got to find my wife and that overrides everything else. She could be in danger.'

'Do the police know of her disappearance?' Rosa asked, treading carefully into what, she knew, might turn out to be a minefield.

'Not yet. I decided to speak to you first.' He fiddled for a moment with the signet ring on his little finger and seemed to be undecided what card to play next. Eventually he said, 'I don't believe in beating about the bush, so professional confidence or not, may I ask what my wife came to see you about? I hope you can see that it's a legitimate and wholly relevant question in the circumstances.'

'I still can't answer it.'

'Did she tell you anything that might bear on her disappearance?'

'Look, Mr Henshaw,' Rosa said after a moment's rapid thought, 'why don't you tell me the circumstances of her disappearance and then I'll decide whether I can help you.'

'All right,' he said, in a none too pleased tone, 'if that's the way it has to be. I've been abroad on business for the best part of a month and when I got home at the end of last week, Evelyn was missing. She spent the first part of my absence at our flat in town and then went back to Briar's End. She stays there most of the time as she doesn't really care for London. Anyway, I got back and she wasn't to be found either at the flat or at Riverview Court. Moreover, there were no messages as to where she had gone. I phoned around, but nobody could offer any clues to her whereabouts.'

'Would she have been alone in the house at Briar's End?' Rosa asked with an innocent expression.

Ralph Henshaw gave her a sharp look. 'Yes,' he said, with a distinct note of aggression. 'We don't have any live-in staff and as far as I know she didn't have a friend staying with her.'

'And you have no idea where she is?'

'None. That's why I'm here. I hope you can help me.'

'Has she ever disappeared before?'

'Yes, but never for more than a couple of days. I'm afraid my wife rather enjoys drama. She acts out fantasies that bear little relation to reality.' He gave Rosa an impatient look. 'You doubtless know the story of our marriage, that we'd both been married before and she was already a widow when we met. I'm sure she told you all that.'

Rosa met his gaze, but said nothing.

'All right,' he said with an impatient shrug, 'it's clear my wife came to see you, but you're not going to help me because of so-called professional confidence. Evelyn may be in danger, but that obviously doesn't matter to you provided you stick to your rules. I hope for your sake that you won't have anything on your conscience.'

Rosa bit her tongue, but determined not to respond to the charge. Not yet, anyway.

'What makes you think your wife could be in danger?' she asked.

'Because she can act in a very irrational way at times. I told you just now she can live out fantasies. Unfortunately, she's been getting worse not better.'

'Has she seen a doctor?'

'It's very difficult to get such people to a doctor. They don't admit there's anything wrong with them.' He gave Rosa a pleading look. 'I'm quite sure, Miss Epton, that this interview wouldn't have got thus far if you didn't know something. I implore you to bend your rules and tell me what it is.'

'I assure you I don't know anything that'll help you find your wife. I have no idea where she is. She made an appointment to see me because she had watched me on a television programme and . . . apparently liked the look of me.'

Ralph Henshaw listened intently. 'I imagine she told you about my first wife's death. It was one of those tragedies that strike suddenly at a family. I've always felt that Evelyn knew rather more than she ever let on. Indeed, I'd go as far as to say she's had Jean's death on her conscience ever since.'

Rosa blinked as she tried to hide her surprise. 'What exactly were the circumstances of your first wife's death?' she asked.

'We were spending the weekend with Evelyn at Briar's End. I had to go up to town on business on the Saturday and the two women decided to drive down to the coast. It was a glorious day and Jean always enjoyed a swim in the sea, though she wasn't a particularly strong swimmer. I got back to Riverview Court around seven, and about an hour later Evelyn turned up alone. She was in a terrible state, almost incoherent. Anyway, her story was that Jean had gone into the water for a last swim when the current dragged her out to sea and she went under. It was a lonely bit of coast and there was nobody else around to go to her rescue. Evelyn can't swim at all. She drove home in an absolute panic and was absolutely distraught. She begged me not to tell the police that she and Jean had been together, as she couldn't face being questioned. We sat up half the night deciding what to do. I tried to persuade her that telling the truth would be the best course, but she only became more distraught. In the end we informed the police that Jean had got up early on Sunday morning and vanished into thin air.'

'Was her body ever recovered?' Rosa enquired.

'Further along the coast, wedged between two rocks. But that was several weeks later.' He paused. 'It's no wonder that Evelyn now carries a guilty conscience around. I'll probably never know what happened down on the beach, but there's no doubt it unhinged her mind.' He paused again and added bleakly, 'We married about a year after Jean's death. We'd grown very fond of each other and our secret had become a bond.'

The question was, which secret? Hers? His? Or one yet to be revealed?

'I have to find out what has happened to my wife,' he went on, breaking in on Rosa's thoughts. 'I had hoped you'd be able to help me . . .'

'Was she in touch with your son or daughter while you were away?' Rosa asked as she sought to steer the interview to her own advantage.

'Ah, she mentioned Christopher and Anthea, did she? The

answer is, no, she didn't. They're not on the friendliest of terms. I'm afraid Anthea is a rather jealous person. She's more like me than her brother is. He was always his mother's boy.'

'So what do you think may have happened to her?' Rosa asked.

'As I keep on saying, I hope you can tell me. Or, rather, that you can give me some clues following her visit here.' He fixed Rosa with a particularly hard stare. 'You see, I can't think why she should have come and seen you unless it was about me. And the fact that you're refusing to tell me anything confirms my belief.' When Rosa remained silent, he went on, 'If Evelyn mentioned Christopher and Anthea, I imagine she also dropped Fran's name into the conversation. She's my business associate. She and Evelyn have never liked each other, of which you were doubtless made well aware.' His tone was sardonic and Rosa could readily believe there was no love lost between the two women.

That, however, didn't help solve her own immediate problem. What to do next? The difficulty was she had nothing to bite on and felt as if she was wrestling with shadows. She had been told two conflicting stories, either of which might be true, but most probably were not. Ulterior motives could not be discounted. One option was to write to Mrs Henshaw and say she regretted being unable to accept her instructions further. End of matter. But that would be a craven course to take at the very moment action was required of her; namely to investigate the disappearance of her client. That was precisely what Mrs Henshaw had come to see her about; her adumbrated disappearance, with the supposition that her husband would have killed her. And now she had disappeared and the husband in question was sitting opposite Rosa and watching her with a distinct air of calculation.

Suddenly he got up. 'I won't take up more of your time, Miss Epton. I imagine you're a busy person, just as I am, and I don't believe in wasting time, my own or anyone else's. If my wife should get in touch with you, please ask her to contact me.' He walked to the door. 'I can find my own way out.'

A moment later he had departed, leaving Rosa to speculate on the real reason for his visit.

That evening when she told him what had happened, Peter said, 'You're being lured into a snakepit, little Rosa. I don't like it at all. They're using you.'

Chapter Four

Rosa had time to ponder these words over the next few days. There was no further news of Evelyn Henshaw and her husband had departed as abruptly as he had appeared. If she was to fulfil his wife's commission, she had to try and think of a way of initiating enquiries which would not land her in immediate embarrassment – if not something worse.

It was on the fourth day after Ralph Henshaw's visit that Rosa's phone buzzed and Stephanie announced in her most dispassionate tone, 'I have Miss Henshaw on the line, will you take the call?'

It was getting to be like a game of Happy Families, Rosa reflected, except that the Henshaws couldn't have less resembled their cheerful fictional counterparts. Miss Henshaw could only be Anthea. But what did she want?

'Yes, put her through, Steph,' Rosa said.

'Miss Epton, my name's Anthea Henshaw,' a brisk, self-assured voice said a few seconds later. 'I probably shouldn't be calling you, but I felt that I must. My father tells me that he came to see you the other day concerning his wife's disappearance.' Rosa noted the disdainful reference to her father's 'wife', rather than admit to having a step-mother. She went on: 'Evelyn's a tiresome, neurotic woman and I wouldn't want you to waste your time on her. I told my father you wouldn't be able to help and there was no point in creating a fuss. She'll turn up again when it suits her. She just wants to make herself interesting.' She paused. 'That's really all.'

'Does your brother share your view?'

'Christopher? He's lucky. He's blissfully happy with a new wife and baby. I'm very fond of my brother, but . . .' She let the sentence tail away. 'He hasn't been in touch with you, has he?' she asked suspiciously.

'No.' Anthea Henshaw had spoken without any hesitation and

with a note of venom she had done nothing to hide. Rosa felt that at any moment the call would end abruptly and she would find herself at the end of a dead line. 'Perhaps you'd give me your address,' she said. 'I'd like to have it, should I need to get in touch with you.'

'I can't think why you should.'

'Nevertheless . . . And after all, it's you who's instigated this call.'

'All right. I have a flat in Chiswick. Got a pencil handy?'

Rosa wrote down an address and telephone number. 'I work at an advertising agency in the West End, but I'd sooner you didn't call me there, so I won't give you the number. Sorry to have bothered you, but I wanted to give you a proper perspective to Evelyn's disappearance.'

Anthea might only be in her twenties, but Rosa had the image of a tough, self-confident girl who was in full control of her life. She wondered if she had a boyfriend and whether he allowed himself to be bossed around. She found it impossible to fit a face to the voice that came over the telephone. On the spur of the moment she reached for the telephone.

'Did you have any conversation with Miss Henshaw, Steph?' she asked.

'Not much, why?'

'I wondered if you formed any idea as to her physical appearance?'

'A bit like me,' Stephanie said after a pause, 'but dark, not blonde, and with a large pair of spectacles to keep clients in their place.'

Rosa laughed. 'You make her sound formidable.'

'If you ask me,' Stephanie went on, 'the Henshaws are the sort of people who deserve each other.'

Rosa thought this probably applied to most of the firm's clients and their relatives.

Chapter Five

Bob King, landlord of the Red Squirrel in Briar's End, decided further steps were necessary to find out what had happened to Stefan, his part-time member of staff.

It was five days since he had put in an appearance at the pub and Bob's efforts to make contact with him at Riverview Court had failed. There never seemed to be anyone at the house to answer the telephone.

Stefan was not only the best of his bar staff, but was also reliable, sending word through when he was unable to come. Moreover, Bob owed him money for overtime he had put in the previous week and wanted to clear the debt.

Nobody had seen him about the village and Bob was . . . well, curious. It seemed so out of character. Thus on the Thursday of the week when Rosa received a phone call from Anthea Henshaw and was still in a state of indecision as to what she should do next, Bob decided he would go up to Riverview Court between afternoon closing and evening opening. It was a pleasant day and the walk would do him good.

He shouted up to Pauline, who had retired to the bedroom, that he would be out about an hour and received a shout back that he took to be acquiescence to his leaving the pub. The two midday servers had finished work and there was only Mrs Dovey clearing up in the kitchen.

The Henshaws didn't use his premises and the nearest he had been to their house was to gaze at it from the bifurcation of the track that led to Spangler's Farm and Riverview Court. This time he proposed going up to the front door. Or maybe the back one. He wasn't too sure of what protocol required, nor particularly worried.

The gate at the end of the drive was closed, but not locked. He had half-expected it might be electronically controlled from the house and that he would find a video camera trained on his approach. Many of the big houses in the district were protected these days by devices whose cunning was only equalled by that of those intent on circumventing it.

Anyway, it was only three thirty in the afternoon and not an hour when you'd expect all the security alarms to be on red alert. Unless, that is, the house was empty with everyone away.

He walked up the drive and reached the front of the house. It had a deserted air and was without any sign of life. Nevertheless, he approached the main door and rang the bell. After doing so a second time without avail, he stepped back and walked toward the corner of the building. The downstairs windows had curtains drawn across them, which seemed to indicate that the occupants had not merely gone out, but were away. It was possible that Stefan lived in the stable wing, separate from the rest of the house, but after walking right round the building he was satisfied that there was no one anywhere about. He stood with his back to the house and gazed across lawn, flowerbeds and lake to a small beech wood. There was not a soul in sight and Bob let out a perplexed sigh. Was Stefan as reliable as he'd thought? Or had something sinister happened to him?

As he stared across the garden a large dog broke cover from the wood and came running across the garden. A man shouted at it, but it took no notice. Reaching the lake it did a belly flop into the water and began swimming around in joyful circles. As its owner came nearer, Bob recognised him as somebody who lived on the edge of the village and who came into the pub from time to time, Trevor somebody-or-other. Bob decided it was time to melt away. He had no wish to have to explain his presence in the garden.

Unfortunately he was too late. The dog had clambered out on the nearer side of the lake and was bounding toward him barking proprietorially and drenching everything within several feet.

'Bacchus, come here!' his owner shouted to no avail.

Bacchus paused within a couple of yards of Bob, as if to decide whether he was friend or foe. His tail was swishing energetically from side to side, but his bark sounded anything but friendly.

'Oh, it's you, Bob,' the out-of-breath owner said. 'Bloody dog, I've only had him a couple of weeks and he's never been properly trained. He's as obedient as a runaway tractor, but he won't bite you. I'd only just let him off the lead and he got through the hedge and into the Henshaws' wood. He obviously remembered the lake from last time and then he saw you.' He glanced up at the house. 'It doesn't look as if there's anyone at home.'

'I don't think there is,' Bob King said, feeling less uncomfortable than he had when first detected. 'I just came along to deliver something,' he added quickly.

Bacchus, meanwhile, plainly saw no future in standing around while people talked and cantered back to the lake.

'He disturbed a duck over in the reeds last time. That's why he made a beeline for the lake today. Thank goodness he didn't catch the bird. It took off like a plane propelled from the deck of an aircraft-carrier and was airborne faster than it had ever been before. Luckily the family were all out that day, too.' He turned and glanced at his dog which was indulging in various aquatic exercises. 'He ought to have been born with fins rather than legs. Well, I'll be off. Reckon we'll leave the same way as we came.' He frowned. 'Don't think I was deliberately trespassing, Bob, because I wasn't. There's a lane on the further side of the wood. Leads up round the back of Pond Mead Farm.'

'I know.'

'That's all right then. I wouldn't want you to think I take liberties on other people's property. It's Bacchus who behaves as if he owns the whole countryside,' he added indulgently.

Bob watched Trevor whatever-his-name retire across the lawn. Every five yards or so he turned and bellowed at Bacchus who was still splashing about at the end of the lake which was partially overgrown with reeds and other verdant plant life. Eventually the dog crawled inelegantly out, shook himself vigorously and rather surprisingly decided to join his master. Bob, who was witnessing the scene, noticed that before racing off the dog dropped something from its mouth. It was something that glinted in the afternoon sun and he wondered what the dog could have found in the muddy water. Before beating his own retreat, he walked across to the edge of the lake where the animal had been exploring. On the ground lay a plastic wallet, rather the worse for wear after immersion and being chewed by Bacchus. It was lying upside-down and had a silver backing, which had caused it to glint in the sun.

Bob stooped down and picked it up. Inside the plastic wallet was a pass, admitting the bearer to St Giles' Polytechnic, wherever that might be. But what interested Bob was the name of the holder of the pass: Stefan Michalowski – and beside the printed name a clearly recognisable photograph of his part-time barman.

He stared at the document in his hand and shivered. Then he peered into the opaque water at his feet, which had been stirred up by the dog. Once the mud had settled, he should be able to see more. Meanwhile he decided to fetch a stick with which to prod. The water was only about two feet deep at that point with a shallow, slippery bank where Bacchus had struggled out.

Looking about him he saw some long bamboo canes propped against a wall at the back of the house. One of those would be just the thing. He walked over and chose the stoutest.

By the time he returned the sediment had settled and he was able to see the bottom. He lowered the stick through two feet of water into the soft mud below it. The stick penetrated a further eighteen inches before striking something resistant. He withdrew it and performed the same operation a foot to the right with the same result. Once more, this time to the left, and the stick went in further without obstruction. Nevertheless, there was definitely something there. Moreover, it was something on the soft side. Not a sheet of metal or a slab of stone. Perhaps, an old mattress. Or worse . . .

There was only one way to find out and that was to remove his own shoes and socks and trousers and get into the lake. He knelt down and put a hand in the water, which was colder than he had expected. He would probably be making a fool of himself, but at least there would be nobody to witness it. If anyone returned to the house while he was groping trouserless in a few feet of dirty water, he would . . . He realised he didn't know what he would do, but he recalled an uncle who had fought in World War II and was full of battlefield aphorisms saying that when you came face to face with the enemy you didn't have time to think, you acted. It was hardly a comparable situation, but act he would too.

Stripping off his lower garments and clutching a tuft of grass, he stepped into the water. He felt his feet sinking into squelching mud before coming to rest on something. His toes told him it was clothing, a woollen garment with buttons. There was a moment of panic when his big toe got caught in a buttonhole and he had to tug it free. A moment later he hauled himself out and feverishly pulled on his clothes over his dripping limbs. He tore out grass to wipe his feet which were covered in slimy mud.

It wasn't the mud that filled him with revulsion, but the fact that one of his feet had touched a human body.

PC Lipscomb was something of a castaway, though a contented one. At a time when village constables had all but disappeared and their stations closed, Briar's End police station had remained open and PC Lipscomb was a visible presence. Everyone in the village knew him and he knew everyone. If he was an anachronism in modern policing, nobody was going to complain.

He had just finished his tea when the phone rang.

'It's Bob King, Phil, can you pick me up at the pub? I think I've found a body.'

'Only think you have, Bob? It's best to be sure about things before you set the law in motion.'

Lipscomb was always wary of hoaxes, particularly on the part of those who frequented Bob King's establishment. If there was ever any trouble in the village, it usually originated there.

'I am sure, Phil. If you'll pick me up, I'll explain.'

'Where is this body?'

'In the Henshaws' lake.'

'I'll be with you in five minutes,' Lipscomb said.

As they drove together to Riverview Court, Bob explained what had taken him to the house earlier in the afternoon and his gruesome discovery.

'We'll soon find out what it is,' Lipscomb said. He was in his mid-thirties and had been born in the district and was a true country copper. All he wanted in life was to be left where he was.

'Do the Henshaws tell you when they're going to be away?' Bob asked.

PC Lipscomb shook his head. 'The house is fitted with burglar alarms, but they ring over at divisional headquarters. Thank goodness they do. With the number of times they go off when they're not meant to, I'd be driven mad if they rang at the station. Some of them are so sensitive, it only needs a butterfly to trigger them off.' He paused. 'I've not seen Mr Henshaw about for several weeks. He's abroad a lot and when he's in this country, he spends most of his time at their flat in London. Mrs Henshaw's mostly here. Then, after all, it's her home. There was all that business when his first wife disappeared and later turned up drowned. We'll probably never know what exactly happened there. Just as well for somebody, I'd say,' he added grimly.

'I presume you knew Stefan?'

'He always seemed a nice enough lad.'

'I shall miss him in my pub. He was a good worker and got on well with the punters.'

'You don't want to jump to conclusions,' Lipscomb said, as Bob was getting out of the car to open the drive gate.

A few minutes later he was showing the officer where he'd made his discovery.

PC Lipscomb peered into the murky water as if it were a crystal ball, then reached for the bamboo cane and began to prod cautiously into the mud.

'I'll go and fetch my tackle from the car,' he said after a while. 'You can give me a hand.'

Five minutes later they returned to the lake armed with rope, a length of chain and an iron hook resembling a ship's anchor. It took fifteen minutes to assemble the equipment to PC Lipscomb's satisfaction.

'OK, let's see if we can lift whatever it is,' he said as he lowered the hook into the water on what he hoped was the farther side of the object.

They watched it sink about eight inches into the mud and stick. Lipscomb pulled on the rope until it was taut.

'It's caught on something,' he remarked. 'Hold me round the waist, I don't want to slip in.'

Bob King did as he was bidden and the officer tugged hard on the rope.

'Something's giving,' he said hopefully.

Quite suddenly, there was a squelching noise and he fell backwards, pushing Bob to the ground before collapsing on top of him.

Caught on the end of the hook was a human arm. As they stared in horror, it slithered off the hook and disappeared beneath the water.

'I'd better get through to headquarters,' Lipscomb said. 'You wait here and guard the scene.'

Bob nodded. 'Can you let Pauline know where I am? She'll have to open.'

'Leave it to me. I can't tell her what's happened or your customers'll be trooping along here for a free show.'

After Lipscomb had driven away, Bob King retired to the house where he sat down with his back to a wall and from where he could observe the lake. Though not unexpected, he had still been shocked by their discovery and felt more secure with the solid house at his back.

It was an hour before Lipscomb returned. His car was followed by a van from which half a dozen officers emerged.

'This is Detective Chief Inspector Greer,' he said, introducing the man who had got out of the car with him and who resembled the smoother sort of bank manager portrayed in a TV advert.

DCI Greer gave Bob a warm smile as if eager to give him an overdraft and shook hands. Two of the officers had meanwhile put on fishermen's waders while the others carried various pieces of equipment to the water's edge. Lipscomb indicated the spot where the body was believed to be and Greer said, 'OK, lads, go to it.'

Half an hour later the body of Stefan Michalowski lay on dry land. It would have been recovered sooner but for the lumps of iron with which it had been weighted.

Bob turned away as he saw the face. At first it had been coated in mud and slime, but then after photographs had been taken one of the officers had poured water over it from a plastic can. The features were grossly contorted, the eyes, as lifeless as discoloured marbles, were protruding, and his skin was the shade of an over-ripe plum. Round his neck was a piece of sashcord pulled so tight that it had bitten deep into the flesh.

'Asphyxiated by a ligature before being tipped into the lake,' Greer remarked. 'At least, that's how it looks. And just to make sure he didn't come floating to the surface, his murderer weighted the body.' He turned to Bob King. 'Can you definitely say it's the member of your bar staff you knew as Stefan?'

Bob nodded dumbly, too shocked to venture into speech.

'Right, we'll go back to the station and you can tell me everything you know about him. For once, we have a solid starting-point, which isn't always the case with bodies fished out of lakes and rivers.' He glanced across at the house. 'Funny that everyone's away. Or isn't it?'

Chapter Six

In a corporate sense the staff at Snaith and Epton were as intelligent and well-informed as any small group of people you could meet. Robin Snaith read *The Times* every day, Rosa the *Independent* and Stephanie the *Daily Telegraph*, while remaining a supporter of the Labour Party. As for Ben, he stayed with the tabloids, and was therefore, not surprisingly, the most likely member of staff to pick up the gossipy bits about the firm's clients and its ongoing cases.

It was the day after the discovery of Stefan's body that Ben's paper had a short paragraph under the heading, 'Weighted Body in Lake Death'.

'Here we are in the news again, Miss E,' he said cheerfully, indicating the piece with a jab of his finger.

Rosa took the paper and read the item. It ran:

The body of a young man has been dredged from a picturesque lake in the extensive grounds of a house at Briar's End. It had been heavily weighted and had sunk into the soft mud that covered the floor of the lake. It is understood that the owners of the property are away and that the police are anxious to question them. Anyone who has any information is asked to phone Briar's End 54321 where an incident room has been set up . . .

'It doesn't actually mention our client's name or that of the house,' Rosa observed.

'I know, but you're not in any serious doubt about it, are you, Miss E?'

Rosa was not, but didn't wish to jump to conclusions with Ben's alacrity.

'Thanks, Ben,' she said. 'I'll make an enquiry or two. Meanwhile, if you see anything further, let me know.'

'Will do, Miss E,' he said. He reached the door and paused. 'Like me to call the police? I could find out what's what in a tactful sort of way. Might save you embarrassment.'

'It's OK, Ben, I want to think how best to make an approach.'

Rosa had considerable respect for Ben's ingenuity in winkling out information, but felt this was not an occasion to delegate. A few minutes later, she asked Stephanie to get her the Briar's End number.

When a voice answered, Rosa gave her name and said she was the solicitor of Mr and Mrs Henshaw of Riverview Court. This, she considered, was more or less true, though she was herself uncertain whether more *or* less at that particular moment. The voice asked her to hold on and a few moments later a different voice came on the line.

'Detective Sergeant Wells speaking, I understand you're calling about the discovery of a body at Riverview Court, is that right?'

Rosa's question had been answered and Ben's assumption confirmed, but she could hardly say thank you and ring off.

'Yes, I saw something in one of the morning papers and wondered what had happened?'

'Do you have any information that'll assist the police?'

'I'm afraid not.'

'But you did say Mr and Mrs Henshaw were your clients, can you tell us where to find them? So far our enquiries have failed.'

'They have a flat in London — '

'Mr Henshaw's travelling abroad and we've not been able to get in touch with him,' Sergeant Wells broke in. 'Neither his son nor his daughter know his whereabouts.'

'He has an associate . . .'

'Miss Gifford, you mean,' Wells broke in again. 'She's gone with him.'

'Oh.'

'But we're very anxious to trace Mrs Henshaw. Do you have any idea where she is, Miss Epton?'

'No. I've not been in touch with her for quite a while.' She could hardly tell the police she had met her only once previously and the reason for her visit. Equally, she couldn't mention Ralph Henshaw's only visit without being drawn into an awkward interrogation.

36

'Perhaps you could say exactly why you phoned?' Sergeant Wells said in a chilly tone.

'Because of this piece I saw in the paper,' Rosa said and faltered.

'If I may say so, Miss Epton, I get the impression you're on a fishing expedition.'

This was so palpably true that Rosa couldn't immediately think how to reply. Sergeant Wells went on, 'If you *do* receive any information which could help us, you have our number. Meanwhile, I'll log your call.'

It may have been her imagination, but she felt a slight note of menace in his final remark.

The call had not gone well and she reflected that Ben could have handled it better. She had, at least, found out that Ralph and Evelyn Henshaw were missing from home and were being sought by the police. What she had hoped to learn was the police theory surrounding the discovery of Stefan's body in the lake, but his name hadn't even been mentioned.

As she put down the phone, she wondered what to do next. After a few moments' thought, she realised her options were either to dismiss the Henshaws from her mind or to pick up the challenge. As she could no more abandon the Henshaws than a good dog can turn its tail on an enticing scent, the challenge was irresistible. And that meant another visit to Briar's End.

'I agree,' Peter said when she told him that evening of the latest development. 'Bob King is bound to know something and he seemed a helpful sort of guy. Let's drive down on Saturday.'

'I think it might be better to phone him first,' Rosa said slowly. 'It'll be impossible to get him on his own if the pub's crowded. I could call him this evening after closing time. I'm sure he won't mind.'

'Meanwhile, let's go somewhere cheap and cheerful for a meal,' Peter said.

'I thought I was going to be feeding you this evening,' Rosa remarked.

Peter shrugged. 'It'd save you dirtying your pots and pans.'

Rosa was naturally thrifty where Peter was happily extravagant. She knew he had thrown in the word 'cheap' only to undermine her resistance. They had dined at an expensive restaurant the

37

previous evening and she was apt to baulk at any suggestion of eating out two nights running.

In the event they ate cheerfully, but not particularly cheaply, at an Italian restaurant near Rosa's flat. It was after eleven o'clock when they returned.

'I'll phone him now,' Rosa said, pulling the telephone on to her lap. 'Is that the Red Squirrel?' she asked when a female voice answered.

'Yes.'

'Mrs King?'

'Yes.'

'I'm Rosa Epton. A friend and I had lunch at your pub two or three Sundays ago.' She took a deep breath. 'I'm the Henshaws' solicitor.'

'You'd better speak to my husband,' Pauline King broke in brusquely. 'He's been answering more questions about what's happened at Riverview Court than he's been selling pints of beer.'

Rosa heard her shout her husband's name, and after a door slammed in the background he came on the line.

'Bob King speaking, who is that?'

'Rosa Epton . . .' Rosa once more introduced herself.

'Yes, I think I remember. Your friend was oriental-looking.'

'That's right.'

'I suppose you saw me on TV?'

'Not actually, Mr King, but . . .'

'We've been besieged by the media ever since Stefan's body was fished out of the lake.' He paused. 'I take it you knew it was me who found it?'

'The paper I read didn't mention that,' Rosa said in a tone of apology.

'Oh, well, I'd better start at the beginning then . . .'

When, twenty minutes later, Rosa put down the phone her curiosity had been more than satisfied, for Bob King had not spared her a single grisly detail.

In rather less time than it had taken Bob, she passed on what he had told her to Peter, who had sat patiently nursing a drink while she had been glued to the telephone.

'What do I do now, Peter?' she asked in a despairing voice. 'Who's killed who and why? It's like grappling in shadowland.'

'You could get in touch with Christopher Henshaw. He's the only member of the family who's not been in touch with you. It could be he can throw light on his family's curious behaviour, though I suppose murder is more evil than curious,' he added after a pause.

Rosa shivered. Peter is right, she thought. From the moment Evelyn Henshaw arrived in the office and wove her extraordinary tale, a feeling of evil had never been far away. The smell was unmistakably there, even if its precise source lay hidden.

Chapter Seven

A further three days went by and Rosa felt that she was still groping in the dark. With Ben's help she had traced Christopher Henshaw to an address in Hertfordshire. When she called the number, the phone was answered by a confident-sounding girl who announced, 'I am Swedish au pair, you want Mrs Henshaw?'

'Actually, I wanted to speak to Mr Henshaw.'

'He is away and Mrs Henshaw is out for the evening. You wish to leave a message?'

'No, I'll call again later. When will Mr Henshaw be home?'

'I cannot say.'

The reply could be interpreted either as genuine ignorance on the girl's part or in obedience to her employers' instructions not to give information about the family's movements to strangers. Rosa thought the latter was more likely.

She was about to ring off when the girl said, 'Who is it speaking?'

'My name's Rosa Epton and I'm a solicitor.'

'I will tell Mrs Henshaw you called,' she said, making it sound almost a threat.

It was two days after that she received a call out of the blue from Ralph Henshaw. Rosa had by now given up leaving messages for Christopher.

'You've got to help me, Miss Epton,' he said in a tone verging on panic. 'I'm at Briar's End police station. They're saying I killed this young man who was found in our lake. Can you come immediately?'

Rosa had often been required to think fast, but never faster than on this occasion. Her immediate thought was that she couldn't possibly represent both husband and wife, if she believed Evelyn Henshaw's story. In truth, however, she was a long way from believing it and the husband's version of past events didn't

40

postulate the same conflict of interest as his wife's. She was glad now that she had refused to accept the cheque Mrs Henshaw had proffered as a retaining fee, for that removed a major inhibition to her diving headlong into the whirlpool. Challenge and tough options made her adrenalin flow and this one was going to involve her in a way that had seemed impossible a short time before. All this flashed through her mind with speed of light, so that she was able to answer his question without obvious hesitation.

'Yes, I'll be with you in a couple of hours.'

'Bless you, Miss Epton. And thanks.'

Robin Snaith was taking a couple of days off and Peter was flying to Paris that afternoon to confer with an Arab client who took over a floor of the Crillon when he was there. She was glad that Robin was away, as she knew he wouldn't approve of what she was doing. He would have sighed and murmured about the professional ethics aspect and then told her to do what she wanted. Well, she was, but without any preliminary lecture. Moreover, she was confident she would be able to steer a course that didn't land her in trouble. In a sense she would be killing two birds with one stone, representing Mr Henshaw and discovering things about his wife.

It was just after five when she reached Briar's End police station. Whereas on her previous visit it had looked like a small detached house with a neat front garden, with only a blue lamp labelled 'Police' to distinguish it from its neighbours, there were now several vehicles crammed into its drive, one of which was a van with a tall radio aerial.

Rosa parked on the verge outside and walked up to the entrance. The front door was open and she could see a number of shirt-sleeved officers to-ing and fro-ing inside.

One of them noticed her and called out, 'Phil, you've got a customer.'

PC Lipscomb appeared from somewhere at the back and came to the door.

'Can I help you?' he enquired.

'I believe Mr Henshaw is here,' Rosa said.

'Was, not is. He left an hour ago.'

Rosa frowned. 'Can you tell me where he is now?'

'Why do you want to know?'

'I'm his solicitor.'

'Miss Epton?'

'Yes.'

'He said you might be turning up. He's been taken to divisional headquarters at Utwell. Afraid we don't have the facilities here for holding people in custody. Have to lock them in the downstairs loo until they can be fetched. Utwell's only half an hour's drive. You know the way?'

Rosa shook her head.

'Go back to the London road, turn left and then second right. You can't miss it.'

'What's the name of the officer in charge of the case?'

'Detective Chief Inspector Greer.'

'One other thing,' Rosa said as she turned to go. 'Where was my client arrested?'

'At the airport. He'd just flown in from Lisbon.'

The police station at Utwell was easily recognisable, a long, low building with a lot of reinforced glass and the word 'Police' in a blue glass panel over the entrance.

Rosa braced herself before walking in. It was a situation in which the police always had the whip-hand and Rosa was used to being kept waiting indefinitely before being admitted behind the scenes to see a usually dejected client. Other times she was given immediate attention, with a cup of strong tea thrown in and was led to where the client was being held as if she was a special visitor calling on a dying patient. On these occasions she was rightly suspicious.

She had barely taken in her surroundings when a figure came through a frosted-glass-panelled door.

'Miss Epton? I'm Detective Sergeant Wells. If you remember I took your call when you phoned Briar's End police station the other day. I don't recall your mentioning you were Mr Henshaw's solicitor.'

Rosa gave him what she hoped was a disarming smile. 'The truth was that I wasn't absolutely sure at the time whether he was my client or not.'

Sergeant Wells raised a sardonic eyebrow.

'Mr Henshaw has given us the impression he would need you at his side even if he had only parked on a single yellow line.'

'Oh, well, a good many honest people are thrown into confusion when confronted by the police.' She gave a short laugh. 'After all, which of us doesn't have a guilty conscience?'

42

'I for one, Miss Epton, but then I'm not one of your clients.'

Rosa decided that Sergeant Wells must have taken a dislike to her as a result of the earlier phone call when he had accused her of being on a fishing expedition, and that it would be a waste of time trying to obliterate that memory. Latent antagonism toward defending solicitors was obviously part of his armour.

'Has my client been charged?' she asked.

'He's being questioned by Detective Chief Inspector Greer.'

'About the body you fished out of the lake?'

'And about the whereabouts of his wife.'

'Are the two things supposed to be linked?'

He gave her a disdainful look. 'Fishing again, Miss Epton?'

'I spend my life doing it,' Rosa said with a touch of asperity. 'It's part of my job, just as it's a part of yours, so I don't know why you need to adopt such a disparaging tone.'

A few minutes later she was shown into a small interview room. Ralph Henshaw was sitting at a table, which was bare apart from a few sheets of blank paper and an empty coffee cup.

He looked up and his face broke into a craggy smile. 'They brought me here just after I'd told you I was at Briar's End. Bravo for finding me.'

His experience didn't appear to have deflated him, though Rosa thought she perceived a certain wariness in his manner that she had not previously noticed.

'I've not made any damaging admissions to the police, which I'm sure will be a relief to you, Miss Epton. I imagine they'll be releasing me shortly and I'd like you to ginger them up. I want to get out of this dreary hole.'

The note of panic she had detected in his voice when he had phoned and asked her to come to his aid had vanished. Presumably, he was now satisfied the police knew less than he had feared. If that was a fair assumption, Rosa could see that it also had ominous implications.

It was time to ask a few questions of her own.

'I take it Chief Inspector Greer hasn't finished interviewing you?'

'He said something about having a short break, though I can't think what else he wants to ask me.'

'While we're waiting to find out, there are a few things I'd like to know. First and foremost, who is Stefan Michalowski?'

'I'd like to know that too,' he said.

'Are you saying you don't know who he is?'

'That's exactly what I'm saying,' he said in a tone that challenged Rosa to contradict him.

'He worked as a part-time barman at the Red Squirrel in Briar's End.'

'So I'm told.'

'The landlord understood he was a research student and that he was living at Riverview Court.'

'It's news to me. Or was until the police told me.'

'But you must have known about him?'

'I'm telling you I didn't.' He sighed. 'Look, Miss Epton, will you believe me if I tell you I'd not been down to Riverview Court for at least a couple of months. I'd spoken to Evelyn on the phone, but I hadn't seen her. To tell you the truth our marriage was all washed up. Things came to a head over Christmas. I was still fond of her after a fashion and I was especially worried when she disappeared as I knew she was capable of behaving irrationally. That's why I came to see you.'

'You found out that she had been to visit me?'

'Yes.'

'How?'

'I think I told you that I found your name and address on a piece of paper in her handbag. It was a question of putting two and two together and for once making four.'

'But you said just now that you never went back to Riverview Court when you returned on that occasion?'

'So?'

'Where was the handbag?'

'Where?' He frowned for a moment. 'In the flat, of course. She often left things there.' It was as though he had safely navigated a sudden dangerous corner and he gave Rosa a quietly triumphant look.

'Are you still worried about her?'

'What an extraordinary question! Of course I am. More than ever now that the police seem to think her disappearance may be associated with this Polish chap's death.'

'I imagine,' Rosa said, 'that they think you may have killed Stefan because he was flirting with your wife.'

'Yes, there's the suggestion,' he said. 'And a bloody silly one it is.'

After what Rosa herself had witnessed, it didn't seem all that silly. He had obviously denied all knowledge of Stefan's existence as a first line of defence. Any admission to the contrary would have been offering the police a powerful piece of leverage. On the other hand, it was a bold lie, if lie it was, and he must be confident it couldn't be disproved.

'I suppose you've heard nothing further from my wife?' he said, breaking in on Rosa's thoughts.

'Not a thing.'

'I wish to God I knew what had happened to her,' he said with a note of vehemence.

If he genuinely didn't know, Rosa could understand that he would be anxious to find out. What she was much less certain about was his motive.

'Your daughter called me after your visit to the office,' Rosa remarked, loosing off a trial balloon.

'What did she want?' he asked suspiciously.

'She didn't think anyone should be too worried about your wife's disappearance. She suggested it was just a piece of play-acting . . .'

'I hope so,' he broke in. 'I think I told you that Anthea and Evelyn had never got on.'

'I was going to add,' Rosa observed, 'that that was before the body was found in your lake.'

'I don't think that will have changed Anthea's mind. What else did she say to you?'

'Nothing. Her only concern seemed to be that nobody should waste time puzzling over what had happened to Mrs Henshaw. Tell me, was your wife given to drama? Some people attract it like magnets. And if it isn't there to be attracted, they create it.'

'Outwardly Evelyn was a conventional middle-aged woman . . .'

'But?' Rosa prompted, when he stopped abruptly.

'What are you getting at, Miss Epton?' he said, giving her a sudden suspicious stare.

'Did she alter her looks or change her style according to her moods, for example?'

'Yes, but not in any dramatic sense.'

'Used she to give herself a fresh hairstyle from time to time? A lot of women do.'

He pursed his lips. 'I suppose so. I'm afraid I didn't always notice.'

No wonder your marriage went on the rocks, Rosa thought to herself.

'What was the colour of her hair?' she asked.

'Ordinary . . . something between blonde and brunette.'

'Was she ever ash blonde?'

He looked startled. 'I'm sure I'd have noticed,' he said. 'No, you can take it from me, she was just mouse brown.' He paused. 'Well, you saw her, so you tell me what was the colour of her hair.'

'She was wearing a wide-brimmed hat when she came to my office. It was difficult to gauge the colour of her hair.'

'Aren't we straying some way from the reason for your visit here, which was to protect my interests while I was interviewed?' His tone carried a note of annoyance.

'From what you've told me, the interviewing may be over. For the time being.'

'Then perhaps you'd go and find somebody and demand my release.'

'And?'

'And what?'

'Because they let you go today doesn't mean the matter's over. The police are investigating a murder, a murder on your property, not to mention your wife's disappearance, so they're bound to want to see you again.'

'I suppose so,' he said grudgingly.

'It's a certainty. What's less certain is whether I represent you next time.'

'You're not going to desert me, are you?' he said in a complete change of tone. 'I appreciate your being here and I want you to go on representing me while this whole affair is being cleared up. I don't want my own solicitor involved in this.'

Rosa wished she could foresee what the clearing-up might involve, but no crystal ball was going to help her do that. It was a bizarre case, but one which intrigued her more than most. A conflict of loyalty might yet arise, but until it did she thought she could properly act for Mr Henshaw, while not forgetting his wife's curious instructions to her and being mindful that her husband would see the advantage of getting his wife's solicitor on his side.

The door opened abruptly and Detective Chief Inspector Greer appeared. He introduced himself to Rosa and gave her the sort of smile that bank managers give to dubious customers.

'You're free to leave, Mr Henshaw,' he said. 'Meanwhile, our enquiries will continue and I shall want to see you again later. You're not planning any further trips abroad in the near future, I hope?'

'I often have to travel at short notice,' Henshaw said.

'Not such short notice that you can't get in touch with me first, I hope. We may *also* want to see you at short notice,' he added pointedly. He stood aside to let them leave. 'And you will let us know immediately, won't you, if you have any news of your wife?'

Rosa had not looked forward to having Ralph Henshaw's company on the drive back to London, but felt obliged to offer him a lift. After all, the police had whisked him to Briar's End and on to Utwell from Heathrow and she imagined his car would, at best, still be in one of the airport carparks.

She was both surprised and relieved when he said, 'Thanks, but I'm all right for transport. One of the officers who came to the airport drove it for me so I can head straight for the flat.'

'Was Miss Gifford on the plane with you?'

'Fortunately, she flew back yesterday. It was bad enough being led away in front of all the other passengers, I wouldn't have wanted her to be involved.'

A note of anger had again surfaced and Rosa guessed that his temper simmered permanently at the end of a short fuse.

'I'll keep in touch with you,' he said, as they parted outside the station.

As she drove home, Rosa tried to marshal her thoughts and reassess her opinion of Ralph Henshaw. He seemed to regard Stefan's death as more of a nuisance than anything else. He showed no sign of regret, let alone sorrow, and appeared to see the discovery of a body on his property as he might that of an abandoned car which had run into his gate-post.

It was difficult to believe he was as ignorant of events as he professed. But then, of course, he was unaware of what Rosa and Peter had witnessed on their Sunday outing to Briar's End. Rosa decided that, for the time being, it was a card she would keep up her sleeve.

It was shortly after she and her client had left the station and gone their separate ways that DCI Greer called a conference.

'We're going to dredge that lake,' he announced to his assembled officers. 'It's my feeling there could be another body there.'

Chapter Eight

As soon as Rosa arrived in the office the next morning she called Bob King at the Red Squirrel. It was just after nine o'clock. She hoped he hadn't overslept and that it wouldn't be answered by a tetchy Pauline. It was with relief that she heard Bob's voice on the line.

'I should be grateful if you could tell me a bit more about Stefan,' she said after a brief exchange of niceties.

'I've told the police everything. What is it exactly you want to know?'

'How long had he been in the village?'

'Not much more than a month, if that. I've got the date written down somewhere if I can find it. Do you want to hold on while I have a look? There's so much paper lying around, I can never lay my hands on anything. Trouble is,' he went on plaintively, 'Pauline normally keeps my desk tidy, but she hasn't had time recently . . .'

Rosa got the impression that the temperamental Pauline was being less than usually cooperative. In any event she wasn't interested in the precise date Stefan had begun work as a part-time barman.

'Did he just come in and ask for a job one day?' she broke in.

'Yes; said he was a student staying up at Riverview Court and was looking for a temporary job to help his finances. It so happened that one of my bar staff, Pete Reeper from the neighbouring village, had gone into hospital and so I was ready to take someone on.'

'Did he have any experience?'

'He said he'd worked in a bar previously. Anyway, I could see he was a quick worker and he had no difficulty mastering the till. He also had a nice personality.'

'Did you think it odd that he was living at Riverview Court?'

'Not at the time. It's a huge house and I thought maybe he was being given board and lodging – well, lodging, anyway – in return for his keeping an eye on the place.'

'Did you ever see him and Mrs Henshaw together?'

'Mrs Henshaw never came near the Red Squirrel.'

'What about in the village together?'

'No, never.'

'Did Stefan talk about Mrs Henshaw?'

'Not to me, he didn't.'

'I wonder if he did to any of your customers?'

After a slight pause Bob went on. 'As you can imagine, there's been a good deal of speculation among my regulars, but it seems that young Stefan, friendly as he was, didn't give much away about himself. He did tell one customer that he'd been living in London before coming to Briar's End.'

'Did he say why he moved?'

'I think he just wanted to be somewhere quieter. Somewhere he could do his studying without the distraction of a big city.' He paused. 'He also told a customer that his parents had gone back to Poland, but he didn't know whether they'd stay there. He'd been born in England and had been to Poland once on a holiday, but to him it was a foreign country, though he could speak a bit of the language.'

'Was there ever any suggestion that he was Mrs Henshaw's toy boy?'

'Don't think anyone gave it that much thought.'

I bet they did, Rosa reflected. 'Didn't you?' she asked.

'What went on up at Riverview Court was none of my business. I only ever saw Mrs Henshaw driving through the village and I've not spoken more than half a dozen words to her since I've been here.'

'Is there anyone else in the village who might be able to give me further information?'

'You could try Mrs Santer. She worked for Mrs Henshaw, cleaning and that sort of thing.'

'Was she working there when Stefan took up residence?'

'She was there right up to recent events.'

'Can you tell me where to find her?'

'You'll find her in the telephone book. I don't know her address offhand.'

It was apparent from his tone that Mrs Santer was no particular friend of Bob King. Or maybe he just didn't wish to share the limelight with her, even though the police would certainly have interviewed her.

Rosa thanked him for his help and added that she looked forward to her next drink in his pub.

Glancing at her watch, she decided she would have to dash in order to get to court in time.

'I hope to be back in a couple of hours, Steph,' she said on her way out. 'Meanwhile, could you find me the phone number of a Mrs Santer who lives in Briar's End?'

'Santa as in Santa Claus?' Stephanie enquired.

'No, as in banter and canter.'

In the event her case never came on, her client having gone on the run, and she was back in the office soon after eleven o'clock.

'There are two Santers in Briar's End,' Stephanie announced. 'N. Santer and V. Santer. Which one do you want?'

'I've no idea, Steph. My hope is that there's someone at one of the numbers who works, or used to work, at Riverview Court. Do you think you could find out?'

'Male or female?' Stephanie enquired briskly.

'Female.'

'I'll see what I can do.'

Rosa went along to her office and had barely unpacked her briefcase when her phone gave one of its short, imperious buzzes.

'Mrs Nellie Santer is the person you want,' Stephanie said. 'Shall I try her number?'

Rosa held on while the connection was being made and was rewarded when a female voice came on the line.

'Is that Mrs Santer?' she enquired.

'This is Mrs Santer speaking,' the voice replied with a touch of primness.

'My name's Rosa Epton, Mrs Santer, and I'm a solicitor acting for Mr and Mrs Henshaw.' She reckoned Mrs Santer would be unlikely to question the doubtful ethics of her representing both husband and wife. 'I understand you worked at Riverview Court?'

'That's right.'

'Did you know the young man who lodged there and who was found drowned in the lake?'

'Stefan, you mean? I used to see him about and he'd say hello, but that's about all.'

'I suppose you used to clean his quarters?'

'No, he always did that himself. I never went near his bedroom.'

'How did he and Mrs Henshaw get on?'

'She was the lady of the house and he was a lodger who had a room above the coach-house.'

'It seems odd that Mrs Henshaw would have taken in lodgers. She can't have done it for the money.'

'I got the impression she knew the family and did it out of the goodness of her heart.'

'May I ask you a personal question, Mrs Santer, did you like Mrs Henshaw?'

'She never did me any harm.'

Rosa realised from the evasive nature of the reply that there was no point in pursuing the question.

'Have you worked for her for a long time?'

'About two years. Mrs Davies, who was her previous help, died suddenly. She'd worked for Mrs Henshaw for about fifteen years. She thought highly of the first Mr Henshaw.'

'Used you to meet the present Mr Henshaw?'

'Hardly ever saw him. He used to come down at weekends when I wasn't there. I met his daughter once or twice. Probably shouldn't say this, but she struck me as a bossy sort of girl.'

'I gather she didn't get on with her stepmother.'

'Mrs Henshaw was a funny woman in some ways.'

'What ways?' Rosa asked, hopefully.

'She never liked me to go into her bedroom. Said she preferred to look after it herself. Always made her own bed, she did.'

'What about when Mr Henshaw was in the house?'

'Since I worked there, he's always had his own bedroom. I used to keep that clean.'

'So they didn't sleep together?'

'No.'

'In what other ways was Mrs Henshaw a funny woman?'

'She could be different things to different people, if you get my meaning. She could get into terrible moods which would last for days. No wonder her husband spent so little time down here. Mind you, she never did me any harm.'

'Used she to have many visitors at the house?'

'Visitors to stay, you mean? Not since she remarried.'

'Did she have any close friends?'

'There was a Mrs Upjohn she used to talk to on the phone

quite a lot. I think she was a widow. She lived somewhere outside London. Bromley direction.'

'Did you ever meet her?'

'No. She never came down to Briar's End while I was there. I don't think she drove a car. But she and Mrs Henshaw used to have lunch together in London.'

'It sounds as if she led a rather lonely life,' Rosa remarked.

'She did quite a lot of painting,' Mrs Santer said vaguely. 'They weren't the sort of pictures I'd want to hang on my walls, but they occupied her.'

'What sort of pictures were they?' Rosa asked with curiosity.

'Coloured shapes and things like that. Personally, I like a nice bit of scenery, but that wasn't her style.'

'Did she seem worried or upset before she went away?'

'Not that I noticed. Sometimes I didn't see her. She'd be upstairs in her bedroom or in the room where she used to paint.'

'Which room was that?'

'It was above the coach-house and looked out over the garden.'

'Near where Stefan slept?'

'Yes.'

'Do you have any idea what's happened to her?'

'If you want my opinion she's playing up.'

'Playing up?' Rosa echoed. 'How do you mean?'

'Like a child drawing attention to itself.'

'You don't think she had anything to do with Stefan's death?'

'Stefan was a foreigner,' Mrs Santer observed darkly. Rosa waited for her to explain her enigmatic comment, which she eventually did. 'It's my guess he was killed by one of his own people. Someone who was looking for vengeance. Poles can be very hot-blooded,' she added, as if that clinched her view.

'Do you have any evidence to support what you're saying?' Rosa asked.

'It's what Stefan himself told me. He said his father was very angry that he wouldn't go back to Poland with them and told him he was betraying his roots.'

It was obviously a theory you either took or left. Rosa left it and shortly afterwards rang off after thanking Mrs Santer for talking to her. She now knew a bit more about Evelyn Henshaw, but not much and certainly nothing that explained what had happened to her. She was about to go out for a cup of coffee and a sandwich when she decided to call Mrs Upjohn and follow up that line of enquiry. There was only one Upjohn in the telephone directory who fitted the description and Rosa dialled the number on her outside phone.

'Is that Mrs Upjohn?' she asked when a female voice answered.

'Vera Upjohn speaking. Have you called to make an appointment, dear?'

Rosa tried in the split second available to envisage what sort of appointment one might seek with a lady who spoke in a tone of such exaggerated refinement, but failed.

'I understand you were a friend of Mrs Henshaw and often used to meet her for lunch?'

'I don't know where you got that from, dear, I never had lunch with her in my life. I don't have lunch.'

'But you were a friend of Mrs Henshaw?'

'Of course I was. Poor Evie, I knew something dreadful was going to happen and I did warn her. I just hope she took my warning. Are you ringing with news?'

'For news, rather than with it,' Rosa said, looking for something to clutch at in suddenly uncharted waters. 'I gather you used to see her quite often?'

'Yes, dear, she'd been one of my regulars for years. She first visited me after her friend went missing and was found drowned. I just hope it's not what's happened to Evie.'

'Forgive me, Mrs Upjohn, I'm not exactly clear for what purpose she visited you?'

'For readings, of course, dear. I read cards and palms. I also do a bit of phrenology. I have genuine powers, I'm not one of your end-of-pier charlatans. And I don't dress like a gypsy out of *Carmen*,' she added emphatically.

'You say that you knew something dreadful was going to happen to her,' Rosa said cautiously. 'Was that because of something she told you?'

'It was my last reading of the cards, dear. It was like seeing huge black clouds in the sky which tell you a storm is approaching.'

'And you warned her?'

'Of course I did, dear, but Evie didn't always listen, even though she continued coming back to me.'

'How did she react to your warning?'

'Very seriously.'

'Did she express any fears of her own? About her safety or well being, for example?'

53

'She didn't have to, dear, I could see it in the cards.'

'Did the cards give any indication as to what might happen to her?'

'You probably don't understand, dear, they're not like a telephone answering-machine. They can only be read by an expert and they need interpretation.'

'And how did you interpret your last reading for Mrs Henshaw?' Rosa enquired earnestly.

'That her life was about to take a sudden turn; that things were about to change dramatically and would never be the same again.'

'Could it not have been that it was about to take a turn for the better—'

Mrs Upjohn tut-tutted. 'I've told you, dear, I could only see storm clouds ahead of her.'

'Did she ever mention a young man named Stefan to you?'

'I'm not sure,' Mrs Upjohn said. 'Who is Stefan?'

'He lodged at her house in Briar's End.'

'I told her more than once that unless she was absolutely frank with me, my readings were bound to suffer. Why are you telling me about Stefan, dear?'

'I just wondered if she had ever mentioned him.'

'Well, I can't remember,' Mrs Upjohn said evasively.

'Did she talk about her husband?'

'Oh, yes, she talked about him all right. And about his mistress.'

'Mrs Santer, who was her cleaning woman, told me that she believed you were Mrs Henshaw's closest friend,' Rosa remarked.

'That's nice, dear, but it doesn't mean that we ever had lunch together. I'm afraid that was one of Evie's little deceptions. Probably didn't want anyone to know that she used to come and consult me. And between you and me, dear, she was always on the phone. So much that I used to add something to her bill for the time we spent talking.'

'Do you have any idea what's happened to her?' Rosa asked, aware that their conversation had to finish sometime.

Mrs Upjohn breathed heavily down the line.

'It all depends on whether she managed to free herself from her environment before it was too late. If she did, she may be in hiding. If not, I fear the worst.'

Rosa reflected that it could have been put more simply. Either she's alive or she's not. It was a viewpoint that couldn't be faulted, but was equally unhelpful in its Delphic quality.

'If she's in hiding, would you expect her to get in touch with you?' Rosa now asked.

'Of course, dear. I know poor Evie'll need my help – provided she's still with us.'

Chapter Nine

'Somebody must be able to tell us who Stefan Michalowski was,' Chief Inspector Greer said in an aggrieved tone. 'He can't just have sprung from nowhere and have departed this life at Riverview Court without someone knowing all about him. And if someone does know all about him, why doesn't he or she come forward and tell us?'

'Presumably Mrs Henshaw could,' Detective Sergeant Wells observed.

Greer glanced at him. 'If you can't be more helpful than that, go and pick buttercups.' He gazed across the lawn at Riverview Court where the lake was being dredged by a team of officers who were working behind screens which had been erected to frustrate prying eyes. 'I'm sorry, Keith, I didn't mean to snap, but I've never known a case with so many elusive threads. Tell me again exactly what the polytechnic said about him.'

'That he was a post-graduate student who worked from home and wasn't required to put in more than the occasional appearance. He already had his BA.'

'Sounds a curious arrangement to me,' Greer broke in.

'It seems St Giles' Polytechnic has a lot of what you might call absentee students, sir,' Wells said, and continued: 'His supervisor said he was a pleasant youth, but didn't play any part in the social activities on offer. He didn't have any close friends . . .'

'And yet he got on well with the customers of the Red Squirrel,' Greer observed.

'You can get on well with people without making bosom friends of them, sir.'

'I'm aware of that, Keith, but there must have been somebody in whom he confided,' Greer said in an exasperated tone. '*And* how the hell did he get to know Mrs Henshaw . . . and where the hell is she?' He glanced sourly at the placid waters of the lake where three officers up to their thighs in water were probing with long steel rods. 'If she is in the lake, her body's probably near the edge. It would have been tilted in, just as his was. You don't row boats out into the middle of a lake to tip a body overboard, unless you're strong. And *have* a boat. There's no sign of any boat, and if she'd been dumped in the Thames, the tides would have washed her up by now.' He turned back to Sergeant Wells, who was standing patiently at his side. 'How many addresses did this polytechnic place have for him?'

'Like I said, sir, just the one in Shepherd's Bush. Mrs Clifford – incidentally she's Polish by birth, but married a man from Trinidad who died last year – Mrs Clifford lets out rooms to students and Stefan lodged in her house for eighteen months. He departed about a year ago, but didn't leave a forwarding address though he looked in from time to time to see if there was any mail for him.'

'Why didn't he say where he was moving to?'

Wells shrugged. 'I don't know, sir, but he didn't. He doesn't seem to have received many letters, anyway.'

'But he never told anyone at the polytechnic he'd left Mrs Clifford's house?'

'Apparently not.'

'And he turned up in Briar's End a month or so before his death?'

'Yes.'

'So where was he living between leaving Mrs Clifford and arriving here?'

'Search me, sir.'

'I'd sooner not. But somebody must know and we're going to find out.'

A dour silence descended, broken eventually by Sergeant Wells.

'Doesn't it strike you as odd, sir, that Mr Henshaw professes complete ignorance of Stefan?'

'It's not the only thing that strikes me as odd. Why was Stefan living here, for example, so far from the college?' He paused. 'Though I suppose his ignorance isn't totally implausible, given that he and his wife seem to have gone their separate ways and that he largely kept away from Briar's End.'

'Even so, sir, I'd have expected him to have at least been aware of Stefan's existence.'

Greer nodded gloomily. 'This case is chock-full of unfulfilled expectations.'

'Do you think Mr Henshaw's first wife's death has any bearing on what's happened?'

'I'll tell you in the morning. I've got the file out and propose reading it this evening.' He stared at the figures patiently exploring the floor of the lake. 'Come on, Mrs Henshaw,' he exhorted, 'give us a break.'

But no break came and as light began to fail the operation was called off.

'She could still be down there somewhere,' Greer observed stubbornly, 'it's the logical scenario. Husband discovers wife and toy boy carrying on behind his back, murders them both and heaves their weighted bodies into the lake. But for that nosy dog, toy boy would never have been found and the assumption would have been that Mrs H and Stefan Michalowski had gone off together.' He glanced at Sergeant Wells. 'You can't fault that for logic, can you?'

'No-o,' Wells said in a far from convinced tone, and then added: 'One presumes that the murders – or, at any rate, Stefan's – were committed in the house, and that he was then transported to the lake . . .'

'There are a couple of wheelbarrows in the coach-house yard and it's my bet that one of those was put to use. As for the weights that kept the body down, there's a mass of scrap iron in the corner stable.'

Sergeant Wells frowned. 'If it was Mr Henshaw – or whoever it was for that matter – how did he manage to kill both of them without number two raising the alarm?'

'I'm not suggesting they lined up for execution,' Greer said. 'In fact they were almost certainly killed separately with the second victim being unaware of what had happened to the first.'

Wells nodded thoughtfully. 'Could be,' he said in a cautious tone.

'Can you think of anything better?'

'Not at the moment, sir.'

'It's my further belief that Stefan whatsit was taken completely by surprise. The cord was looped over his head from behind and pulled tight before he could begin to struggle. If I'm right about that, it points to his having known the person who killed him and to his not having suspected anything.' He paused and his jaw

58

dropped. 'That means it could have been Mrs Henshaw. In that event she's not lying at the bottom of the lake at all, but is more likely to be sunning herself on a foreign beach kitted out in everything from a trendy bikini to a brand new identity.'

'She didn't sound the sort of person to wear a bikini, sir,' Sergeant Wells remarked. 'And what motive would she have had for killing Stefan?'

'The age-old motive of a woman scorned. Her boyfriend had become bored with her and was setting his sights elsewhere.'

'We've no evidence of that, sir.'

Greer sighed. 'We've very little evidence of anything, Keith, except of a brutal murder, full stop. In default of forensic being able to suggest where the murder took place, it's my guess our Polish friend was killed in one of the disued stables. Because he was asphyxiated one wouldn't expect to find blood, and because the stables are an untidy mess, one isn't going to be able to detect signs of a scuffle or anything of that nature. Anyway, the murderer could have had plenty of time to clear up after he'd disposed of the body. Or bodies.'

'Put like that, sir, I can't see Mrs Henshaw having had the strength to strangle a healthy young man, manhandle his body into a barrow and wheel it across fifty yards of lawn to the lake where she tipped it into the water.'

'You've left something out.'

'What's that, sir?'

'The bits of scrap iron she stuffed in his pockets,' Greer said with a faint smile. 'But who's to say she didn't have an accomplice?' Before Sergeant Wells could answer, the chief inspector went on, 'The one element this murderer had on his side, which is denied to most, was time. After the deed was done he had all the time in the world to make his getaway.'

'It certainly looks as if Mrs Henshaw took a suitcase of clothes with her.'

'Or her murderer staged things to make it appear that she had,' Greer observed in a wry tone. He went on, 'Whether Mrs Henshaw is a murderess or a victim is a matter of speculation for the moment, but I know one thing for sure, I didn't take to her husband. Not one little bit, I didn't. When we have something further to go on, we'll really put him through the shredder.'

'And I didn't like that woman solicitor of his,' Wells said with a sniff.

'Rosa Epton? She's certainly tougher than she looks, but I don't think she cheats.'

'Don't worry, I'm not taking any chances with her. Anyway, I don't believe in fraternising with the other side.'

Chief Inspector Greer felt quite ready to fraternise with anyone if it would help him solve the case.

Chapter Ten

Rosa and her partner Robin Snaith frequently went days without catching more than a glimpse of one another. She would be in court and he in the office and vice versa.

He had recently been defending a doctor who was up before the General Medical Council's disciplinary committee on a charge of professional misconduct. The case had troubled him considerably and the burden of representing someone whose professional career was at stake had oppressed him. In the five days that the hearing lasted, Rosa had seen him only once. He was coming in one evening as she was leaving and he had looked grimly preoccupied.

It was therefore with delight that she observed his relaxed expression when he came into her office on the day after she had been down to Utwell.

'Over, is it?' she enquired.

'Yes, they let him off.'

'Well done. You must feel relieved.'

'I do. I always believed the allegation was false, but I was far from sure I'd be able to persuade the committee. Fortunately my bloke turned out to be a better witness than I'd expected and the complainant was so obviously a vindictive woman that even I was confident in the end.' He paused. 'But there's always such an alarming element of touch and go in our job. Trying to achieve justice is like rummaging around in a bran tub.' He gave Rosa a sardonic smile. 'Though one has to admit that most miscarriages of justice involve guilty persons being acquitted. And don't start telling me it's infinitely better that ten guilty men should go free than that one innocent person should be convicted. I've always been cynical about that piece of pious flannel. Anyway, how are things going in the Henshaw world?'

Rosa brought him up to date with everything that had happened and waited to hear what he would say.

'It sounds as if you could have impaled yourself on the horns of a professional dilemma. Mr and Mrs Henshaw are in obvious conflict and yet you've accepted instructions from both of them. How are you going to talk yourself out of that?'

'I'm not sure that I do act for Mrs Henshaw. I've not had a word from her since her one and only visit to the office and I've not accepted any money from her. Thank goodness.'

'Just as well you refused her offer of a down-payment,' Robin observed.

'I did so for the very reason that I hadn't made up my mind how to handle the matter. I thought she'd probably be in touch with me again, but she hasn't been.'

'What do you think has happened to her?'

Rosa gave a helpless shrug. 'I haven't the slightest idea. She may be alive, she may be dead. All I do know is that I'm less and less inclined to believe the story she told me when she called here. Parts of it may be true, but I suspect those are the parts that don't matter. She and Ralph Henshaw can't both have told the truth about his first wife's death, with each in effect accusing the other.'

'Neither of them sound particularly creditworthy,' Robin remarked, 'so what are you going to do?'

'I'll get in touch with Ralph Henshaw and suggest we have a conference. Then before we meet I'll make a list of pertinent questions to put to him.'

'Supposing, in the mean time, that Mrs Henshaw pops up and says she's gone into hiding because she fears for her life, what'll you say to her?'

'I'll have a few pertinent questions for her as well, the first being who was Stefan Michalowski and what was he doing at Riverview Court?'

Robin looked at her with a thoughtful expression. 'I wish you luck. I think you're going to need it. Incidentally, have you had any contact with Frances Gifford?'

'Not yet.'

'She's not been in touch with you?'

'I imagine she's deliberately staying in the background, but I have it in mind to call her.'

'She'll probably give you another slant on life with the Henshaws,' he observed wryly. 'Doesn't Mrs Henshaw have any family you could approach?'

'Only a sister who lives near Nice. Mrs Henshaw said they weren't close and did little more than exchange Christmas cards.'

'Nevertheless she might have heard from her sister in the present circumstances.'

'Ralph Henshaw told me he'd phoned his sister-in-law, but that she wasn't at home. I gather she works for an art dealer and does a lot of travelling.'

Robin got up and moved toward the door.

'Take a day off from thinking about the Henshaws and come down to lunch on Sunday. If Peter's free, bring him with you.'

'That sounds a nice idea,' Rosa said. 'I'm seeing Peter this evening and I'll ask him.'

'Is he still gallivanting about the world on behalf of wealthy clients?'

'More than ever.'

Robin gazed out of Rosa's window at the back of the warehouse which filled the view.

'I'd still sooner be in our work,' he said.

'So would Peter. One sheikh is very much like another, whereas our clients and their problems are as varied as liquorice allsorts.'

Rosa always enjoyed visiting the Snaiths, who lived about twenty miles west of London. She liked Susan who was Robin's cheerful, easy-going wife and had known the two children since they were babies. She knew, too, that Peter got on well with the family, and that Katie, in particular, who was now twelve, regarded him as a real fun person. David, who was two years older than his sister, was always impressed by Peter's knowledge of the current pop scene, something in which his father couldn't even pretend to be interested.

When she met Peter that evening and mentioned the invitation, he said great. Later he said, 'Why don't we fly down to the south of France the weekend after next and look up Mrs Henshaw's sister? Who knows, we might bump into Mrs Henshaw herself.'

'It's a long way to go on such a tenuous hope,' Rosa said doubtfully.

'That's settled then,' Peter said firmly. 'I'll make reservations tomorrow.'

'But anything may have happened by the weekend after next,' Rosa protested.

'Doesn't matter if it has, the south of France is still a nice place for a weekend,' Peter replied cheerfully.

Rosa invariably put up initial resistance to his more extravagant suggestions, only to succumb when she remembered how much she had enjoyed all the previous occasions they had taken off together. Her resistance, which was born of natural thriftiness (even when somebody else would pick up the bill) plus a sense of caution, was never long a match for Peter's grandiose plans.

At eight o'clock the next evening Rosa pressed the front door bell of a renovated mews house not far from the river in Chiswick. It reacted with a brisk and officious sound which she could clearly hear on her side of the door. It didn't waste time being melodious and was what Rosa would have expected if she had given it any thought.

The door opened and a tall girl stood looking at her without any sign of pleasure.

'Miss Henshaw?'

'Yes.'

'I'm Rosa Epton.'

The girl frowned for a moment. 'Of course, you're the solicitor I spoke to on the phone. Is there something you want?'

'I'd like to have a talk with you.'

'Well, all right, I suppose you'd better come in,' she said with a minimum of grace.

Anthea Henshaw was not only tall, but had a long neck. Her dark hair was cut with geometric precision with a straight fringe in front and near bob at the back. She was wearing a tailored pair of black slacks and a black silk blouse with a high collar. She wasn't pretty, but definitely had style, Rosa reflected as she followed her up the stairs which led straight from the front door. She made a casual movement to close a door at the top, but not before Rosa had noticed a large double bed. The sitting-room overlooked the mews at the front and was decorated entirely in black and white. Black leather sofa and chairs and a white carpet. The walls were white with black polka dots. A large abstract painting on the wall that faced the window consisted of black and white shapes and in their centre a sinister-looking crimson orb that gave the impression of being about to burst. A gleaming sports trophy stood between two black and white photographs on the mantelpiece; they showed Anthea, alone on the river, sculling during Henley week. She had obviously once been a very successful rower.

Anthea Henshaw sat down in one of the black leather armchairs and left Rosa to follow suit.

'What do you wish to talk about?' she asked in a tone which combined resignation with arrogance.

'Your father and your stepmother.'

'I think it's disgraceful that the police detained my father at the airport the other day. It was quite unnecessary and extremely heavy-handed. But then we know that the police can behave with as much finesse as rampant rhinoceri when they choose.' She switched her gaze from the window to Rosa. 'My father told me he sent for you.'

'It wasn't unreasonable for the police to have wanted to question him,' Rosa said, determined not to show her pique at the observation she had been sent for. 'After all, the body of a murdered man had been discovered in the lake at Riverview Court and your stepmother had disappeared.'

'They'd do better looking for her than harassing my unfortunate father. I told you on the phone that she was at best an unstable neurotic.'

'And at worst?'

'A grade-A bitch.'

'Have you always disliked her?'

'Yes.'

'Have you any idea where she could be?'

'None.'

'Not even if it would help your father?'

She gave Rosa a cold, angry look. 'Of course I want to help my father.' She paused and added, 'Even if it means finding out what's happened to his wife.'

'He seems genuinely worried about her.'

'Of course he is. Not because he loves her, but because nobody likes to be involved in the sort of mystery her disappearance has created. She's done it on purpose. A typically spiteful and malicious act.'

'You don't believe her disappearance is related to the death of Stefan Michalowski?'

'I've no idea. I choose not to think about it.'

'Have you any knowledge of him?'

'No.'

'That's what your father said too, and yet somebody must know who he was and what he was doing staying in the house?'

'You'd better ask his wife if and when she turns up.'

'It's only one of a good many questions she'll have to answer,' Rosa said. 'Meanwhile, don't you agree it's an extraordinary state of affairs? Your stepmother vanishes and the body of a young man is fished out of the lake and there isn't anyone who purports to know a thing about him?'

Anthea Henshaw gave a shrug of indifference.

'It may be your job to speculate, but it's not mine. I've made it clear what I think of my stepmother and I don't mind if I never see or hear anything of her again.'

'Do you get on with your father's partner, Frances Gifford?'

'Fran's all right. She has both her feet on the ground and knows what she wants out of life. And she's good at her job.'

Rosa didn't enquire whether that included being her father's mistress.

'I'd like to interview her. Do you think your father would object?'

'Why not ask him?'

'It seemed more tactful to take soundings first.'

Anthea's features managed a small smile, though it didn't extend to her eyes, which remained as clear and chilly as a cat's.

'I'm afraid you must sound elsewhere, Miss Epton,' she said, glancing rather obviously at her watch.

Rosa decided to take the hint. There was nothing to be gained by extending her visit. She had learnt quite a lot about Anthea Henshaw just by meeting her and seeing where she lived.

'I won't accompany you downstairs. Slam the front door behind you,' Anthea said.

Rosa saw that the bedroom door had swung slightly open again. Enough to reveal the large double bed she had noticed earlier.

There was certainly no evidence of a live-in boyfriend, but that didn't mean anything.

As she drove home Rosa pondered which way to turn next in the maze the Henshaws had lured her into. Though Christopher Henshaw seemed to be outside the immediate circle of deceit and intrigue, she still wished to meet him. By the time she did he would have been briefed by his father and sister about what to say and, more likely, what not to say, but she felt it important to form her own view about each of the members of the Henshaw clan. And that included Frances Gifford.

It so happened that not long after Rosa got back to her flat that evening, the lady in question was driving into Briar's End. She had taken a circuitous route to avoid the main village street, and parked well away from the padlocked gates of Riverview Court. Walking carefully up to the gates, she made sure no one was around before producing a key from the pocket of her suede jacket. The police and Scene of Crime officers would have departed with their evidence long since, but she couldn't be too careful. Closing the gates as quietly as possible she then walked the remaining fifty yards up to the house.

Though she had not seen a soul since driving past the road sign which announced Briar's End, it was still necessary to take every precaution. But she had now done the trickiest part, which involved parking the car and unlocking the main gate, and was confident she had not been detected. It was too chilly an evening for even the most ardent young lovers to have been out sampling the alfresco delights of damp moss and dripping trees. Rain had unforeseen blessings.

She produced two further keys and let herself in. She was carrying a flashlight and used its beam to get her bearings, being careful not to direct it near the windows.

Reaching the top of the stairs she paused to readjust her ears to the silence. Apart from the occasional creak that all old houses are prone to, which is their own sort of tummy rumble, there wasn't a sound. She tiptoed across the landing and entered Evelyn Henshaw's bedroom. The first thing she did was to draw the curtains across the windows just in case anyone should spot the dancing beam of her flashlight from the lane that bounded the estate at its farthest limit, the same lane along which Bacchus and his master had been exercising when the dog broke away and entered the garden.

Evelyn Henshaw's dressing-table stood between two high windows, and once she had drawn the curtains she knelt in front of it and opened the shallow top drawer on the right-hand side. Reaching to the very back, she felt the key she was looking for and withdrew her arm. Next she turned her attention to a small writing desk set against a wall running back from the left-hand window. It had a sloping front of red tooled leather backed by four oblong drawers, two upper and two lower. Three of the drawers opened at her touch, but the bottom right-hand one was locked. She quickly opened it, however, with the key she had taken from the dressing-table drawer. She directed the beam of her flashlight into its interior and let out a quiet sigh.

Ten minutes later she was leaving Briar's End as surreptitiously as she had arrived. In her handbag was the object of her visit. A flat, black notebook with a label on its front carrying the inscription:

Evelyn Henshaw
Private Journal

Chapter Eleven

Rosa woke up with a start from the dream she had been having in which Ralph and Evelyn Henshaw each had hold of one of her arms and were tugging in opposite directions. They had both shrunk in size and she felt she should be able to shake them off quite easily. But the more vigorously she shook her arms the tighter they clung to her. It was at this point she woke up and discovered that one of her arms was dangling over the side of the bed while the other was clutching a corner of the pillow. She lay back and massaged the arm that had been dangling until it slowly came back to life, evidenced by acute pins and needles up and down its whole length.

She glanced at her bedside clock and saw that it was just after three. She wished Peter was lying beside her, and reflected ruefully that he had wanted to take her out the previous evening but that she had demurred and had gone to visit Anthea Henshaw instead.

She turned over and tried to compose herself for a few further hours of sleep. She didn't mind the Henshaws occupying her daytime thoughts, but had no wish to dream about them when she went to bed.

The rest of the night passed peacefully and she awoke, as she normally did, just before her alarm went off at seven o'clock. She was in the office by eight fifteen reading through the papers she needed for court. One of her more regular clients had been charged (yet again) with creating a disturbance at the home of his mother-in-law where his estranged wife had taken refuge.

Having worked out what she could say on his behalf to a world-weary magistrate who had heard everything before, she decided she had time to call Ralph Henshaw's office. The phone was answered by a girl who obligingly told her that Mr Henshaw wouldn't be in that day, but that she could speak to Mrs Gifford if she wanted.

Rosa did want. Indeed, she couldn't be better pleased, for it was Frances Gifford she really wished to see.

'Good morning, Miss Epton,' a firm but courteous voice said a moment later. 'I know your name, though we haven't yet met.'

'I'd very much like to have a talk with you, Mrs Gifford. Will you be in this afternoon?'

'I shall be, but wouldn't it be better if I came to your office? Ralph is away today, but Sandra can hold the fort for an hour or so.'

Rosa was somewhat taken aback by Ralph Henshaw's alleged mistress sounding so agreeable to a meeting. She had expected to hear claws being sharpened, instead of which there had been gentle purring. It put her on her guard.

On her guard or not, she was further disarmed by the appearance in her office of a smart woman with a pleasant expression. Frances Gifford was wearing a well-cut trouser suit, plum-coloured, and a frothy yellow chiffon scarf at her neck.

Stephanie had announced her arrival on the phone and a few moments later Ben had shown her into Rosa's office.

'Mrs Gifford to see you, Miss Epton,' he said ceremoniously, giving Rosa a sly wink as he retired from the room.

Fran Gifford settled herself in the visitor's chair and faced Rosa with the confidence of someone being interviewed for a job she felt certain of getting.

'It was good of you to go chasing down to Briar's End at such short notice. The last thing Ralph expected when he came back was to be detained at the airport. The whole affair has become a nightmare; first, Mrs Henshaw's disappearance, followed by the discovery of this young man's body in the lake.'

From her tone, the two events were obviously related.

'Did you know Mrs Henshaw well?' Rosa asked.

'No. I used to speak to her on the phone from time to time, usually to transmit messages from her husband, but we seldom had occasion to meet and I don't think I'd seen her at all over the past year.' She met Rosa's gaze head on. 'The fact was she took an immediate dislike to me which increased as her marriage deteriorated.'

'I confess to wondering why she and Mr Henshaw ever got married,' Rosa observed.

Fran Gifford nodded slowly. 'I think Ralph persuaded himself that they should – how can I put it? – should pair up after his first wife's tragic death. It was never what you would call a love match.'

'Did you know his first wife?'

'Good gracious, no. I became his secretary only after her death. His nerves were shattered at the time and I was able to give him the support he needed. Needed in his work, that is,' she added quickly.

'I suppose he's talked about his first wife's death?' Rosa said.

'Yes. He's always told me what he told you. He has no evidence, but he very strongly suspects that Evelyn was responsible. If not wholly, at least in part.'

'And yet he married her!'

Fran shrugged and turned away. 'I can't answer for Ralph,' she said sharply.

Her expression defied Rosa to do any probing of her own.

'So what do you think has happened to Mrs Henshaw?' Rosa enquired.

'I think she killed the young man and has fled.'

'You don't believe she herself has been murdered?'

'Who by?'

'Her husband, perhaps?' Rosa said tentatively.

'Ralph had no reason to kill her.'

'Not for her money?'

'Not for anything.' She sighed and went on, 'Evelyn was a complete neurotic. She created fantasies and lived them out.'

'That wasn't the impression she gave me the only time we met.'

'Of course not. Everything was calculated to provide the effect she wanted.'

'It sounds as if she'd have made a very good actress,' Rosa observed drily.

'She was one.'

Rosa was thoughtful for a while as she gazed at the composed and self-assured figure sitting in her visitor's chair.

'What can you tell me about the young man whose body was found in the lake?'

'No more than Ralph could tell you. Which is nothing.'

'Somebody must know more about him than has been disclosed so far. For a start, how he came to be staying at Riverview Court?'

71

'I assure you *I* have no idea,' Fran Gifford said, fastidiously removing a small piece of thread from the lapel of her jacket.

'Do you know Mr Henshaw's two children?' Rosa enquired.

'Christopher phones his father quite often and we talk when I happen to take his calls. As for Anthea, she's got a good job and has a fairly full life. In some ways she's your dedicated professional woman.' She gave Rosa a small smile. 'Perhaps you're one yourself, Miss Epton?'

'I hope not. I like my job, but it's not the be-all and end-all of my life.'

'I believe you have a solicitor boyfriend?' Fran Gifford said in a slightly teasing tone.

Rosa gave her a look of surprise. 'Yes, Peter's a solicitor, but how do you know?'

'A cousin of mine met you both at a party a few months ago and told me about you. My cousin's name is Helen Wright, but her name won't mean anything to you. I don't recall the name of the party givers.'

'I'm afraid I can't help either,' Rosa said icily, not too pleased at the manner in which the disclosure had been made. 'You were telling me about Anthea.'

'I'm afraid poor Anthea isn't very lucky with men. She has a way of frightening them off. She's had a number of boyfriends in her life, but they don't last.'

'Does she have one at the moment?' Rosa enquired with curiosity. What she had just heard didn't conflict with her own view of Anthea Henshaw, though she wondered which had come first, the chicken or the egg? Was it her manner that frightened men away or was her manner the result of being rejected?

'No, she hasn't had anyone dancing attendance since Mike,' Fran replied, then looked embarrassed. 'I shouldn't be talking about her in this way. She's a great girl and very close to her father.' She gave Rosa a deprecating smile. 'Was there something in particular you wanted to see me about?' she asked.

Rosa shook her head. 'I just wanted to have a general talk. The more people I talk to, the better picture I have of the background to what's happened.'

'I'm afraid it must be a somewhat confusing picture.'

'Yes, but I hope it'll become clearer as bits fall into place. I confess that at the moment it's rather like looking at the loose pieces of a jigsaw puzzle and wondering which fits where.'

'I do assure you that Ralph has told you the truth,' Fran said. 'Evelyn Henshaw is a mischief-maker through and through. She can be completely unscrupulous and vindictive with it. I don't expect you to take my word for it, but I do urge you to be on your guard when you're dealing with her.'

Fran Gifford seemed to take it for granted that Evelyn Henshaw was still alive. Possibly because she didn't want to face up to the alternative, namely that her partner's wife was dead.

Rosa was used to discovering fresh facets to a client's nature, but it seemed almost as if Evelyn Henshaw was something different to everyone who met her. The question was, which was the real person? Was it the woman in the intimidating hat who had calmly declared that her husband was going to murder her, as he had done his first wife? Or the woman with ash-blonde hair holding hands with the young man mowing the lawn? Or any of the other malign, mendacious Evelyn Henshaws that had been conjured up for Rosa's inspection?

Chapter Twelve

Fran Gifford entered the dining-room of the Henshaws' London flat with a mug of coffee in each hand. She walked across to the table where Ralph Henshaw was sitting with his wife's journal open in front of him.

'Did Evelyn always keep a journal?' she enquired as she put down one of the mugs within his reach.

'What was that?' he murmured in a preoccupied tone.

'I asked if Evelyn always kept a journal.'

He glanced up. 'No, she only began after Edward's death. He was considerably older than her and was something of a Svengali in her life. At least, that's always been my impression, though I never knew him. He died several years before Jean and I met Evelyn on a cruise . . . But I've told you all this before. Anyway, I think the journal was her way of exorcising him.'

'Surely that can't be the only volume if she's been keeping it all these years?' she pressed.

'It's not. I was hoping you might find others in your search.'

'I only looked where you told me. Where do you think the others are?'

'They must be hidden somewhere in the house.'

She gave him a quizzical look. 'Do you really mean to say you've never read them?'

'The fact I knew she kept a journal was purely accidental. I assure you she never left them lying around for anyone to read.'

'But you were her husband, Ralph!'

'So our marriage certificate indicates,' he observed sourly. 'She never used to write up the journal when I was around. She did once mention that she kept a journal of her thoughts and impressions, though it was for nobody's eyes but her own.' He glanced down at the open notebook. 'I imagined that writing it was like going into the confessional, but I'm not so sure on the evidence of this volume.'

'What period does it span?'

'Only the last few weeks before she . . . disappeared.' He flicked the pages over. 'You can see it's a fresh book. She didn't write something every day, only, it seems, when the spirit took her.'

'Does she refer to her Polish friend staying at the house?'

'She's disappointingly coy on that subject. It's as if . . .' His voice tailed off.

'As if she had a guilty conscience,' Fran said for him.

He shrugged. 'There could be other reasons,' he remarked vaguely.

'Such as?'

'She didn't record anything that might tell against her.'

'What's the final entry?' Fran enquired after a thoughtful silence.

'It was obviously written several days before things happened. There's no reference to bodies in the lake or anything like that.'

'Does she mention going to see Rosa Epton?'

He turned back a page. ' "Went to see a solicitor of the name of Rosa Epton," ' he read. ' "Told her of my fears about Ralph and asked her to keep a watchful eye on things. She's a shrewd young woman, but I think I impressed her with my sincerity. We'll see." '

'Like I've always said, she's a complete neurotic and about as sincere as a six-times-married Hollywood star.'

Ralph Henshaw sat silently frowning at nothing in particular and Fran went on, 'How did you know where she kept this ever-so-private journal?'

'I once opened her bedroom door when she was locking it away. She was so absorbed in what she was doing she didn't see me standing there and I quickly withdrew before she became aware of my presence.'

'It doesn't seem that my burglarious exploit has been as helpful as we'd hoped,' she remarked.

For answer he got up from his chair and walked across to the settee where she was sitting. Flinging himself down beside her, he put an arm round her shoulders and pulled her against him.

'If it weren't for you, I think I might sink.'

'You're no more likely to sink than a cork tree,' she replied unsentimentally. 'What you have to concentrate on is staying one move ahead of the police. And of the Epton woman.' She disengaged herself from his arm. 'So what do you propose next?'

'Find out where Evelyn kept the earlier journals. I shan't have an easy mind until I know what she wrote about Jean's death.'

'It may be no more significant than what she's written about her Polish friend.'

'Maybe not, but I've got to know.'

Fran Gifford gave him a searching look. Though she had become his mistress, it was, for her, more a practical measure than an affair of the heart. Nevertheless, they still had a common interest. Survival.

At about the same time, and on the other side of the park from the Henshaw flat, two other people were sitting together on a settee. One difference was that Rosa made no attempt to escape from Peter's encircling arm. She had gone to his flat for supper, and they were relaxing with a sense of well-being induced by an excellent meal. Rosa wasn't a bad cook, but Peter was in an altogether superior class.

He drew her closer to him and gave her a soft, sensuous kiss behind the ear. Rosa didn't exactly purr, but her reaction was much the same as that of a cat being stroked in a favourite place.

'Happy?' he enquired.

'Ask a silly question and you're liable to get a silly answer.'

'I know the answer, anyway.'

'How?'

'By the dreamy look in your eyes. They say everything.'

Rosa gave a soft laugh. 'If you're that clever, tell me who murdered Stefan.'

'Definitely not Mrs Henshaw,' he said, kissing the tip of her nose.

'How do you know?'

'It's not a woman's crime.'

'There's no such thing these days. Women can be as handy as men with pistols and knives and all manner of blunt instruments.'

'They don't strangle people.'

'Who says they don't? Given the right circumstances they're perfectly capable of strangling someone.'

'But not of transporting a heavily weighted body across twenty yards of lawn and tipping it into a lake.'

'I agree it would depend on the size and strength of the woman, but it's not impossible.'

'Could Mrs Henshaw have done that?'

'I wouldn't rule it out.'

'And Fran Gifford, what about her?'

'Same answer.'

'Could Anthea Henshaw?'

'Ditto.'

'I've run out of women.'

'Wouldn't you like to know whether I could have?' Rosa asked, giving him a quick kiss on his cool, smooth cheek.

He stared at her as if wondering whether he ought to register shock at the question.

'Well?' she said.

'I don't like to think you'd ever be capable of committing a murder,' he remarked solemnly.

'Don't you believe that everyone has a flashpoint when they could kill another human being?'

'Possibly, but I also believe that most people are blessed with adequate self-control which keeps them from murderous attacks on their own kind.'

'The murder rate is always increasing,' Rosa observed. 'Moreover, most murders are not committed by people running amok. Forget what the law says about *mens rea*, the fact is that the majority of murders are wholly unpremeditated in the lay sense. The flashpoint is reached and the next moment there's a body on the floor.'

'You're not suggesting that Stefan was killed on the spur of the moment?'

'I wouldn't have thought so. My guess is that it was well and truly premeditated.'

'And I still say it wasn't a woman's crime,' Peter said stoutly.

'Then who was it?'

'Ralph Henshaw is the obvious person. He had motive and could easily have created the opportunity.'

'And what do you think has happened to his wife?'

'I think she could also be dead. Murdered by her husband.'

'If you're right, Peter, why should Stefan's body have been put in the lake and hers disposed of in some other way?'

'In the first place we can't be certain that her body *isn't* in the lake. The fact that the police haven't found it only proves they haven't looked in the right spot. And secondly I don't suggest they were necessarily killed at the same time or at the same place. In fact, common sense dictates that they weren't. Once *one* was out of the way, the murderer could turn his attention to the other.'

'But if Evelyn Henshaw *is* still alive, she must certainly be in danger. I mean, one must assume she fled because she knew what had happened and that she'd be next on the list.'

'In that case,' Peter said, slowly, 'the crunchpoint could be approaching and you'll have to decide which of them you will represent. Evelyn or Ralph? Ralph or Evelyn?'

'Have I got myself in a terrible mess, Peter?' Rosa asked in a worried tone.

He picked up one of her hands and tenderly kissed the palm. 'It's not like you to agonise over things that may never happen, little Rosa,' he said.

'No, but this time . . .'

'Is no different from a lot of other times. Anyway, I thought your interest had been fully aroused by the Henshaw goings-on.'

'It has, but I don't like to feel I may suddenly find myself out of my depth.'

'Don't worry, I'm an excellent swimmer.'

Rosa snuggled up against him and he drew her protectively into his side.

Chapter Thirteen

Detective Chief Inspector Greer had had his evening meal at home and decided to go along to force headquarters and look through his in-tray. For the past four days he had concentrated his efforts trying to solve the murder at Briar's End while working out of divisional headquarters at Utwell, where he had established a base.

It was around nine o'clock and the complex of modern buildings that housed the Chief Constable, his supporting officers and an ever-increasing amount of technical equipment, was largely silent.

Duty officers, plus a few conscientious extras (or those escaping their wives), were working away at cluttered desks, but the general air was that of a school which had broken up for the holidays.

Greer was just passing the end of a corridor that was slightly less institutional-looking than its neighbours when a door opened and he found himself staring at Mr Armstrong, the chief constable, dressed in dinner jacket with a white carnation in his button-hole.

'Ah! The very man! Do you have a spare ten minutes?'

'Yes, sir.'

'Well, come along to my office and tell me about your enquiry. I'm due at a mayoral reception in half an hour, but I've been wanting to get in touch with you.'

Greer followed the chief constable into his executive suite, accepted a whisky and sat down. The chief constable meanwhile began polishing his shoes and brushing imaginary dust from his shoulders.

'It sounds as if you've got a tough nut to crack,' the chief constable observed pleasantly. 'At least the press has lost interest for the time being and you don't have them under your feet. Tell me, first, what's happened to Mrs Henshaw?'

Greer sighed, took a large gulp of whisky and relaxed.

'I wish I knew, sir. From all accounts she was a very strange lady who was capable of unpredictable behaviour.'

'You say *was*. Do you mean that you think she's dead?'

'I didn't mean to imply that, sir. Maybe she still *is*.'

'Surely there'd have been a sighting of her by now if she were still alive?'

Greer nodded gloomily and took another swig of whisky.

'Except that if people put their minds to it, they can make a very good job at disappearing.'

'Even middle-aged ladies?'

'Even middle-aged ladies, sir, who have a toy boy in tow.'

'I could understand that if she and the toy boy had taken off together, but they didn't.' The chief constable picked up Greer's glass and reached for the whisky decanter. 'Incidentally, what about this Stefan person, he must have a background, what is it?'

Greer's expression became even more glum.

'We've traced his parents who upsticked and went back to Poland over a year ago. They live in a suburb of Warsaw and somebody from the consular division of our embassy paid them a visit. They were shattered by the news of their son's death, but weren't much help. They told the chap from the embassy that Stefan had been born in England and felt none of the ties that had drawn them back to Poland. They said he wasn't very good about writing letters and that the last one they'd received had been about six weeks previously. He had then been living somewhere in London, but they weren't sure of the address . . .'

'You mean they didn't know it?' the chief constable broke in.

'Apparently not, sir. Because he moved around a bit, they always wrote to him care of a small Polish travel agency in Acton. They said he was popular amongst his friends and had a succession of girlfriends, none of whom had lasted very long.'

'Did they provide any names?'

'Yes, sir. Val, Betsy and Jenny or Joanie seemed to be the best they could do.'

'But no surnames?'

'Not one, sir. Although they'd lived in England for over forty years, they'd never really become assimilated. They always spoke Polish together, and though they had a good understanding of English they were not at ease speaking it.'

'Did they know anything about their son being at Briar's End?'

'They had never heard of the place, sir. Nor of anyone named Henshaw.'

'What about his polytechnic friends?'

'The ones we've spoken to liked him, but were totally uninquisitive about his background. He didn't talk about it and they didn't ask questions.'

The chief constable nodded. 'I think that's a feature of much of today's youth,' he said with a sigh. 'I asked my daughter the other day about a young man she'd brought to the house. He was a likeable enough chap, but when I later enquired of her what his father did and what was his brother doing in Canada – he'd mentioned that à propos something or other – she looked at me in astonishment and said she hadn't the faintest idea.'

'We have managed to trace one of the girls, sir, through a tip from someone at an old address,' Greer said, picking up the threads of his own story. 'Betsy Summer. She slept in his bed for about six weeks last summer, but left it when, as she put it, he wanted to experiment. She reckoned he was over-sexed.'

'So she got out while she could, eh? Was she able to help over the other girls?'

'She thought Val might be a French girl who had now gone back home, but she had never heard of Jenny or Joanie. She said there'd probably been a good many others in his short life.' He paused. 'One thing she did say which was interesting was that he was ready to use his bed to assist his social advancement.'

'Hence Mrs Henshaw?'

'Exactly, sir.'

'But you've no idea how he came to meet her?'

'Not yet, sir.'

'What did the village think of this set-up?'

'They used to see very little of Mrs Henshaw. She didn't mix or socialise and even Mrs Santer who was her daily help didn't really know her. Michalowski worked part-time at the Red Squirrel. He got on well with the punters who knew him as a research student earning a bit of extra money, but he seems to have been adept at evading any awkward questions. Mind you, sir, that's hardly surprising in the circumstances. He wouldn't have wanted it to be known he was no more than a gigolo.'

The chief constable gave Greer a surprised look. 'Not often one hears that word these days,' he observed.

Greer blushed. 'Sorry, sir . . .'

'Oh, don't apologise! It's a perfectly good word and I'm sure it describes what Michalowski was. If so, being murdered was no more than an occupational hazard.' The chief constable glanced at his watch. 'I'll have to be off in a moment, but I'm glad I saw you. I wanted to be brought up to date.'

Greer gulped down the remainder of his drink and got up.

'I hope you'll enjoy your evening, sir,' he said.

'Don't worry, I shan't,' the chief constable replied. 'At least *you're* not obliged to attend functions you'd sooner give a miss. I often think back to the days when I was a young PC on the beat in the Met. I won't pretend they were the happiest of my life, but one didn't have to attend mayoral receptions looking like a penguin.'

Greer gave him a non-committal smile. All he knew was that he wouldn't mind swapping his own office for the chief constable's executive-style suite, nor his car for the chauffeur-driven vehicle now waiting outside. Least of all he wouldn't have minded swapping salaries.

With these thoughts he made his way back to the reality of an overflowing in-tray and an office that was as inviting as a plate of cold left-overs.

Chapter Fourteen

Vera Upjohn had fully expected to have heard from Evelyn Henshaw, either by one of the accepted means of communication or via the supernatural, but no message had reached her by either of these channels.

It wasn't simply that Mrs Henshaw was her most reliable client who always paid promptly and without demur – though that did earn her favoured treatment – as the fact that she was genuinely worried about what had happened to her. She liked Evelyn Henshaw in a way that a doctor establishes a special rapport with one of his patients. She wouldn't have expected her to disappear without a word, and even if she had been obliged to flee for her life there had certainly been more than enough time for her to get in touch. On this basis Mrs Upjohn could only assume that she must be dead. Hence her attempts to tune in to the supernatural. But the supernatural remained obstinately silent, despite her efforts to entice even the briefest of emanations.

It was three days after Chief Inspector Greer's interview with the chief constable that she decided she had to do something. She didn't have anyone coming until evening and then only an old gentleman who always overstayed and finally produced a dozen reasons for not paying the full consultation fee. If she had not been so professional, not to mention so soft-hearted, she would have barred the door to him or given him the shock of his life as she peered into what always appeared to be a placid future. She hoped in vain that he would become as bored with her readings as she was, but so far without any sign of success.

After a lunch-time plate of spaghetti bolognaise and two glasses of red wine, she drew the blinds in her always stuffy sitting-room and got ready for a siesta. First, however, she lit a few joss-sticks and switched on a small table-lamp whose shade was draped in red. She then sat down in a rocking-chair and fell quietly asleep while trying to make a long-distance call to the kingdom of the supernatural.

When she woke up, she felt strangely disorientated. She was thirsty, but didn't have the energy to get out of the chair and fetch a glass of water. She just lay back and stared drowsily about her. She knew she had had a long dream, but couldn't for the moment recall it. Evelyn Henshaw wasn't part of it and yet it concerned her. Sometimes it took her ages to remember all the details of a dream. Sometimes she never could. Those were the most frustrating occasions.

Slowly recollection seeped into her conscious mind. Mr Henderson, her next client, had figured in the dream. He was running away from something and kept on looking back over his shoulder with horror. For a tiresome old man in his mid-seventies he ran surprisingly fast. He was running away from a red glow and calling out something as he ran.

Mrs Upjohn frowned in a concentrated effort to relive the dream. Yes, that was it, Mr Henderson was running toward her extended arms and calling out the name, Evelyn.

She sat up with a jolt. It could only mean that Evelyn Henshaw was somewhere behind him, out of sight, and that her own arms were extended to her, not to Mr Henderson. That made sense. The fact that the two participants had never met each other in real life was irrelevant. She knew them both.

The red glow might have been a brilliant sunset or even a fire, though nothing she could do would bring it any clearer.

By now she was fully awake and heaved herself out of the rocking chair. She must get a drink of water. Reaching the kitchen she flopped into a chair and poured herself a glass of wine from the half-empty bottle. Wine was always better than water.

Staring rheumy-eyed out of the window at the blank side of the next-door house, she called out, 'Evie, Evie, speak to me, Evie, wherever you are.'

It was only later she realised that her dream had been prophetic.

Chapter Fifteen

Bob King, licensee of the Red Squirrel at Briar's End, switched off the saloon-bar lights and retired through the door that led to the private quarters.

Another day was over and he was more than ready for bed. His wife had already gone upstairs. But first he had a duty to perform. An evening ritual one might call it, and Ferdinand, his wife's dachshund, stood by the side door to remind him in case he should forget.

He didn't really mind taking the dog out, except when it was raining, when, fortunately, Ferdinand wasn't too keen either on wasting time searching for smells and getting wet.

But this was a dry, balmy evening in mid-May and both man and dog sallied forth in uncomplaining spirit. The route was always the same, dictated by Ferdinand, who was a creature of habit. They turned left along the main road, which was deserted at that hour of the night, and walked as far as the lane which led to Riverview Court. At that point Ferdinand would turn for home and Bob was ready to follow suit.

Bob, for his part, enjoyed the quietness and all the country smells, while for Ferdinand there was always the hope of coming across a rabbit or disturbing a game bird that was unwisely nesting too close to the road. Neither creature was ever in any risk of being caught, but each gave Ferdinand a sense of his own superiority.

They had just reached the turn-round point when Bob stopped and peered ahead. Something funny was happening at Riverview Court. There was a sudden dull explosion, followed by a sharp crack. Even as he stared in the direction of the house he saw a long tongue of flame shoot out of one of the first floor windows.

Leaving Ferdinand to his own devices he ran toward the entrance. The main gate was padlocked, but he clambered over without too much difficulty. As he tore along the drive, it was clear that the whole house was well and truly alight. There was no sign of human life, however; nor was there a car parked outside. It must have been an electrical fault, he thought, as he made a wide detour to reach the main lawn and examine the aspect of the house which contained most of the windows. From the edge of the lake he looked back, half-expecting to see someone standing at a window about to jump for safety. But the windows were either glowing or billowing smoke.

He felt a movement at his feet and looked down to find Ferdinand claiming his attention. Stooping down he scooped up the small dog and tucked him under his arm.

Maybe he should have phoned for help immediately instead of going to investigate. In the event it probably wouldn't have mattered what he did. Nothing could have saved the house.

By half-past midnight there wasn't a soul in Briar's End who was asleep. Those who had gone to bed early had been woken by the successive waves of sirens and flashing blue lights as fire engines and police cars followed each other to the scene of the fire.

Most of the men and quite a few of the women joined the procession, many of them accompanied by excited children.

Bob King, who had taken Ferdinand home and explained things to his wife, returned to the house. Pauline had scornfully rejected his suggestion that she should accompany him.

By the time he arrived back at Riverview Court the front drive resembled carnival night. PC Lipscomb was doing his best to control the crowd, which was generally well-behaved. Only a few village teenagers were out to flout authority and get in the way, but they quietened down after one of their number had his hair singed by a spark.

After Bob had had a word with PC Lipscomb, he walked on and reached the front of the house where fire appliances and police cars were parked in an anarchic log-jam.

'I'm Bob King,' he said to a plain-clothes officer standing beside a police car. 'I was the first person on the scene.'

The officer looked at him sharply. 'So tell me about it,' he said. 'I'm Detective Sergeant Wells.' When Bob had finished speaking, the officer asked, 'And you're quite sure you didn't see anyone at all?'

'Certain. I'd thought there might have been somebody trapped inside, but there wasn't a sign of human life.'

'And you didn't see anybody outside?'

'No.'

'Or hear a car being started?'

'No.' Bob gave a thoughtful frown. 'If someone had been trapped inside, their car must be around. It could be in the stable yard.'

'Who says they must have come by car?'

'They'd hardly have walked. Not late at night in a lonely area like this.'

'Probably not. But we're in the early stage where nothing can be taken for granted.'

'I suppose you'll be notifying Mr Henshaw of the fire?'

'He may already know,' Sergeant Wells observed, shooting Bob a sidelong glance.

'There've been some funny goings-on recently,' Bob remarked in a ruminative sort of way.

'And Riverview Court has had more than its fair share of them. A darned sight more.' Wells paused. 'In fact, one might say that being burnt down is all part of a pattern.'

'The real mystery is what's happened to Mrs Henshaw.'

'I was hoping you might tell me something.'

'Afraid not.'

'Surely the punters at the Red Squirrel must have been airing their views?'

'Oh, there are rumours enough, but they're nothing more than speculation. The fact is that though she'd lived in the village for a good many years, nobody really knew her. She took no part in village life and became almost reclusive after her first husband's death. Then after the business involving the first Mrs Henshaw people shrank from her company. At least, that's what I've been told. It happened, of course, well before Pauline and I arrived in Briar's End.'

'OK, OK,' Sergeant Wells said impatiently, 'but what about this Stefan chap? He worked for you, you knew him.'

'I've told your people all I know. He was efficient and got on with the customers. I couldn't have asked for more.'

'But damn it, he must have told someone what he was doing at Riverview Court.'

'He was a research student and found it a quiet place to work.

He did odd jobs around the garden in return for his board and lodging.'

'It doesn't make sense,' Wells remarked testily. 'How did he get to know Mrs Henshaw in the first place?'

'He hinted that there was some family connection—'

'I know what he hinted,' Wells broke in, 'but it still doesn't make sense, with Mr Henshaw denying all knowledge of him and nobody coming forward with any information.'

Bob shrugged and turned to move away. He didn't see why he should stand there and be the butt of Sergeant Wells' exasperation.

The fire was by now under control, though it would still be some time before a proper search of the house could be made.

Nobody appeared to doubt that arson was the cause, but that merely postulated more questions than it answered.

A young uniformed officer came hurrying over to where Sergeant Wells was standing in the headlights of one of the fire appliances. He said something to him and pointed round the corner of the house. Wells hastened away with the young officer at his side.

Bob King was left wondering what was up and decided to hang around a bit longer in the hope of finding out. He didn't have long to wait.

He was still standing a few yards from where he and Sergeant Wells had been speaking when the same young officer appeared in front of him.

'Mr King?' he asked breathlessly. Bob nodded. 'Sergeant Wells would like a word with you, sir. Will you come with me?'

'What's happened?'

'They've found a body.'

Keeping a safe distance from the house from which occasional smouldering spars of wood were still falling, they reached the further side and the relatively unscathed stable yard.

'Where are we going?' Bob asked as he tried to keep up with his younger companion.

'It's in one of the sheds.'

'But the fire hasn't affected there,' Bob said in a puzzled tone as they approached.

'Sergeant Wells'll explain,' the PC said, his mission almost accomplished.

A moment later Wells appeared in the open door of one of the sheds that lined the further side of the yard.

'Ah, there you are! We've found a body and I'm hoping you may be able to identify it.'

'Why should I be able to identify it?' Bob asked with a sudden hard lump in his throat.

'Just take a look, that's all.'

Bob followed Sergeant Wells into the shed. At first he couldn't see a thing, then the beam of a flashlight was focused on a bundle-like object on the floor.

'Ready?' Wells asked and focused the light on the end of the bundle where a matted head protruded.

Bob turned away, feeling physically sick.

'Recognise him?'

'Yes, it's old Joshua,' Bob said in a shaken voice.

He followed Wells out of the shed into the yard which was inches deep in water from the firemen's hoses and reeked of smouldering debris.

'Let's get out of here,' Wells said, leading the way back on to the lawn, 'then we'll be able to breathe again. Sorry to have dragged you into that, but Lipscomb's gone back to the station and I wanted someone with local know-how.' He took a deep breath of cool night air. 'Who's old Joshua?'

'He's a tramp who comes and goes in Briar's End. When he's here he'll come round to our back door and we give him food. He may do that three or four days running, then he disappears for a month or more. Presumably does his rounds of other villages.'

'When did you last see him?'

'Earlier today when he came begging.'

'Did he ever come into the pub?'

'No, fortunately. Never even attempted to. He was a smelly old bugger and would have driven out all my other customers. It was an unwritten rule which he kept to.'

'Do you know where he normally slept?'

'Anywhere he could lay his head.'

'Well, he chose the wrong place last night,' Wells observed sardonically.

'I suppose he knew Riverview Court was empty.'

'Very likely, but he didn't know he was going to get in the way of an arsonist.'

'It looked as if his head had been bashed in.'

'It had.'

'I wonder why the arsonist went to that shed?' Bob said with a shiver.

'That's one of the easier questions to answer,' Wells remarked. 'It's where the paraffin was kept.'

Detective Chief Inspector Greer was awakened at six o'clock in the morning and told of the fire at Riverview Court.

'When was it?' he asked aggressively, angry at being woken up, but angrier still that he had been sleeping while the case of which he was in charge had taken a convulsive turn.

'I think it was around midnight, sir,' the officer on the line replied.

'Why the hell wasn't I told sooner?' he demanded to know, but went on quickly: 'Oh, never mind, I suppose it's not your fault.'

The officer, who was merely passing on a message in reporting the matter, mouthed 'sod you, too' as he disconnected.

Forty minutes later Greer arrived at the scene where he found Sergeant Wells talking to the officer in charge of the fire brigade team.

'Sorry to drag you out, sir. As a matter of fact, I was wondering if you were going to come.'

'I'd have been here sooner if anyone had bothered to let me know,' Greer remarked sourly.

Sergeant Wells gave a puzzled shake of the head. 'But I asked somebody to send you a message, sir, hours ago.'

'Well, I never received it. But never mind about that for the moment, tell me what's happened.'

Wells did so and concluded, 'Obviously someone came with the intention of setting the house alight, hence his visit to the paraffin shed where Joshua woke up to discover what was happening and was killed for his pains. The arsonist then set fire to the house and made off.'

'Any clue as to the motive?'

'Not yet, sir. We've not yet completed a search of the place, but my guess is that somebody was intent on destroying evidence of some sort and decided to burn the house down.'

'A bit drastic,' Greer observed.

'Depends on the nature of the evidence. Perhaps it couldn't be removed and had to be destroyed. It doesn't seem to me, sir, that we need look very far for the culprit.'

'You mean, Ralph Henshaw?'

'He sticks out like a rabbi in a packed mosque.'

'We'd better haul him in,' Greer said. 'He's certainly got a few questions to answer.'

'With luck there'll be even more by the time we lay our hands on him.'

But when later that morning two officers arrived at the flat off Bayswater Road, they were unable to obtain any answer either to the doorbell or to prolonged heavy banging.

A visit to Ralph Henshaw's offices near Paddington proved equally fruitless. A notice informed anyone who was interested that it was closed for the day.

The morning papers that day had carried brief reports of the 'mysterious' fire at Riverview Court and of the discovery of a man's body in one of the out-buildings. Most of the papers further reported that neither the cause of the fire nor of the man's death had yet been established and that both matters were under police investigation.

As usual Ben had spotted the report and was waiting to thrust his paper at Rosa as soon as she arrived in the office. For once, however, she had read it in her own paper, though she still accepted Ben's to see if it said anything different.

When she reached her room, she asked Stephanie to call Ralph Henshaw at his flat, and when this evoked no reply, to try his office.

In neither case was she any more successful than the two police officers, who had made personal visits at both sets of premises.

Until she knew more about what had happened she didn't wish to call the police, as this could be embarrassing if they began asking *her* awkward questions. She also pondered phoning Bob King, but again decided not to do so for the time being. Though he seemed friendly enough, she had no evidence as to exactly where his loyalties lay and she didn't want her quests after information relayed to third parties, especially not to the police.

It was toward the end of the morning, which she had spent at her desk catching up with paper work, that Stephanie announced she had Mr Ralph Henshaw on the line.

'Put him through, Steph,' Rosa said, with unusual eagerness. It was not that he had suddenly become a favourite person but that her curiosity had been further fired by the newspaper reports she had read.

'Miss Epton? When can I see you? It's urgent.'

'Where are you?'

'In London.' He might as well have said 'in Africa', Rosa reflected.

'Do you wish to come to the office?' she asked.

'No.'

'I could probably come and see you at your flat . . .'

'Out of the question. We must meet somewhere anonymous, where we're not known.'

'Make a suggestion,' she said, with a touch of impatience.

'The lobby of the Cumberland Hotel,' he replied after a pause.

'All right, I could meet you there at six.'

'I'd prefer an earlier time. Why don't we say three?'

'I'm in court all afternoon, six is the earliest I can manage.'

Intrigued and curious as she was, Rosa didn't intend throwing everything overboard just to accommodate Ralph Henshaw.

'All right, six,' he said reluctantly and rang off.

Later, on her way to the meeting, she bought an evening paper to see if there was a fuller report of the fire. By then, however, news had moved on and events at Riverview Court had been displaced by reports of a particularly gory murder in leafy Wimbledon and of a baronet who had held police and bailiffs at bay in a siege of his modest semi-detached in Dulwich. The latter piece boosted interest by mentioning the name of a rock star who lived nearby and of an MP's wife who had once been married to the baronet.

In the circumstances, Rosa thought it fortunate that the fire at Riverview Court had escaped the spotlight. If someone had done a bit more homework, it would almost certainly have been considered more newsworthy.

The hotel lobby was a seething mass of tourists, booking in, checking out and being marshalled into groups for their next piece of entertainment.

She was gazing helplessly around when Ralph Henshaw materialised at her side.

'I saw you come in,' he said. 'I've got a table over in a corner. The waiter promised to hold it for me.'

As she followed him across the lobby, she cast him a covert glance. The chin was as aggressive as ever, but there were dark pouches beneath his eyes which she had not previously noticed. Later, when they were sitting down and he had ordered drinks, she observed that the eyes themselves were red-rimmed. He looked as if he had lost a night's sleep and Rosa wondered with foreboding what she was about to hear.

Sitting forward in his chair and lowering his voice, he said, 'The police are looking for me, that's why I didn't want to come to your office; I also know they've been to the flat.'

'I take it this is in connection with the fire at Riverview Court?' Rosa said.

'You've read about it?' Rosa nodded and he went on, 'Did you know that a man's body had been found?'

'Yes. Who was it?'

'God knows! Some old tramp who thought he'd found somewhere safe to shelter, I imagine. Tough on him!'

'Why should anyone have wanted to burn the house down?'

'Who says they did? It could have been an electrical fault or some form of spontaneous combustion.'

Rosa shrugged. 'I assumed it was deliberate. Isn't it your assumption, too? If not, why are you so keen to avoid the police?'

He gave her a foul look, which reminded Rosa that he was not somebody who liked being crossed.

'I suppose it's natural the police wish to interview me,' he said stiffly. 'That's where you come in, I refuse to meet them without my lawyer being present.'

'I think,' Rosa said slowly, 'that you had better begin by telling me what you know about last night's fire. First of all, where were you at the time?'

'I had supper at the flat and went out around eight thirty to meet a business associate. I got home just after eleven.'

'Were you alone in the flat before going out?'

'Yes.' His expression challenged Rosa to query his answer.

'And where did you meet your business associate?'

'At the Cavendish Hotel in Jermyn Street.'

'I take it that, if necessary, your meeting and the time you spent at the hotel can be corroborated?'

'Certainly. I'll give you the name of the man I met, if you want.'

'Later, perhaps. Can anyone confirm that you were in the flat before going out?'

'I left my unwashed supper things in the sink. They'll still be there.'

'That doesn't really corroborate anything, except that somebody had a meal and didn't wash up.' Rosa paused and decided to bite the bullet. 'Was Miss Gifford at the flat yesterday evening?'

'She was earlier, then she went out to see some friends.'

'What time would that have been?'

'She left the flat about six thirty.'

'Where do her friends live?'

'I've no idea. I don't pry into every corner of her life, but I've no doubt she'll tell you if you ask her. Are all these questions necessary?' His tone was belligerent.

'They're questions the police will ask you, so I'd like to know the answers in advance,' Rosa said briskly. 'There's just one more for the moment, when did you first hear about the fire?'

'Mrs Santer, the cleaning woman, phoned around midnight to say that Riverview Court was on fire. She took it upon herself to call as she didn't know if anyone else would let me know.'

'And that was the first you knew about it?'

'Yes. If you don't believe me you can speak to Mrs Santer yourself.'

Ignoring the gibe, Rosa said, 'And what did you do?'

'I packed an overnight bag and left the flat. In the light of past events, I knew the police would come looking for me and, as I've already said, I preferred to meet them in my own time and not theirs.'

'Have you any idea who might have started the fire, assuming that it was deliberate?'

'None,' he replied, curtly.

'Have a guess,' Rosa said, nettled by the crude unhelpfulness of his response.

'I'm not here to play guessing games,' he said. 'What I want you to do is arrange a meeting with the police and accompany me to it. Can you do that?'

'Yes, I'll call Detective Chief Inspector Greer and fix a time.'

'Is there any reason why it shouldn't be held on my patch?'

'I think it would be better if we drove down to Utwell. I don't necessarily believe in accommodating the police, but on this occasion I'm sure it would be best.'

His expression was one of distaste. 'If you say so,' he remarked.

'Yes, I do. After all, you don't want them looking for you and detaining you on sight.'

'They'd have no right to do that.'

'You may say that, but I doubt whether it's their view.' She paused. 'After all, you've been avoiding them and they're bound to ask you why.'

'I've told you why. It's because of their previous behaviour in detaining me at the airport. It was a thoroughly high-handed action on their part.'

Rosa decided not to argue further about the propriety of police conduct on that occasion. She knew from experience that it was generally her more autocratic clients who complained the loudest when the police behaved out of line. Not that she thought the police had on this occasion. She was, moreover, sure that Greer would want to know why Henshaw had not immediately got in touch with him as soon as he heard of the fire.

Her certainty about this was confirmed when an hour or so later she called the chief inspector from home to arrange the promised meeting.

'Oh, so your client has surfaced, has he, Miss Epton?' he observed in an anything but friendly tone.

'He's been in touch with me and wants to help you in any way he can,' Rosa said in a tone of studied professionalism.

'It's a pity he didn't get in touch with me immediately, instead of going to ground for the best part of twenty-four hours,' Greer observed unpleasantly. 'Ah, well, I expect he had his reasons . . .'

Rosa remained silent. She was under no obligation to respond to such taunts. She had warned Ralph Henshaw what to expect and though silence would also be one of his options, it was scarcely a viable one in the circumstances unless he wanted to spend longer than necessary assisting the police with their enquiries, as the euphemism describes it.

As Rosa sat beside Ralph Henshaw in his Jaguar the next morning, her mind was occupied with thoughts of the interview that lay ahead. Her client was in an uncommunicative mood and that suited her. They were due to meet Detective Chief Inspector Greer at ten thirty at divisional headquarters in Utwell.

Henshaw had denied all knowledge of the fire before being phoned by Mrs Santer. Rosa hoped he had told her the truth, but didn't have one hundred per cent faith in his word. But what concerned her more were the cards held by the police. Perhaps they didn't hold any; on the other hand they might lead with an ace, followed by a second. It was not knowing that made her edgy. One thing lawyers disliked more than anything was having surprises sprung on them. It was often a client's own fault if his lawyer was ambushed, but that didn't make it any better.

'Is there anything you want to ask me before we get there?' she asked, when the first signpost to Utwell appeared.

'I can't think of anything,' he said. 'I just hope we're not going to be kept hanging around. There's very little I can tell the police and I have better things to do than answer the same stupid questions over and over again.'

'Maybe, but I advise you not to show it,' Rosa remarked. 'If you're stroppy, the police'll be doubly stroppy. And they have the whip hand, anyway.'

He frowned angrily. 'I'll do my best to control myself,' he said in a grudging voice.

'Good. Incidentally, who knows you're driving down to Utwell today?'

'I told Fran, of course, as she'll have to look after the office while I'm away. And I spoke to my daughter before picking you up this morning.'

'Did either of them offer any views about the fire?'

'Anthea wondered if my wife mightn't be hanging around intent on mischief—'

'That strikes me as most unlikely.'

'Me, too, though possibly for a different reason.'

'Meaning what?'

He appeared momentarily flustered. 'My daughter can be a bit melodramatic, especially where her stepmother's concerned,' he said with a sudden dismissive shrug.

'But you have no reason to believe your wife had anything to do with the fire, have you?'

'Of course not.'

'And you've no idea where she is?'

He shot her an angry sideways look. 'You still believe I've killed her and disposed of the body, don't you?'

'I've never said that.'

'No, but you've thought it. I can tell.' In an abrupt change of mood, he let out a heavy sigh. 'Not that I blame you. I just wish you'd try and see, however, that I'm the real sufferer as long as my wife's disappearance remains unsolved.'

Rosa couldn't think of a suitable comment, so said nothing. She wished she could see into Ralph Henshaw's mind. It didn't matter that she felt neither warmth nor sympathy toward him for she often had clients who fell into that category, but it was rare for her to have one about whom she had so many jagged doubts.

It was almost as if Greer and Sergeant Wells had been watching out for their arrival. Henshaw had barely parked his car in a space labelled 'Official Visitors Only', when Greer appeared at one door and Wells at the other.

'I don't think you strictly come within the definition,' Greer observed, sardonically, 'but leave it here all the same. We'll go up to my office.'

They followed him through a side door of the building with Sergeant Wells bringing up the rear as if to cut off any attempt at retreat.

'Well, Mr Henshaw,' Greer said when they were seated on either side of his desk, 'what can you tell me about the fire at Riverview Court?' Before Henshaw could reply, he added, 'And don't say "nothing", because I shan't believe you.'

Henshaw's chin came out like a steam shovel about to go into action.

'I'm afraid I know nothing that'll help you,' he said with disdain.

'So why are you here?'

'Because I realised you'd want to interview me.'

'Why didn't you get in touch immediately?'

Henshaw shrugged as though the question was unworthy of answer.

'I like to do things in my own time.'

'Was it because you had something to hide?'

'No.'

'Why then?'

'I've already answered that question.'

'Try again.'

Henshaw sighed. 'If I'd set my own home on fire, I'd hardly be offering myself for interview.'

'That doesn't follow at all. By now you've had time to arrange things, to destroy evidence and perfect your alibi. Yes?'

'Yes, but it's not true.'

'Where were you when somebody put a match to Riverview Court?'

'I was in London the whole of that evening. I've already told Miss Epton my movements.'

'Now, tell me.'

He did so, giving Chief Inspector Greer an identical account to the one he had earlier given Rosa.

'So, as soon as Mrs Santer phoned around midnight to tell you your home was on fire, you packed a bag and scarpered? Why? Sounds pretty suspicious to me.' He glanced at Sergeant Wells who added a judicial nod.

'I can't help how it sounds, it's the truth,' Henshaw observed with as much dignity as the circumstances allowed.

'And where did you go and hide yourself?' Greer enquired in his quietly hectoring tone.

'I went to a bed and breakfast place near Paddington.'

'Address?'

'Twenty-two Shoreham Crescent, W2.'

'Stayed there before?'

Henshaw hesitated and frowned. 'Yes.'

Greer gave Sergeant Wells a nod which caused him to get up and leave the room. Rosa, meanwhile, sat silent and watchful. Unless an interviewing officer stepped badly out of line, she generally reckoned it was better not to intervene; certainly not to give the impression her client needed any protection from fair questioning. And Ralph Henshaw seemed better able than most to look after himself.

'Any news of your wife?' Greer asked with total suddenness.

Henshaw blinked as though a bright light had been shone into his eyes. 'No, none.'

'Ah, well, I'm sure there'll be news sooner rather than later. You must hope that, too?'

'Of course.'

'Great strain on you, not knowing whether she's still alive,' Greer remarked in a tone that was just short of being a sneer.

Ralph Henshaw, to Rosa's relief, remained silent.

Greer, meanwhile, went on, 'I understand you have a grown-up son and daughter? Have they not been able to throw any light on recent events? Your daughter, for example, you've doubtless discussed things with her?'

'You're on a fishing expedition, officer. I don't blame you for that, but you're wasting your time.'

It was Greer's turn to sigh. 'So much of what we do in the course of an investigation turns out to be a waste of time.' He paused and added, 'But I don't regard questioning you as falling into that category. Far from it. Try and see it from my point of view. A valuable house is burnt down. A clear case of arson, says the fire brigade. Not only is the house badly damaged, but a dead body is found. Not burnt, mark you, but with a battered skull. So we look immediately for the owner of the house. His wife has already disappeared and may have been murdered. But now the owner has vanished, too. Why, I ask myself?'

It was at this moment that Sergeant Wells returned to the room and whispered into Greer's ear. Rosa, who had never particularly taken to Wells, liked even less the expression of smug triumph that had settled on his face. Greer listened intently before focusing his attention back on Henshaw.

'So, George Peachey is an old friend of yours?'

'I don't know what you're talking about.'

'George Peachey who runs the bed and breakfast establishment in Shoreham Crescent.'

'Oh, *him*! Yes, I know him.'

'Know him well, I understand. Did national service together and have been friends ever since?'

'None of which is a crime as far as I know,' Henshaw said, angrily. He glanced at Rosa sitting beside him. 'How much more of this do I have to put up with?'

'With as much as I deem necessary, Mr Henshaw,' Greer replied before anyone else could speak. 'Perhaps you'd like to have a word with Miss Epton before we go on. I don't know what advice she's given you so far, but she may care to update it. You can go along to the interview room.' He turned to Sergeant Wells. 'Show them the way, will you, Sergeant?' Looking toward Henshaw again, he went on, 'You're in very deep water, Mr Henshaw. Very deep indeed.'

'That officer's an animal,' Henshaw observed when the door of the interview room had been closed and he and Rosa were alone.

It was a cheerless room with a single high window letting in daylight. Four hard chairs were set round a wooden table on which rested a tape-recorder. Rosa made sure it was switched off before speaking. As she shared a number of the police doubts about her client, she felt herself in a more than usually invidious position, but the time had long passed when she could possibly withdraw from the case. In any event her interest had been aroused too far to contemplate such a step.

'But I'll not be brow-beaten,' he added as he glanced about him with distaste. 'How much longer is this likely to go on?'

'The police can hold you for up to nine hours without charging or releasing you, then for a further nine hours after a review of the situation by a senior officer not involved in the investigation.' She paused. 'After all, they are investigating a murder, as well as a case of arson.'

'I thought it was two murders,' he remarked, savagely. 'Not to mention every other crime that's been committed in the country in the past month. I'm their prime suspect for the lot.' He paused and stirred restlessly on his chair. 'Just tell me what I have to do to get out of this place as soon as possible.'

'I'm afraid there's no short cut,' Rosa replied. 'If you stand up and say you're leaving, they'll think of a reason to hold you. All you can do is sweat it out and hope to be released at the end of the day. If they had enough to charge you immediately, they'd have done so. Just hang on to that thought.'

Henshaw nodded with an angry, grudging expression.

A few minutes later Sergeant Wells appeared in the doorway and suggested a resumption of the interview. As they walked along the corridor on their way back to Greer's office, Rosa glanced out of a window which looked down on the yard where Henshaw had left his car.

The doors of his Jaguar were open and two young officers in overalls appeared to be spring-cleaning the interior. Rosa immediately realised that this was no benign favour or act of courtesy, but a search for evidence. Fortunately, her client was too pre-occupied with his own dark thoughts to have observed what was going on.

It had been Rosa's hope that sooner rather than later Chief Inspector Greer would realise he had met his match and would bring the interview to an end. It was a hope that depended on his not having enough evidence to do anything else. But now she felt somewhat less sanguine. She realised that the police were frustrated by their failure to solve any of the mysteries that had broken out in the Henshaw ambience and that their determination to achieve a breakthrough was in no way diminished. She also realised that Ralph Henshaw was their prime target and would remain so until their suspicions were diverted elsewhere.

Her own feeling was that he was guilty as suspected or was covering up for somebody. Somebody such as Fran Gifford, who had been acting on his behalf as he wouldn't have wanted to run the risk of being seen in the area himself. That certainly made sense and Rosa didn't doubt that Fran would have been ready to accept the risks for the man she loved. But why had she been dispatched to Briar's End to commit such a monstrous crime? For some people arson provided a form of sexual satisfaction and the arsonists often hung around to witness the excitement of the developing blaze. That would hardly have applied in Fran's case, assuming it were she: in fact, the only purpose of the fire would have been to destroy vital clues; clues to what had happened to Evelyn Henshaw and, who knows, to the events surrounding the death of the first Mrs Henshaw. If this were a plausible line of reasoning, it showed that the death of the unfortunate Joshua was an irrelevance. He had got in the way and had had to be expunged. It also indicated something about the mentality of the murderer. A person who was both determined and ruthless.

As she followed her client back into Greer's office, she found herself staring at the back of his head. His strong, firm neck seemed to exude virility and determination in a manner she had not previously noticed. Probably because, seen from the front, it was his chin that served the same purpose.

'Anything fresh you want to tell me?' Greer enquired when they were seated. He cast Rosa a hopeful glance as if to give the interview a kick-start.

'Nothing,' Henshaw remarked and stared stonily out of the window. He turned slowly back to face his interrogator. 'I have nothing further to tell you and I demand to be released unless you want to get a writ for unlawful imprisonment.'

Rosa's heart sank. Henshaw was in enough trouble without adding truculence to his armoury. Moreover, as she had already told him, the police held all the trump cards. She leaned across and placed a hand on his forearm.

'Cool it,' she mouthed when he turned his head in her direction.

Chief Inspector Greer, meanwhile, watched them with an air of quiet satisfaction.

'I'm afraid there's no question of your being released,' he said. 'It's much more likely you'll be charged . . .'

At that moment the telephone on his desk rang shrilly and he nodded at Sergeant Wells to answer it.

'Who wants to know?' Wells asked after listening for half a minute. Turning to Greer he said, 'It's his daughter wanting to know if he's here.'

Greer put out a hand and took the receiver. 'Miss Henshaw, is it? Yes, your father is here, helping police with their enquiries . . . What? . . . Yes, she accompanied him . . . They're both in my office now . . . Why are you so anxious to know? Is it because you have knowledge of something we don't? If so, share it with us.' Greer's tone was dangerously smooth. 'No, I'm afraid you can't speak to him . . . How long will he be here? I'm afraid I can't answer that, it largely depends on him . . . By all means, come down to Utwell. I can't promise you anything, but I've been wanting to meet you . . . Fine. Take pot luck, as the saying goes.' He replaced the receiver. 'That was your daughter, Mr Henshaw,' he said with a faint note of relish. 'I gather she had only just found out you were here. I'd have thought you'd have told her where you were going.' When Henshaw set his mouth in a firm line which would have required a can-opener to prise his lips apart, Greer went on, 'Did you tell Mrs Gifford you were coming here?'

'That doesn't strike me as a particularly relevant question, Chief Inspector,' Rosa broke in.

Greer stared at her as if her presence had slipped his mind. He seemed about to argue the point, but then shrugged and turned his attention back to Ralph Henshaw.

'As I was saying, I'd hoped the recent break would have given you time to consider your situation more fully, but it seems not. I don't know what advice Miss Epton has given you, but it's clear that you're not going to help the police solve any of the crimes that have taken place at Riverview Court. In those circumstances, we'll break off this interview and meet again later.' As Henshaw jumped to his feet, Greer added, 'I didn't say anything about your release. I don't know whether Miss Epton proposes to hang around, that's up to her, but you can go and kick your heels in a police cell. And before you start threatening me with writs, you can check with Miss Epton that I'm within my rights. It's sometimes forgotten that the law also bestows rights on the police, though we're less clamorous about ours than the Council of Civil Liberties and their ilk are about yours.'

Rosa decided it was time to intervene. Interviewer and inter-viewee were building up a head of steam. At the moment Greer was in the better position to show his frustration. He could throw taunts which Henshaw was unable to match, though she feared that at any moment he might lose his control and say something which might afford him temporary satisfaction, but have the ulti-mate effect of tying a boulder round his neck.

'I'd like to have a quick word with my client,' she said.

'I thought that was what we had a recent break for,' Greer observed in a not too agreeable tone. 'OK, go ahead, we'll all look the other way.'

Rosa got up and brought a reluctant Henshaw to his feet. They walked into a corner of the room where she whispered urgently into his ear.

On returning to their chairs facing Greer's desk, she said, 'My client would like to make a written statement. He's told you that he was in London at the time of the fire and knew nothing of it until Mrs Santer called him. I think it's time that was recorded.'

Greer pulled a face. 'Is that all?'

'Are you refusing Mr Henshaw the opportunity of making a written statement?' she asked, with studied surprise.

'No, I just hope it isn't a waste of time.'

'Whose time are we talking about?' she enquired gently.

'Does he wish to write it in his own hand?' Greer's tone was heavy with boredom.

'Why not? It's always the safest way.'

'Perhaps you'll ensure, Miss Epton, that it's not full of irrel-evances. You know the matters to which he should address his mind and I rely on you to keep him on the rails.' He turned to Sergeant Wells. 'You'd better go back to the interview room and get started,' he said, as though washing his hands of what was about to take place.

Ralph Henshaw seemed uncertain whether to add his own tup-penceworth, but, in the event, followed Sergeant Wells out of the door.

'May I have a word with you, Miss Epton?' Greer said, as Rosa was about to follow suit. 'This daughter of his who phoned earlier on, do you know her?'

'I've met her. Why do you ask?'

'She sounded considerably het up on the phone.'

'That's hardly surprising. Any daughter who's fond of her father would be upset in the circumstances.'

'It was more than upset.' He was silent for a few contemplative seconds, before giving Rosa a look that invited her to contribute a further view. All he got, however, was an impatient shrug. Rosa had formed her own judgement of Anthea Henshaw after visiting her at the flat in Chiswick and had no intention of sharing it with Chief Inspector Greer.

She turned toward the door. 'Shall I find my client in the same interview room as before?'

'Yes, I'll show you the way,' Greer said, jumping up from his desk as if suddenly mindful of his manners.

As they came into the corridor, Rosa looked sidelong out of the window to see if anyone was still examining Ralph Henshaw's car, but the yard was deserted.

'May I ask why you suddenly advised your client to make a written statement?' Greer enquired, as they made their way up a short flight of stairs to the interview room. 'It seemed to come out of the blue.'

Rosa gave him a bland smile. 'That's the nicest thing you've ever said to me.'

Greer's expression instantly changed. 'In here,' he said coldly as he opened a door.

One of Rosa's virtues, where her clients were concerned, was that she never forgot whose side she was on. Though she never gratuitously set out to antagonise the police, she always resented being patronised or being expected to react with the trained obedience of a circus animal. She declined to jump through any of their hoops unless it suited her, and should an officer crack a whip in her vicinity she could bare her teeth as effectively as any Rottweiler.

Henshaw's statement was unadorned and to the point.

Sergeant Wells read it through with a sour expression.

'Is this all you want to say?' he asked.

'There's nothing else to say. I wish to leave.'

'I'm sure you do, but for the time being you're our guest.' Wells walked across and opened the door. Without a backward glance he left the room, speaking briefly to the young detective constable standing in the corridor outside.

'At this rate, we'll all die of old age before anything happens,'

Henshaw remarked, glancing impatiently about the room. 'Can't you speed things up?'

'I'm afraid not. They know their rights and they clearly intend to take their time. It's all part of a war of attrition.'

'I call it a bloody scandal.'

Rosa stared at him with a thoughtful expression. She never ceased to wonder at the different ways her clients reacted to the situation. Some became wobbly jellies and could hardly put their minds to any use at all. Others lost the faculty of rational thought through sheer anger and their sense of outrage. Others again, and Ralph Henshaw fell into this category, seemed incapable of grasping the seriousness of their plight.

Watching him pace about the small room, occasionally sitting down only to jump up again immediately, Rosa decided there was no point in trying to learn anything fresh from him. She was certain he could tell her a great deal more if he wanted, in particular about the death of his first wife and the disappearance of his second. She was equally certain that the police were determined to charge him with at least one of the serious crimes that hung over his head. They'd like to charge him with the lot, but would be satisfied with one for starters.

The door of the interview room suddenly opened and Chief Inspector Greer stood there. He half-turned and said, 'Your father's in here, Miss Henshaw. As fit as when you last saw him. We don't beat up our prisoners at Utwell.'

Rosa doubted whether he meant that you had to go to other stations for that, but kept the thought to herself.

Anthea Henshaw stepped inside the room and came to a halt.

'Are you all right, Father?' she asked in a tight voice. 'I was worried about you.'

'There was no need for you to have come,' he replied in an equally stiff tone.

As Rosa listened to this formal exchange of greeting, she wondered why Anthea *had* chosen to come. Her father could clearly have done without his daughter's visit, which had visibly upset him, and she, having arrived, didn't seem to know what to say. At least, not in front of an audience. She looked as statuesque as Rosa recalled from their previous encounter. She was several inches taller than her father and a good deal thinner.

'Now you know he's all right and all in one piece, I'm afraid I must ask you to leave, Miss Henshaw,' Greer said. 'It may be possible for you to talk to your father later.' He turned to Sergeant Wells. 'Take Miss Henshaw along to your office and find out what she can tell us . . .'

'I can't tell you anything,' Anthea said fiercely. 'I'd like to speak to my father alone.'

'He has a solicitor looking after his interests. I take it you know Miss Epton?'

For the first time Anthea looked in Rosa's direction. 'Yes, we've met,' she said, giving Rosa a small token smile. 'If you won't let me talk to my father,' she went on, turning back to Greer, 'I'd like to have a word with Miss Epton.'

'By all means. We'll leave you to have it here.'

The three men had barely departed from the room when Anthea flung herself down on to one of the chairs.

'I was so worried about my father that I just had to come,' she explained. 'But the police needn't think that *I'm* going to help them in their enquiry, because that's the last thing I'll do.' She gave Rosa a fierce look. 'What's my father told them?'

'Simply that he has no knowledge of who started the fire or did any of the other things under investigation.'

'My father's tough,' she observed. 'They won't be able to break him down.'

'The trouble is,' Rosa went on, 'that his denials become more threadbare all the time. If he persists in saying, "don't know, can't help" to everything they ask him about, he'll not do himself any good.'

'It's that bitch of a wife,' Anthea said furiously. 'She's the cause of everything that's happened. I'd like to . . .'

Though Rosa waited, the sentence remained unfinished. After a while she said, 'What can you tell me that'll assist your father? He's in deep trouble.'

Anthea's gaze darted about the room like an angry insect. All she said, however, in a venomous hiss, was, 'My bloody stepmother!'

'Why are you so certain she's still alive?' Rosa asked with a curiosity that kept coming to the surface.

'I just am,' Anthea replied and added abruptly, 'Oughtn't you to be with my father?'

Rosa stared at her dispassionately. Presumably she had friends, but Anthea was a strange girl: certainly not one with whom one felt immediately at ease.

'Yes, I'd better go and see what's happening,' she said, standing up and moving toward the door.

Before she got there, however, it was flung open and a triumphant-looking Sergeant Wells stood on the threshold.

'Your client's about to be charged, so you'd better come,' he said, addressing Rosa.

'Charged with what?' Anthea shouted. 'He's not done anything. How can you charge him?'

A woman police officer stepped past Wells and came across to where she was sitting white-faced and rigid.

Rosa hurried after Sergeant Wells along the corridor.

'What are the charges?' she asked as she tried to keep up with him.

'Arson and murder. But that's only for starters.' He threw her a triumphant look. 'I reckon you're going to have your work cut out with this one.'

So did Rosa, though it was the last thing she was going to admit to Sergeant Wells. For her the battle was just beginning.

Chapter Sixteen

It was two hours later that Rosa headed for home, leaving a dour and grim-faced Ralph Henshaw at the police station.

Anthea had departed earlier; indeed had disappeared unnoticed without a word to anyone.

Greer explained that he couldn't allow Rosa to drive away in Henshaw's car as he wished to have it thoroughly examined and she, for her part, refrained from saying what she had seen earlier through the window. He did, at least, offer to have her driven to the nearest main-line station and Rosa accepted.

'He'll be up before the magistrates tomorrow morning, Miss Epton. Will you be coming down?'

'Most certainly.'

'We'll be asking for a formal remand in custody.'

'I'll still be there.'

'I'm afraid you'll hardly be home before you're turning round to come back.'

'It's happened before,' Rosa remarked.

It was around eight thirty when she reached her flat and her only thought was to have a long soak in a hot bath. First, however, she listened to messages on her answering machine. There was one from Stephanie asking her to call the office first thing in the morning if she wasn't proposing to show herself. The other three were all from Peter, who had flown to Zurich earlier in the day and was going to have to stay there overnight. She had just played back message number three when he called in person.

'Are you all right?' he asked anxiously. 'I thought you'd run away.'

'I'm exhausted and frayed round the edges, but otherwise as lively as a bottle of fizz that's gone flat.'

'What you need, little Rosa, is a strong drink and a hot bath.'

'If you listen you'll hear the bath water running.'

'I can't hear any bottles gurgling.'

'I'm glad or I'd have worried about your ears. When will you be back, Peter?'

'Tomorrow. I'll come round in the evening.'

Rosa thought of all the work piling up on her desk in the office and said, 'I'd like that more than anything.' Blowing a kiss down the line she rang off and sat back with a contented sigh.

Suddenly she remembered her bath water was still running.

Utwell Magistrates' Court was next to the police station and had been built at the same time. A subterranean passage joined the custody cells in each building and was generally regarded as an extravagance they could have done without, given the small amount of use it received. In fact, Ralph Henshaw was the first person to be taken from the one building to the other for over three weeks. But then it was a generally law-abiding neighbourhood.

Prisoners remanded in custody were normally detained in the court cells until transferred to an appropriate prison. But he had been an overnight guest of the police. Even if the tunnel was put to infrequent use, the custody officer appreciated it in wet weather.

The court itself had every mod con devised by those who had never spent any part of their lives in court. It had tip-up seats that made it sound like an unruly classroom, an air-conditioning system that nobody seemed able to adjust to the needs of the day, sloping surfaces from which papers slithered in avalanches and an amplifying system that boomed and emitted tropical bird whistles at its own chosen moments.

Rosa arrived an hour before the court was due to sit and parked her car in a space reserved for barristers and solicitors. Beneath this legend somebody had added their own comment which had been smudged in an unsuccessful attempt to erase it. It read 'and other toadies'.

The legal profession, she mused, was apt to arouse strong feelings amongst those who tangled with it.

She walked next door to the police station and asked to see her client. The officer on duty had not been there the previous day and she was obliged to explain who she was. It seemed that neither Chief Inspector Greer nor Sergeant Wells had yet arrived.

Eventually she was taken down to the cells by an elderly sergeant who resembled an overgrown version of one of Snow White's benign dwarfs.

Henshaw glanced up when his cell door was unlocked and gave her a wry smile, which she took to be a good sign. Somebody had obviously lent him a razor and he looked surprisingly spruce and rested, though a closer look revealed eyes which were bloodshot and tired.

'Do you know, I'm quite looking forward to this?' he remarked.

'To what?' Rosa asked with a puzzled frown.

'To an enforced rest. I gather remand prisoners have everything except their liberty. Food sent in if they want, their own clothes, unlimited visitors, books to read . . .'

'I'm glad you're feeling so relaxed,' Rosa said, taken aback by his remarkable change of attitude.

'It's all yours now,' he said.

'If I'm going to defend you successfully, it has to be a joint effort,' she remarked firmly. 'You have to supply the ammunition.' She paused. 'At the moment I don't have any worth the name.'

He gave her a pacifying nod such as a parent might accord a demanding offspring.

'By the way,' she added, 'your daughter disappeared rather abruptly yesterday evening. Nobody seems to have seen her leave. I gather the police were rather annoyed.'

'She should have stayed away in the first place.'

'Would she have let your son know where you are?'

'You never know with Anthea.'

'And won't Mrs Gifford be wondering what's happened to you?'

'Perhaps you'll call her when you get back to London and tell her what's happened. I'd like to see you again when the court business is over.'

'Of course.'

A few minutes later, Rosa left the police station and walked over to the court. Ralph Henshaw made the same journey below ground.

Although business hadn't started, the court was full of expectant onlookers. Murder and arson were not everyday fare and the presence in the dock of the owner of Riverview Court added further spice to the situation. The fact that Ralph Henshaw wasn't the actual legal owner, but was only married to her, was a nicety

110

that wasn't going to spoil anyone's day. After all, her mysterious disappearance was an exciting ingredient on its own.

As she reached the row of seats reserved for lawyers, an eager-looking man of around forty leaned towards her.

'Miss Epton? I'm Roger Strong from the CPS. I don't think we've met before, but I'm sure we'll hit it off.'

His tone was more hopeful than confident and Rosa gave him a courteous good morning as she began unpacking her briefcase.

'This shouldn't take very long,' he went on. 'Never seen the court so full. Quite a cause célèbre for Utwell. I must say it's an extraordinary story, not that I've heard it all, of course. The police still have a tremendous lot to do before we'll be ready to present our case.'

Rosa acknowledged the information with a small smile. As long as he wasn't expecting her to fall in with everything he proposed, it didn't matter. If he did, he would soon learn that she was no pushover. In fact his eager-to-please manner could indicate that Rosa's reputation as a tough opponent had reached the court before her.

'Miss Epton?' a female voice enquired. 'I'm Heather Hull, the clerk.'

Rosa looked up to find Ms Hull standing over her. She had observed the clerk's name on a board outside and had wondered what lay in store. She hoped not to be confronted by a militant feminist nor yet by a timid female only recently qualified. Ms Hull appeared to be neither. She had burnished auburn hair, pulled back into a soft bun – and the most enormous pair of round horn-rimmed spectacles Rosa had ever seen, which had they not been transparent, would have blotted out most of her face. Her voice had a pleasant lilt which redeemed what might otherwise have been an unfortunate accumulation of excesses.

'We're ready if you are,' she went on. 'Mrs Strickland is in the chair, supported by Major Riley and Miss Tufnell.'

'I'm ready when everyone else is,' Rosa said, feeling that it was required of her to put everyone at their ease. She wasn't used to being treated as a guest of honour in any of the courts she normally attended.

'You want to watch her,' the crown prosecutor whispered in an aside and then quickly slid back to his own seat, only to slither back and add, 'she can be devious, can Ms Hull.'

A great many people who earned their living in magistrates'

courts could be devious. Indeed, most were at some time or another, though it was not a label that any chose to attach to their own conduct. Rosa scarcely had time to ponder the philosophical niceties involved when a female usher called for silence and everyone stood up. Mrs Strickland appeared through a door at the back of the bench attired, Rosa thought, more for a garden party than a morning's work administering justice. Major Riley leaned heavily on a thick walking-stick as he followed her to his place and Miss Tufnell brought up the rear fluttering to her seat with an eager-to-please expression that reminded Rosa of a devoted companion.

Meanwhile Ms Hull had taken her own place immediately below the chairman's eye. Rosa, who was all for female magistrates, nevertheless refused to refer to 'chairpersons' or worse still 'chairs'. To her 'Madam Chairman' was polite and dignified and as acceptable as a good many other oddities of language.

The clerk rose and read out the charges to the court in general and Ralph Henshaw in particular. The dock was immediately behind Rosa so that she was unable to observe his expression. When she did take a quick look, he still had a relaxed air, as though he was quite happy to be providing the morning's entertainment.

As soon as Ms Hull had explained for everyone's benefit that, subject to a prima facie case being established, the charges would be heard by a jury at a crown court and that today's proceedings were a first formal step, Rosa rose.

'Yes, Miss Epton?' the clerk said, in a tone she might have used to a partner on the tennis court who had just poached a shot.

'I'm applying for reporting restrictions to be lifted,' Rosa announced, to an immediate buzz of interest among the assembled reporters who weren't expecting this particular bonus. Normally, proceedings in the magistrates' court remained unreported to avoid the subsequent crown court trial being prejudiced by tendentious comment, even by accurately recorded evidence. No way should future jurors have their minds affected by what they read about a case which they might (against all odds) be called upon to try at some distant future date. It was one of the law's many complacent doctrines and necessitated a belief in nanny always knowing best.

The defence, however, had the right to apply for the restrictions to be lifted and Rosa had decided so to do. It was an unusual application in a case such as the one before the court and Ms Hull was clearly taken back. The three magistrates appeared to wait for guidance from some quarter and Miss Tufnell gave the impression that she would have worn a different dress if she had known. As for Roger Strong of the CPS his lips could be seen moving as if in silent prayer, but more probably in rehearsal of words which the nation's printing presses were poised to spread across the land.

For Rosa, it was a calculated move. Far from being afraid of prejudicing her client's future trial, she hoped that publicity would flush out all the information about him and his family that she was sure was being withheld from her. If she beat hard enough on the drum, somebody would come forward with something. It might not please Ralph Henshaw, but if he didn't like it, he could find someone else to defend him. But she didn't think he would. Therefore so long as he retained her services, she would be in charge. One thing for certain was that she had a fight on her hands and she didn't intend being frustrated by anyone who was notionally on her side. That included the spectre of his second wife, Evelyn, who, it seemed, all the time hovered never very far away.

When invited to address the court, Roger Strong rose from his seat, cleared his throat a couple of times and said he was asking for a remand in custody as the defendant had only just been charged and the prosecution wouldn't be ready to proceed for several weeks. In fact he said everything more than once so that straightforward sentences tended to become inverted the second time round to give them a new look. Well, a new sound, at least.

Rosa later learnt that he had been a none too successful jury advocate to whom the repetition had an allure of its own. To suggest that he also enjoyed the sound of his own voice didn't come amiss.

When her own turn came, Rosa said she hoped there wouldn't be any undue delay on the part of the police and the CPS in substantiating the charges which had been preferred against her client. She would regard it as part of her duty to harry them if she felt procrastination had led to a hardening of their corporate arteries.

Mrs Strickland, from the chairman's seat, listened impassively, but with a distinct alertness, as she waited to say her own piece, which was to remand Ralph Henshaw in custody.

Rosa hurried after him for a final word in the cells before slipping out of the back entrance and straight into a gaggle of newspaper reporters who were waiting by her car.

'We were wondering why you're opting for publicity in this case,' their selected spokesman said. 'Not complaining, mind you, but still wondering.'

Rosa smiled. She wanted publicity and here was an opportunity. 'I'm pleased that my request was granted by the court as I want to smoke out anyone with information. People are often coy about coming forward and I want to make it impossible for them to remain hidden.'

'You believe there's a lot of covering-up going on?'

Rosa frowned. Something warned her to tread carefully. 'Not necessarily any covering-up, but people with bits of vital information about some of the things that have happened.'

'Such as?'

'Who killed Stefan Michalowski and what's happened to Evelyn Henshaw.'

'Have you tried asking your client?' asked a reporter with a sly smile and thinning sandy hair which was greasy like his manner.

'My client knows nothing about either matter, any more than he does about who set fire to his home. All he knows is that it wasn't him.'

'Will you be suggesting that he's been set up?'

'I don't have to suggest anything. He's innocent until he's proved guilty. And he won't be.' She paused and added, 'But I'll certainly need all the help I can get, hence I'll be grateful for anything you print in the hope it may produce answers to some of the questions.'

'And if it doesn't?'

'It will,' Rosa replied, adding to herself, 'It must.'

One of the journalists hung back after the others moved away.

'It's the family that needs digging into,' he remarked, giving her a conniving look. 'At least, that's my opinion. Anyway, good luck. By the way, I'm Adam Chetwynd of the *Valley Monitor*. Circulation thirty-three thousand,' he added with a wink.

As she drove back to London, Rosa felt like a yachtsman embarking on a round the world race in which skill and stamina would be fully tested and the natural elements were not all the voyager might have to contend with.

She had never before appeared in a case of so many confusing threads. Threads which failed to match, but must somehow be made to form a coherent pattern.

Chapter Seventeen

'Where have you been, Christopher? I've been trying to reach you for days. All I got was your wretched answering machine.' Anthea Henshaw's voice was cross and reproachful. 'I did leave messages, but presumably you never got them.'

'I've been away,' Chris Henshaw replied without going into details. 'And Amanda's away, too.'

Anthea was uninterested in the whereabouts of her sister-in-law, whom she looked upon as spoilt and brainless and in a permanently broody state.

Not for the first time since she and Chris had married, Amanda had gone back to her mother taking two-year-old Jason with her. It was her regular flight path in times of stress and her mother, a domineering woman if ever there was one, stood complacently by, waiting for the ultimate break-up of her daughter's marriage. She tolerated her son-in-law, but had yet to say a charitable word about his family.

'Presumably you've seen the papers?' Anthea now went on.

'Yes. The police can't really believe that dad burnt the house down, can they?'

'They've charged him, and with murder, too,' Anthea observed vehemently.

'Murder's crazy. It could only be manslaughter at the most. He didn't deliberately kill the old chap in the paraffin shed.'

'You've obviously not read the papers properly. The man in the shed wasn't burnt to death. He was bludgeoned. That's murder, Christopher,' she added, reminding her brother that she had always enjoyed having the last word. 'Anyway, father appeared in court this morning and has been remanded in custody.'

'Were you there?'

'No. He asked me to stay away. He has a woman solicitor, Rosa Epton, whom I don't altogether trust.'

'What's wrong with her?'

'A bit too pleased with herself.' She paused. 'The point is, Christopher, I think we ought to meet. It's time to show family solidarity. I know you've opted out since you got married, but it's our duty to rally round father.'

'What about Fran, have you been in touch with her?'

'Of course I have. She's frantic.'

Chris Henshaw couldn't see his father's mistress ever becoming frantic. He did not dislike her, but she was far too controlled in her emotions.

'So, when are we going to meet, Christopher?' Anthea asked impatiently.

'It'll be best if I call you back,' her brother said, and rang off before she could protest.

Chris had never got on particularly well with his sister, who had very much been their father's favourite. Indeed, he had married shortly after their mother's death in order to loosen family ties. This had not been difficult, given the possessive qualities of his mother-in-law who had clamped him to her own bosom until her daughter had tearfully related tales of his excessive sexual demands. From that day, Mrs Arnold had viewed him with doubt and suspicion. To her, sex was something to put up with, at the same time keeping it strictly in its place, which was at the bottom of life's agenda.

As for Chris Henshaw himself, he was still deeply in love with his wife and devoted to their small son. Moreover, he looked forward to the arrival of their second child and charitably attributed his wife's neurotic behaviour to her pregnancy. He was surprisingly tolerant of her flights back to her mother and it never occurred to him to make a stand. He had thrown in his lot with her relatives from the beginning and had no regrets. To his own family he remained passively dutiful, and, unlike his sister, had never felt any hostility toward his stepmother, nor toward his father's mistress.

He had hoped that marriage would relieve him of the atmosphere of threatening strife in which he had grown up and which he had hated. He had been fond of his mother and had loathed hearing his parents quarrel, his mother hurrying from the room so that nobody should see her tears and his father tight-lipped and glowering. Anthea had always been on her father's side, which made him automatically take his mother's. It didn't matter where the rights and wrongs lay. In fact, more often than not he didn't know. He realised at an early age that his mother could be an exasperating woman, but that didn't excuse his father treating her like his chattel.

He felt surprisingly unmoved by the fact that his father now stood charged with murder and arson. And there was still Stefan Michalowski's death described so gorily in the press, waiting to be laid at someone's door; for that couldn't be anything other than murder.

The decision he had to make was whether he should get in touch with Rosa Epton and tell her what he knew about his stepmother's disappearance. Despite his sister's plea for family solidarity, he had no wish to be drawn into his father's troubles. Certainly not to make them worse. On the other hand there was such a thing as public duty which could be a handy way of reaching a decision and clearing one's conscience at one and the same time.

'Christopher Henshaw would like to see you,' Stephanie said on the phone not long after Rosa had come into the office the following afternoon.

'When does he want to come?'

'He's here now.'

Rosa blinked in surprise. She had always intended getting in touch with him; indeed, had made at least one unsuccessful effort to do so. And now here he was on the doorstep. Presumably, his father's arrest had given him a sense of urgency.

'OK, Steph, let me just unclutter my desk and then I'll see him.'

Apart from anything else she held the view of most professional people that clients should always be kept waiting, if only to show who was the boss.

Though she could see a faint family resemblance when a few minutes later he was shown into her room, he seemed to lack the spikiness of his sister and the animal magnetism of his father.

Though he had not inherited his father's aggressive chin, the likeness was apparent. He was a generally softer version, his face being dominated by a pair of large grey eyes that gave him a contemplative air which was totally alien to Ralph Henshaw's pugilistic expression.

He was plainly ill at ease. Probably, Rosa speculated, having second thoughts about coming.

'It's good of you to see me without an appointment,' he said, sitting forward on the edge of her visitor's chair. 'But in view of what's happened, I decided I ought to come and see you straight away.'

'You're referring to your father's arrest?'

He nodded. 'That, in particular, but everything else as well.' He swallowed uncomfortably. 'I've never got on particularly well with my father and my sister and I invariably end up arguing. Funnily enough, I like his mistress and I had a rapport going with Evie – that's his second wife.' He paused. 'But, of course, you met her.'

'She was the first member of your family I did meet,' Rosa said with a slight smile. 'You're the last.'

He made a face. 'We must seem an odd lot. A bit like the Addams family, but without their black humour. Well, let's say without their humour. Recent events are certainly black enough.'

He had fallen silent and Rosa decided to give him a gentle push. She was genuinely intrigued to know what had brought him to see her.

'I'm afraid your father's in serious trouble. How serious I shan't know until I've studied the witness statements that'll be served in due course. He denies having anything to do with the fire at Riverview Court or knowing anything about the dead man whose body was found in one of the sheds, but it would obviously assist his defence if there was evidence to support his alibi.' She went on quickly. 'He's told me what he did on the night of the fire and I shall obviously try and substantiate what he's told me. Perhaps you're in a position to help?'

He shook his head. 'I last spoke to him over a week ago before any of this happened. He called me to ask if I had any news of my stepmother. He seemed worried about her disappearance . . .'

'Wasn't that natural? His being worried, I mean?'

'Yes and no. I think he was more worried about Evie's money than about her well-being. After all, Fran had been his mistress for several years and I don't think Evie was ever particularly interested in sex – at least, not with my father.'

'What about Stefan?'

A small, reflective smile flitted across Christopher Henshaw's face.

'I don't think she was ever averse to the odd toy boy in her life. Can you imagine anyone less like a toy boy than my father?'

Rosa couldn't, but decided to leave the question unanswered.

'Get back to this phone call your father made. You say he wanted to know if you had any news of your stepmother?'

'Yes.'

'And what did you tell him?'

'That I hadn't.'

'I take it he phoned *you* because he knew the two of you were on . . . well, speaking terms?'

'I suppose so.' He paused and studied his feet as if they were a new discovery. 'The thing is, it wasn't true.' He looked up and met Rosa's gaze. 'It wasn't true that I'd not heard from Evie.' He reached into an inside pocket of his jacket and produced an envelope. 'I had this about a week after she'd disappeared.'

Rosa could see it bore a French stamp with an Alpes Maritimes postmark. Inside the envelope was a picture postcard of Nice. She turned it over to read:

Dear Chris,
   I am fleeing for my life. If I survive, I'll keep in touch.
   Affectionately, Evie

'Is that definitely your stepmother's handwriting?' she asked.

He nodded. 'Definitely.'

'And you received this about a week after her disappearance?'

'Yes.'

'That means, a week after Stefan's murder,' she said in a thoughtful tone. 'Doesn't your stepmother have a sister who lives in the south of France?'

'Yes. I've tried to get in touch with her on the phone, but there's never any reply. I have not met her and I know she's often travelling.'

'Your stepmother mentioned her when she came to see me. I gathered they didn't keep in close touch with one another.'

'They were still sisters,' Chris Henshaw observed. 'When it comes to a showdown, blood is thicker than water.'

Rosa wondered whether that applied in the case of his own family as well.

'You've heard nothing further from her?'

'Not a word.'

'So it's possible she may still be in fear of her life?'

'I wouldn't pay too much attention to that card,' he said

abruptly. 'Evie has always been prone to dramatise. I only showed it to you as evidence she's still alive.'

'You haven't shown it to the police?'

Christopher jumped as if she had made an improper suggestion. 'No,' he said, vigorously shaking his head. 'The last thing I want is to become involved in their enquiries.'

Rosa looked at him thoughtfully. Whatever his motive, the card was certainly not evidence that Evelyn *was* still alive, but she didn't wish to argue with him. Maybe he was already regretting having shown it to her, suddenly aware that he could be letting down the family. On the other hand perhaps he wanted to assure Rosa that his stepmother *was* still alive and that whatever else his father had done he had not murdered her. But surely he wasn't that naive!

Oh dear, Rosa thought, I'm becoming paranoid about the Henshaw family. Chris Henshaw seems a nice enough person, so don't start seeing some dark and sinister motive behind his visit.

While these thoughts had been chasing each other round her head, he appeared to have sunk into a reverie of his own.

'Did you know Stefan Michalowski?' Rosa asked suddenly.

It seemed to take several seconds for the words to reach the right section of his brain and Rosa was about to repeat the question when he gave her an apologetic smile.

'I'm terribly sorry, I'm afraid I was miles away. I was thinking of Amanda and our small son.'

'I'm glad that you, at least, have a satisfactory family life.'

'Did I say that?' he asked in a tone of surprise.

'I don't think you did, but I assumed it,' Rosa replied, awkwardly.

'I'm deeply in love with my wife and I know she loves me. That should be enough for anyone, shouldn't it?' he said wistfully.

'All marriages have their ups and downs,' Rosa said hastily, as she saw a tear begin to roll down his cheek.

Their meeting had taken a sudden, embarrassing turn.

'I'd better be going,' he said, suddenly jumping to his feet. 'I just wanted to give you Evie's card. It had been on my conscience that I hadn't come forward with it before.' He produced a business card from his wallet and put it on her desk. 'You probably have my address anyway, but here's my card if you need to get in touch with me.'

'You must have given a lot of thought to everything that's

happened; do you think the same person is responsible for Stefan's murder and the subsequent fire at Riverview Court?'

'Look, Miss Epton, I'd prefer not to get drawn into speculation about those matters. I'm sure you understand . . .'

His reluctance could only mean he had a shrewd idea, if not actual evidence, of who was responsible for the grisly sequence of events, Rosa thought. And that in turn meant a member of his own family was involved.

'Did you ever meet Stefan?' she asked, as he retreated to the door.

'I may have done . . . I don't know.'

And with that cryptic remark, he fled from her room and out of the building. Rosa shrugged. He wasn't her first visitor to make an abrupt departure and set her wondering.

When she told Peter about it over dinner that evening, he said, 'I wish you'd never taken on this case.'

'It fascinates and frustrates me in equal measure,' Rosa said, as she popped a slice of cool melon into her mouth. 'Anyway, I couldn't possibly opt out now. I'm fully committed.'

Peter became thoughtful as he tackled his plate of crisply fried whitebait. 'If you're so determined, what's your next move?' he asked, retrieving one of the tiny fish that had fallen off his fork into his lap. He was a fastidiously clean and neat person who hated any fall-out of food on his person.

'That's the trouble, Peter, I'm still trying to find a starting-point. OK, Ralph Henshaw says he's had nothing to do with the events that are the subject of charges, and with luck we may be able to substantiate an alibi . . .'

'In which case he'll be acquitted,' Peter broke in.

'Yes, and the mystery remains unsolved.'

'Your job is to defend him and not to solve extraneous mysteries,' Peter observed in a tone of unusual severity.

'But they're all part of the same thing, Peter. And you're forgetting that it started with Mrs Henshaw asking me to act if anything should happen to her. Well, happen it most certainly did. Stefan was found murdered in her pond and she then vanished off the face of the earth.' She gave Peter a rueful look. 'However you look at it, I'm involved up to my ears.'

'It seems to me that you've jumped into a vipers' pit,' Peter remarked in a far from happy tone.

'If you're likening the Henshaws to vipers, I think you're being unfair. They may lack a certain charm, but, then, so do a lot of my clients. The only charmers who come to me professionally are con merchants.' She gave him a sudden smile. 'The unsuccessful ones come my way, the successful ones are your clients.'

He looked reflective for a moment, then grinned.

'That's a nice thought,' he said. 'Anyway, we'd better decide on your next move.'

'Under the influence of this delicious melon, I already have. I shall go and visit Mrs Upjohn tomorrow. I feel she's the most likely person to have heard something from Evelyn Henshaw.'

'Isn't she a bit dotty?'

'Eccentric perhaps, but that doesn't mean she's not reliable.'

'Don't let her cast any spells over you.'

'If anyone casts spells I hope it'll be me,' Rosa replied, as she studied the Dover sole a waiter had just placed in front of her.

An hour and a bit later they left the restaurant.

'Your place or mine?' Peter enquired, as he slipped an arm round her waist and steered her towards his car.

Chapter Eighteen

Rosa went into the office early the next morning to catch up with work she had neglected while dancing attendance on Ralph Henshaw.

If she had looked for a couple of hours of peace and quiet before anyone else arrived, she had forgotten their faithful office cleaner, Mrs Druce, who went in at six o'clock three mornings a week to vacuum and dust and empty waste-paper baskets. She had vanished by seven thirty and gone to her next job. She was a dour, hard-working and trustworthy woman who had been cleaning the offices of Snaith and Epton for over five years. One could tell when she'd been dusting for she had a knack of putting things back in a different place. Stephanie had once been bold enough to point this out to her. Mrs Druce had listened, nodded and gone on doing it.

She acknowledged Rosa's unexpected arrival without surprise, her only comment being, 'I've done your room, miss,' as she vacuumed her way to Robin's office.

Rosa didn't mind the hum of a vacuum cleaner at a distance, which was rather the same way she felt about bagpipes. She had dug into a pile of work on her desk before realising there was complete silence and that Mrs Druce must have departed. She worked on for a further hour before deciding to go out for a cup of coffee at the sandwich bar round the corner. She was just leaving when Stephanie arrived. It was always a toss-up whether she or Ben arrived first.

'Early bird, eh?' she remarked sardonically. 'Did you beat Mrs Druce to it?'

'I wasn't that early, Steph.'

'You know you're due at South-Western at eleven?'

South-Western was one of the magistrates' courts she attended with regularity.

'Yes, I know. I'll be back in fifteen minutes.' She glanced at her watch. 'I want to call Mrs Vera Upjohn before I leave for court. Perhaps you'd dig out her number for me?'

'Is she the soothsayer lady?'

Rosa nodded and wondered whether Mrs Upjohn would be flattered by the description. Mrs Upjohn's kind were liable to be touchy about the labels people fastened on them.

By the time she returned to the office, the rest of the staff had arrived, including Robin with whom she boxed and coxed and who was just on his way out again.

She waited till ten o'clock and then asked Stephanie to get her Mrs Upjohn's number. She listened to it ringing and was about to replace the receiver when a voice answered.

'Is that Mrs Upjohn?'

'It is, indeed. I'm speaking to Miss Epton, am I not?'

'Yes,' Rosa said with some surprise.

'I recognised your voice at once, dear. I never forget a voice, even if I haven't heard it for years, and you have such an attractive voice.'

Rosa wasn't sure how to acknowledge the compliment, but Mrs Upjohn swept on.

'And now you're phoning to say you've had news of Evie, yes?'

'I'm afraid not. In fact I was hoping you'd heard from her . . .'

'Oh dear, oh dear, this is most worrying,' Mrs Upjohn broke in. 'I thought she was getting in touch with me one day last week, but it turned out to be another faithful friend.'

Rosa didn't like to ask whether alive or departed this life. Mrs Upjohn was apt to regard the distinction as irrelevant.

'Did you read that Mr Henshaw had been charged with burning down their house?' Rosa went on.

'It came to me in a vivid dream, dear. And, yes, I also saw something in the newspaper. Are you sure he doesn't know what's happened to Evie?'

'He swears he doesn't.'

'I must look at the cards again,' Mrs Upjohn said with a sigh. 'And I have one or two other possibilities up my sleeve.'

Rosa thought it best not to enquire what they were. She was about to bring the conversation to an end when Mrs Upjohn spoke again.

'If Evie had come to me sooner, I would have warned her against marrying the Henshaw man. Nobody marries a murderer while she's in her right senses. I'm sorry, dear, I know you're defending him in court, but that can't prevent me speaking the truth. He's a murderer. He killed his first wife. Surely you're aware of that, dear? Evie must have told you.'

Rosa was tempted to say that Ralph Henshaw was equally sure it was Evie who had done that, but the time had not yet come for sharing confidences with the Bromley soothsayer. Fortunately, Mrs Upjohn didn't wait for answers. The artefacts of her trade might offer equivocal advice more often than not, but they always did so with the greatest of confidence. The Delphic Oracle had set a tone still followed by the bands of clairvoyants, palmists, card and tea-leaf readers. People didn't pay good money to be fobbed off with doubts and uncertainty.

'I know you're a lawyer, dear, but I ask you to be very careful in your dealings with the Henshaws. They're very dangerous, as poor Evie has learnt to her cost. At least the fire should have destroyed some of the evil. If they ever rebuild the house I hope they'll be careful not to let the spirits back in again. It's not impossible, at the same time not easy.'

Rosa decided not to follow Mrs Upjohn down this particular path which struck her as leading straight into Alice's Wonderland.

'As for that poor young man found in the lake, he deserved better,' Mrs Upjohn declared firmly.

'Everyone deserves better than to end up at the bottom of a lake,' Rosa observed.

'Not necessarily, dear, but Stefan certainly did.'

'Did you ever meet him?' Rosa asked, remembering that Mrs Upjohn had earlier denied knowledge of him.

'Just the once.'

'You met Stefan?' she said in surprise, thinking their wires had become crossed.

'I've said so, dear. Evie brought him to see me for advice.'

'What was your impression of him?'

'A personable young man, though I'm afraid he didn't take me seriously.'

'In what way?' Rosa enquired, hoping the answer might provide her with a lead of some sort.

'I warned him that his life had hidden surprises in store and that he should be on his guard, but I'm afraid he just laughed, which was foolish of him,' Mrs Upjohn said severely. 'But that's youth for you,' she added in a more charitable tone. 'I wouldn't have seen him, but Evie was very keen that I should and I didn't want to disappoint her.'

'May I ask what he wanted to see you about?'

After a pause Mrs Upjohn said, 'Normally I wouldn't dream of discussing a client's affairs, any more than you would, dear, but seeing that he's no longer with us, and after all the terrible things that have happened, perhaps there'd be no harm.'

It was on the tip of Rosa's tongue to say she was sure the spirits would understand when caution held her back. Mrs Upjohn had already expressed herself censoriously about those who made light of her powers.

'What I'm about to tell you, dear, must go no further,' she now said in a tone of sepulchral solemnity. Fortunately she didn't wait for Rosa's response to this injunction. 'He asked if the girl he had recently jilted was likely to carry out her threat to harm him.'

'Did he mention the name of the girl?' Rosa interrupted.

'It'll be better, dear, if you let me tell it in my own way.'

'I'm sorry,' Rosa said in a suitably chastened tone.

'As I was saying, this girl had apparently threatened him with violence if he left her. Of course, I asked him her name and he told me it was Perdita and that he had known her several months but that she had become increasingly demanding and he had decided to make a break. Also he thought his studies would benefit from a move away from London.'

'Was Mrs Henshaw present?' Rosa asked, deciding to risk further reproof.

'It was Evie who had brought him and she was much more interested in my various readings than he was. As I told you, dear, I'm afraid he didn't take me seriously, which was foolish of him, nice young man as he was.'

Rosa was about to ask for further details of the meeting when Mrs Upjohn said briskly, 'I can't stand here talking all morning, dear. I have a very important client arriving shortly. A very important client, indeed,' she added in case Rosa hadn't heard the first time. Then she heard the phone click.

As she made her way to court, Rosa pondered over their conversation. It had provided her with food for thought, though, as with spinach which boils away to nothing, she felt the same might apply to Mrs Upjohn's discourse.

Chapter Nineteen

Peter reminded her of his offer of a long weekend in Nice.

'We might find out something about Mrs Henshaw,' he added as a bait. 'Doesn't her sister live out there?'

'She has a villa in a village called St Virgile de Var, but nobody's been able to contact her. It's less than ten miles from Nice in the Var valley.'

'You mean, nobody's been able to reach her on the phone, but has anyone actually knocked on her door?'

'I imagine the French police may have done so at the request of our lot.'

Peter clucked impatiently. 'We all know what that means. A bored gendarme ringing the bell once and going away. Incidentally, what's the sister's name?'

'Zena Vitry. I gather her husband died several years ago and they had retired to the south from Paris where he had had a job at the Louvre.'

'Then Nice it is,' Peter said eagerly, 'with Madame Vitry as our special target. I'll book flights and reserve a room at the Négresco.'

Rosa sighed. Nobody was more extravagant when it came to arranging weekend breaks and Rosa had long ceased to make any serious protest. She knew Peter could afford them and the suggestions always came from him so she didn't feel she was on the scrounge.

Thus it was that on a Friday afternoon two days later they caught an afternoon flight from Heathrow to Nice, where the hire car Peter had bespoken was waiting for them.

Rosa hadn't been to the south of France since she had accompanied her older brother and his then fiancée on a camping holiday on the Côte d'Azur. She had been reluctant to tag along and they even more so to take her, but her father, who was liberal in some respects and straight-laced in many others, had insisted from his Herefordshire rectory that it would be improper for brother Robert and girlfriend Barbara to go unescorted.

The trip had not been a success and Rosa was now able to smile as she recalled the number of times they had tried to give her the slip. Her acute sense of self-preservation, rather than any addiction to their company, always managed to frustrate their efforts. However much they tried to lose her, she clung on, hating every moment. So much for the memories of over fifteen years ago.

The hotel now came into view as they approached along the Promenade des Anglais. It was exactly as she remembered it with its baroque cupolas and air of refined elegance. Peter had barely drawn to a halt when their luggage was removed and a commissionaire took possession of the car keys.

'Don't look so nervous,' Peter whispered, as he led the way to reception.

The fact was that Rosa invariably felt overawed by the sheer splendour of such establishments. It was as if she half expected to have her path barred and to be shown politely but unmistakably to the way out. Peter, on the other hand, treated de luxe hotels with the same respect he might show a Wimpy bar.

The boy who had brought up their bags having bowed his way out, preceded by the immaculately dressed young man who had shown them how to switch on lights and open the window on to the verandah, Peter wrapped his arms round Rosa and gave her a long, passionate kiss.

'Happy?' he enquired, leading her by the hand on to the verandah. 'One kiss for "yes" and fifty for "no".'

Later they showered and changed. Rosa wore a white dress trimmed in pale yellow and Peter put on a crisp cream-coloured tropical suit. 'Have you stayed here often, Peter?' Rosa asked casually as she put the finishing touches to her face.

'Why do you ask?'

'Because all the staff seem to know you and kiss the ground you walk on.'

He gave her a beaming smile. 'I know a good many of them. One of my Arab clients always stays here if he can book a whole floor.'

For Rosa the evening passed magically. They dined at a restaurant where food and service were blended to perfection. Afterwards they strolled back to the hotel in the intoxicating evening air.

'Let's go to bed,' Peter said on their return, which is exactly what they did.

As usual he was up before her the next morning and was splashing in the shower by the time she became aware of the new day. She turned over in bed and snuggled up against his pillow. At that moment he came back into the bedroom and after a second's hesitation squeezed into bed beside her. It was another hour before either of them got up again.

Around noon they set off in the car and headed out of Nice in the direction of Colomars up the Var valley. A signpost showed St Virgile de Var as being seven kilometres beyond, apparently halfway up a mountainside. When they got there, the village proved to be little more than a scattering of villas along the narrow, winding road.

'There it is,' Rosa exclaimed, pointing at a villa on their left bearing the nameplate 'Villa Montmorency'. 'It looks pretty deserted.'

'They all do,' Peter observed. 'Either everyone's away or they're waiting to ambush visitors.'

He halted the car directly outside the main gate whose lower half was sheet metal giving way to a heavy iron framework above. There was a bell-push and an answer phone set in the left-hand gate-post. The front of the house could be seen about twenty yards down a drive of overgrown shrubs and cypress trees. There was no sign of life. Rosa got out and went across to discover if the bell produced one. She pressed it hard and kept her finger on it while Peter watched her with wry amusement from inside the car.

Suddenly to her surprise, so much so that she started back a pace, a crackling flow of French spurted from the rusty grille. It was a woman's voice, but was otherwise incomprehensible. It seemed to go on for a long time, but then stopped abruptly as it had begun. Rosa, whose knowledge of French had deteriorated since getting an A-level at school, gave the device a frightened look. Then bracing herself stepped closer and spoke.

'Est-ce que Madame Vitry est chez soi?' she articulated carefully. 'Je m'appelle Rosa Epton, je suis une amie anglaise.' Not strictly true, of course, as she had never met Mrs Henshaw's sister in her life, but stripped of complications, it was the best she could do.

There was an atmospheric crackle and a further incomprehensible flow. Fortunately, she caught the final word. 'Attendez!' Wait, she would. Till the moon rose, if necessary.

A couple of minutes later an old woman appeared coming up the drive toward them. The closer she got, the more cronelike she appeared. She had a scarf over her head and several layers of dark-coloured outer garments.

She made no attempt to unlock the gate, but stood staring at Rosa through the iron bars, as if trying to decide whether she was friend or foe.

'You are English?' she asked suddenly in a harsh voice.

'Yes,' Rosa said keenly. 'I didn't realise you spoke the language. That makes things much easier. Is Madame Vitry at home?'

'No. Away.'

'Has her sister, Mrs Henshaw, been staying here?'

'I don't know,' she said, after an unnecessarily long pause.

'But you do know Mrs Henshaw?' This received a shrug. 'You speak very good English,' Rosa said, hoping that flattery might ease the situation.

The woman shrugged. 'Madame Vitry teach.'

'Have you worked for her for a long time?'

'Forty years.'

'When will she be home again?'

Another shrug.

'Can you tell me how I can get in touch with her?'

'You give message to me. I tell her.'

'I'm staying in Nice and go back to England on Monday.'

'I speak to Madame this evening.'

This seemed the best offer she was likely to receive and she accepted it with an effusion of mercis.

Returning to the car from which Peter had been observing the scene, she searched the pockets for pen and paper.

'She speaks English,' Rosa said, as she delved for materials. 'She's promised to pass on a message to Madame Vitry.'

'Did she say anything about Mrs Henshaw?'

'No, but she didn't react as if she were dead.'

A few minutes later Rosa returned to the gate with the note she had written, using the roof of the car as a desk.

The old woman was exactly as Rosa had left her. Obdurate and patient. She took the note and without looking at it stuck it in a pocket of her capacious skirt. Then with a 'Bonjour, mademoiselle,' she turned and walked back toward the house. Rosa watched her until she passed from view behind a clump of bushes.

There had been something bizarre about the whole episode, but Rosa nevertheless felt satisfied with the tenuous contact she had made.

'You can charge that to expenses,' Peter said cheerfully as they set off again.

'The taxing master wouldn't even find it funny,' she said, recalling some of the battles in the past she had had with taxing officials who vetted her claims for expenses. 'And anyway I thought I was on a free ride.'

'You are, little Rosa. I have a client whose yacht is moored at Cannes. He asked me to bring out some documents which require his signature. He'll be happy to pay for our trip.'

'Really happy?'

'Well, he certainly won't protest.'

'When are you going to deliver these documents?' Rosa asked suspiciously.

'Now. Then we'll drive back along the coast to Nice.'

Peter had a habit of springing on her matters about which he had not said a previous word. She supposed it was a facet of his natural inscrutability. Whenever she asked him why he had not told her earlier, he would give her a surprised look and say that Oriental reticence didn't require one to tell the world everything one was going to do.

'But I'm not the world,' she would protest.

'No, you're little Rosa and I love you very much.'

'Would it be different if I was your wife?' she once asked.

'No, because I'm me and you're you. A legal bond wouldn't change our natures.'

And on that note, the conversation would end. It was a reminder to Rosa that, though Peter had more than once urged her to marry him, she had preferred to keep their relationship on its existing basis. Marriage could be like fitting bars to all the windows, whereas a continuing affair, well-tended and carefully nurtured, was as fresh as a flower-bed after a shower of spring rain. Well, almost!

When they reached the waterfront at Cannes, Rosa looked for

the most expensive yacht on the assumption that Peter's Gulf State client would be its owner.

'How did you know it was that one?' Peter asked.

'I just did,' Rosa said smugly. It was moored some way from the quayside and looked quietly opulent. 'How do we get to it?'

'We don't. The sheikh will be sleeping. He only wakes up in time to come ashore and spend the night at the Casino. There'll be a speedboat moored somewhere along here with one of his aides on board.'

Boat and aide were soon found and after a brief exchange of greetings the documents were handed over. A couple of minutes later, Peter was back in the car and they were driving along the promenade.

'I gather his Excellency was on a winning streak at the tables last night, so he'll be honoured to pay for our dinner tonight. He told Ahmed to tell me.'

'Where are we going to dine?'

'We'll drive over to Monte Carlo. I've already fixed it.'

To Rosa it was a marvellous evening. A superb meal in a sumptuous setting and Peter's company. As much as anything she enjoyed studying her fellow diners. Millionaires accompanied by gorgeous girls who were ready to sing for their supper – and a great deal more beside. Bored-looking old couples who had to spend their money somehow and the occasional gigolo working hard to earn his keep with a blue-rinsed dowager whose husband had passed on his way scattering his wealth behind him.

Rosa found them all a fascinating spectacle. She certainly didn't envy them, for almost each one was an anachronism. Bored and waiting to die in a sea of parasites.

'I wonder what they make of us,' she whispered to Peter as she grappled with a meringue chantilly of indelicate proportions.

'That you're an heiress with perverted taste who has picked up a poor Chinese boy.'

She gave him a sharp look. 'If I thought you really meant that, I'd get up and go.'

'Then, what about that we're on our honeymoon? Anyway, what's it matter what any of them think?'

'It doesn't,' Rosa said a trifle defensively.

'Exactly, so why don't we dance?'

He led Rosa on to the nearly empty floor and pulled her into his arms.

'It's being a wonderful weekend, Peter,' she said softly as he held her to him.

'I'm glad you're happy, because I certainly am,' he said, giving her a quick kiss. He giggled. 'Now everyone'll know we're here on a naughty weekend. For many of the old dears, naughtiness is no more than a memory, but they'll still make the most of it.' He paused and gave her another kiss. 'Luckily, we've got a long way to go before naughtiness is only a dream.'

They drove back to Nice in virtual silence, each sensing that conversation would destroy the magic enveloping them.

'A telephone message for Mademoiselle Epton,' the night porter said as he handed Peter their key and Rosa a piece of folded paper.

Madame Vitry telephoned, Rosa read.

'Did she not leave a message?' she asked, looking up from the piece of paper in her hand.

The porter frowned before taking it from her and reading it.

'This is the message, mademoiselle,' he said patiently. 'Madame Vitry has telephoned.' He peered at it more closely. 'It was at nine fifty hours. If she had said more, it would be here,' he said, shaking the piece of paper as if to see whether any hidden words dropped out.

'She'll probably call you in the morning,' Peter said, smothering a yawn. 'It's too late to phone her now. And, anyway, you don't know where she was calling from.'

'But supposing she doesn't, Peter?'

'We'll decide then what to do,' he said, steering her toward the lift. 'If she hadn't intended trying to reach you later, she wouldn't have left a message in the first place.'

'I suppose not,' Rosa said, in a doubtful tone. 'I just hope she doesn't have second thoughts about getting in touch.'

For once Rosa woke up before Peter the next morning. There was light round the edge of the curtains and she picked up her watch which was on the bedside table. Seven thirty. Peter was sleeping quietly on his side of the bed. He was the most peaceful sleeper God had created. Indeed, Rosa sometimes panicked that he had died he was breathing so gently. She got up and went into the bathroom for a drink of water. She felt unusually thirsty and attributed it to having drunk more than usual the previous evening. She cleaned her teeth and splashed on some toilet water. By the time she returned to their bed, Peter had distributed himself across it diagonally. He always looked so incredibly young when he was asleep. She bent over the bed and kissed him lightly on his upturned cheek. He stirred and she moved away so as not to wake him; but he suddenly put out a hand and pulled her down on top of him.

'You smell delicious,' he said, sleepily.

Rosa sighed and slipped into the space he made for her. 'I wonder what time Madame Vitry will call,' she said.

'I suspected you were wondering something like that,' he murmured. 'But it's too early to think about her. Think about me, instead!'

'Supposing she doesn't phone back,' Rosa said earnestly.

'She will, she will. Trust my instinct. It's now ten minutes before eight and I bet you the phone rings before ten o'clock. Probably between nine thirty and ten. It's Sunday and she won't want to call too early; equally she'll want to catch you before we go out.'

'You sound so confident, Peter.'

'I am. Anyway, seeing that we're both now wide awake, why don't you order breakfast while I take a shower? Or the other way around if you like?'

Their breakfast arrived about forty-five minutes later and they had it out on the balcony wearing dressing-gowns. Orange juice, coffee and croissants, with delicious French butter and strawberry jam.

They had just finished when the phone rang in the bedroom.

'There you are!' Peter said, glancing at his watch. 'Twenty minutes before ten. To the minute like I said. You'd better answer it.'

'You answer it, Peter,' Rosa said in a cajoling tone.

He stepped through the french window into the bedroom. A moment or two later, he called out, 'Madame Vitry wishes to speak to Mademoiselle Epton.'

Rosa jumped from her chair and stepped into the bedroom.

'Is it really her?' she hissed at Peter who was standing by the bedside table holding the phone.

'One hundred per cent.'

Rosa took the phone from him. 'Is that Madame Vitry?' she asked in an unusually nervous tone.

The voice that answered had a chesty quality and lost no time in coming to the point. 'We must meet, Miss Epton. I suggest the Café Marbeuf in the Rue des Cignes at eleven o'clock. Yes?'

'You mean this morning?' Rosa enquired, taken aback by the sudden speed of events.

'Of course. You'll be there, yes?'

'Definitely.'

'À bientôt,' the voice said and promptly rang off.

'My bet is she was at the Villa Montmorency the whole time,' Rosa said turning to Peter. 'Her old servant must have given her a reassuring report. Or . . .' Her voice trailed away.

'Or what?' Peter asked.

'Or nothing . . . it was just a whimsical thought.'

They found the Café Marbeuf without difficulty, a dingy café in a dingy street in the hinterland of Nice.

'She could have chosen somewhere with a bit more charm,' Peter remarked, as they approached it on foot from where he had parked the car. 'She's not at one of the tables outside. I'll have a quick look inside.' A moment later he returned to Rosa's side. 'There's a woman sitting alone at a table in the far corner, who might be Madame Vitry.'

'Let's find out,' Rosa said, walking in ahead of him.

The woman he had mentioned immediately gave her an identifying wave and waited for them to go across to where she was sitting.

'I'm Zena Vitry,' she said, holding out a hand. There was something vaguely familiar about her which was explained when she went on, 'I saw you yesterday when you came up to my villa. In fact we spoke at the gate.'

'Were you the old woman who pretended to be the housekeeper?' Rosa asked hesitantly.

'Some housekeeper! Yes, I was. I wanted to have a squint at you before deciding whether to talk to you. It's a ruse I've adopted on several occasions. I used to be on the stage and was always cast as older women, so there's nothing very difficult in playing the role of my own faithful housekeeper.'

Rosa reckoned the woman sitting in front of her was around sixty. She had not very well dyed auburn hair and a pudgy face that had yesterday been hidden by the head-scarf. Her skin was smooth and soft.

'So you're Mrs Henshaw's sister?' Rosa said in a tone of delighted discovery. 'I've been trying to get in touch with you . . .'

'Too many people have been trying to get in touch with me,' Madame Vitry remarked, sharply. 'The English police, Evelyn's family . . . she only wants my help when she's in trouble.'

'Have you seen her?'

'Yes, she stayed at the villa for a few days. That's as long as we can tolerate each other's company.'

'So she hasn't been murdered,' Rosa observed, more to herself than to Zena Vitry.

'*Hadn't* when I last saw her,' Madame Vitry said in a tone devoid of any sentiment.

'When did you last see her?' Rosa asked.

'About ten days ago. She just took off, saying she still had fears for her life.'

'From whom?'

'Her husband, I suppose.' Her tone was clear enough evidence that she had little patience with her sister's obsessions.

'Where is she now?'

'My guess is somewhere in the mountains.'

'Have you spoken to her since she left the villa?'

'Yes,' Madame Vitry replied, but didn't add to her reply.

'Does she know her husband has been charged with arson and murder?'

'Yes. She is angry that he burnt down her house. After all it was *her* house, not his. She knows nothing about the murder. It was unfortunate.'

Rosa felt it was somewhat more than that for Joshua. Admittedly he was in the wrong place at the wrong time, but he'd done nothing to deserve forfeiting his life.

'How did she know about the fire, and why is she so sure it was her husband's doing?'

'You must ask her that yourself.'

'Are you aware that my introduction to this whole drama was her visit to my office to ask me to watch over her interests should anything happen to her?'

'The trouble with Evelyn has always been her inability to distinguish between reality and fantasy. It was the same when she was a child. I suppose she told you that our mother committed suicide?'

'No,' Rosa said in a startled tone. 'I didn't know that.'

'Well, she did. I was eighteen at the time and Evelyn was sixteen. Our father went off soon afterwards with a much younger woman and we were left in the clutches of an eccentric aunt who used to dance around on the lawn at full moon. Small wonder that we both escaped and married young. François Vitry was fifteen years older than me and worked in the archive department of the Paris Opera at the Palais Garnier.' She let out a reminiscent sigh. 'He was a great Wagnerian. *Tristan and Isolde* would cause tears to stream down his face, not just the Liebestod in Act Three but during the whole of the love duet in Act Two. The sheer uplifting beauty of it. But he loved all Wagner's operas and used to say that his idea of heaven would be listening to one after the other sung by all those wonderful singers of the thirties, Melchior, Flagstad, Leider and the others, with a vast celestial orchestra conducted by Wilhelm Furtwängler.' She paused and for a few seconds gazed into a blissful past. There was a note of asperity when she went on, 'Evelyn, of course, doesn't have a note of music in her. She's the sort who'd dig into a box of chocolates during Brünnhilde's immolation.'

Rosa decided to try and steer her away from Wagner and into matters of immediate concern.

'Was her first marriage a success?'

'Edward doted on her, but she was never faithful to him. I'm afraid my sister found that promiscuity added spice to her life and Edward didn't make any fuss provided she was discreet.'

'I'd like to ask you about the first Mrs Henshaw. I gather she and Ralph Henshaw were staying with your sister when Jean Henshaw met her death? Did Evelyn ever speak to you about it?'

'The sixty-four-thousand-dollar question! How exactly did she come by her death?' Zena Vitry murmured in a musing tone. 'It's a question of believing whom you want. Evelyn has always denied any complicity in Jean Henshaw's death, though it's only latterly that she's actually accused Ralph.'

'Are you aware that he accuses *her* of his first wife's death?'

'Not very chivalrous of him,' she observed airily.

To Rosa, chivalry didn't enter into it, and after a brief pause she said, 'I can see that he may have had a motive for murdering his wife, but I can't think of any she may have had for killing her best friend.'

'If it was my sister who was responsible, I'm sure it was more of an accident than a deliberate killing. Not even Evelyn goes in for murder. They were down at the beach together and something happened and Evelyn came home and spun a story to Ralph Henshaw. Whatever it was, she's been suffering from a guilty conscience ever since. Ralph, who, I suspect, didn't mourn his wife's death, decided to support Evelyn's account of events until they eventually broke ranks and she swung round like a weather-vane and came running to you with her story of her life being in danger; of a husband who had killed his first wife and now had his sights trained on her.' She gave Rosa a hard stare. 'Absolute rubbish and typical of her!'

'What about this young research student who was living at Riverview Court and whose body was found at the bottom of the lake?'

'It was his misfortune to become embroiled with my predatory sister.'

'Have you any idea where she met him?'

'If she's to be believed, it was at some function in London.'

'And do you believe her?'

'I don't believe anything my sister tells me unless it's supported by other evidence. Anyway, so far as Stefan is concerned, she's been evasive and reticent. I knew nothing of him until she turned up on my doorstep asking for asylum and saying her life was in danger.'

'What did she actually tell you?'

'That this young student who had been staying at the house had been murdered and that she was next in line. Or some such melodramatic rubbish.'

'What was your reaction?'

'I told her she could stay and I agreed not to let the authorities know she was there. It was a matter of only a day or so before the police called and asked if I knew where she was. I told them I didn't.'

'Did the English police phone?'

'They phoned and someone from the Sûreté in Nice came visiting. I told them all I couldn't help. Meanwhile, Evelyn kept to the house and jumped a mile every time she heard a footstep outside or a shadow fell across the window. I knew from the English newspapers that this young man, Stefan, had been found in the lake and that Evelyn had disappeared from home. I just wished she hadn't involved me. I didn't know what she'd been up to, and, quite frankly, didn't wish to know. It was a relief when she left.'

'And you've no idea where she is now?'

'She phones me every second or third day, but doesn't say from where. And I don't ask her,' she added firmly.

'Does she speak French?'

'About the same as yourself, Miss Epton,' she said wryly.

Rosa thought it likely that Madame Vitry knew her sister's whereabouts but despite their unloving relationship wasn't yet prepared to divulge it.

'Do you know Frances Gifford?' she asked.

'Ralph Henshaw's mistress? I've met her once. I had dinner with her and Ralph here in Nice. It must have been at least four years ago.' Observing Rosa's expression she went on, 'He was on business in the area and invited me to dinner. He introduced her to me as his business partner, but I assumed she was his mistress.' She met Rosa's gaze. 'I should think she was successful in both capacities.'

'Had Evelyn told you about her?'

'Yes. In a none too charitable way. She didn't say much, but made it clear she would put up with it only so long as it suited her. Evelyn was a great one for storing things away for future use. I'm sure that her husband's relationship with Mrs Gifford was one of them. I don't think Ralph ever realised how devious Evelyn could be. He was a tough amongst toughs, used to getting his own way, and it never occurred to him that anyone could get the better of him. As far as he was concerned he had a wife with money and a mistress who met all his other needs.' She paused. 'But why am I telling you all this? You've met him. He's your client. You must have formed your own judgment.'

'But it's still very useful to hear your views. It's a strange set-up.'

'You know Evelyn used to visit some crazy woman who read tarot cards and told fortunes . . .'

'Mrs Upjohn?'

'Yes, that's the woman. Evelyn used to hang on her every word and pay her fat sums of money to hear all the rubbish.'

'Did your sister tell you about her?'

'Certainly not. Her life was a series of secret compartments and that was one of them.'

'Have you ever met her step-daughter, Anthea?'

'Strange girl,' Madame Vitry said in a reflective 'tone. 'She stayed down here not long after Ralph and Evelyn got married and before the rot set in. She didn't trouble to hide her feelings that she had no wish for a stepmother.'

'Rather impudent of her in the circumstances to come and stay with you.'

'Yes, it was, but typical of her, I later decided. I certainly never suggested a return visit. She was no trouble, mind you, but she gave me the creeps. She may be different now . . .'

'I don't think she's altered much,' Rosa remarked. 'There's obviously a strong bond between her and her father.' After a pause she went on, 'Just to complete the family picture, do you know Christopher, the other sprig of the first Henshaw marriage?'

Madame Vitry nodded slowly. 'He and his wife spent a week at my villa soon after they were married. A nice young couple.'

'The impression I got from your sister was that, apart from exchanging Christmas cards, you and she virtually had no contact. And yet you seem to have met all the members of her new family and know much more about them than you'd have gained from an exchange of Christmas cards . . .'

Rosa paused to see whether Madame Vitry would respond to this bit of kite flying.

'I don't know why Evelyn chose to give you that impression; there's a great deal I don't know about her. But, in fact, she used to phone me and pour out her woes several times a month.' She gave Rosa a small sardonic smile. 'If you want to know, I've never sent her a Christmas card in my life.' She glanced around her. 'I think I'll have another cognac before I go.'

'Of course,' Peter said, jumping to his feet and going over to the counter, where le patron was moving slowly about. He was a depressed-looking man, with a drooping moustache which added to his general air of melancholy. Only one other person had come into the café since they'd arrived and he was sitting at the bar where they exchanged brief snatches of conversation. To Rosa such taciturnity was all rather un-French.

'I think there's one thing I ought to tell you,' Madame Vitry said when Peter returned with her drink. 'My sister had an illegitimate child. I don't suppose she mentioned that?'

'No,' Rosa said in a tone of considerable surprise. 'Was this when she was a young girl?'

Zena Vitry's tone was unmistakably sly and there was little doubt she was relishing her moment.

'It was exactly twenty-one years ago. I should know, the baby was born at my villa. Edward stood by her throughout. He was well over fifty and they'd been married a long time when it happened.'

'Was it a boy or a girl?'

'A boy.'

'And what happened to him?' Rosa enquired intently.

'Evelyn had him adopted. She made the arrangements herself and never referred to the child again.'

'Did she say who the father was?'

'She was totally tight-lipped about that. It's my belief it was a one-night stand, and by the time she knew she was pregnant, she had lost touch with the father. She probably never even saw him again after they'd had their fling.'

'I suppose it's possible; however, did she keep in touch with the adoptive parents? When I say, keep in touch, I mean she knew where to find them?'

Madame Vitry shrugged. 'Of course it's possible. I can only tell you that from the day she and the baby left the Villa Montmorency, she never referred to the child again. And never has.'

'Was your husband around at the time?'

'We were at the flat in Paris and she had the villa to herself. I came down for a couple of nights while she was there, but that was all I saw of her. My husband's old nurse, who was then in her seventies and who looked after the villa for us, tended Evelyn's needs. She died a long time ago now,' she added, before Rosa could ask a question.

'And you've no idea whatsoever about the father's identity?'

'A ship that passed in the night,' she said. 'Knowing my sister, I would assume he was much younger than she. She always had a penchant for younger men, even though she married a much older man. But that was quite different, of course . . .'

'And what about Ralph Henshaw?' Rosa asked with curiosity. 'He's about the same age.'

'Between Edward dying and Ralph marrying her, I imagine Evelyn had a number of sexual encounters of the one-night-stand variety. Then she met Ralph and his wife on a cruise and they became very chummy.' She gave a small shrug. 'There's no doubt that Ralph Henshaw is an extremely sexy character and I'm sure

Evelyn would have been flattered by his attentions. She may also have felt she was getting a bit long in the tooth for the sort of gigolos she used to pick up at tea-time in West End hotels.'

'Did her husband, Edward that is, know what was going on?'

'I don't know how much he knew and I don't know what Evelyn told him. He was absolutely devoted to her and was obviously prepared to overlook her indiscretion, if one can use that euphemism to describe a bouncing baby boy.'

'I wondered if they might have considered keeping it as their own?'

'There's nothing maternal about Evelyn and Edward was too old for changing nappies. Not that he need have had that pleasure.'

'I wonder if Evelyn told him who the father was?' Rosa said thoughtfully.

'I've no idea,' Madame Vitry said in a brusque tone. 'Anyway, he's dead.'

'I also wonder,' Rosa went on, 'how much of the story Ralph Henshaw is keeping to himself?'

'Knowing Evelyn, I should think nothing. She had no reason to tell him and it wasn't the sort of information she'd be likely to spread around. Not even to her new husband.' Her tone was bitter and Rosa could only conclude that the two sisters were bonded together in malice and contempt as much as in anything else. Zena seemed to be the first person that Evelyn turned to when in trouble. Moreover, Zena never seemed to repulse her.

'I must get back,' Madame Vitry said peremptorily. 'Call me before you leave. I may have news, but more likely not.' She adjusted her shawl, which was falling off one shoulder. The gesture was theatrical and Rosa could suddenly see her doing it to effect on the stage.

She shook hands briskly and shouted an au-revoir to le patron as she sailed out of the café and got into an ancient Citroën parked at the kerb.

'L'addition, monsieur,' le patron said hurrying up to their table with the bill. 'Service non compris,' he added firmly.

By the time Peter had settled the bill, Rosa was walking toward their car, trying to assess their visit. The most important thing was the knowledge that Evelyn Henshaw was still alive. At the beginning, Rosa had felt certain she was dead, but as time had gone by without the discovery of her body, she had become increasingly unsure. Evelyn Henshaw's living existence did not, however, solve any of the surrounding mysteries. It merely altered their perspective.

Rosa found she had no difficulty in accepting the picture her sister had painted of her. They were, indeed, an eccentric couple, with Evelyn the stranger. But that could be because they only had the one picture. She imagined that Evelyn might well paint Zena in unexpected colours.

Deep in thought she reached the place where Peter had parked the car to find that he was only a few paces behind her.

'They're straight out of a Pinter play,' he remarked.

'Evelyn and Zena, you mean?'

'Who else!'

'I've been thinking, Peter, I've simply got to see Evelyn Henshaw again.'

'You'll probably end up being more confused than you are now.'

'I've still got to see her. Last time I could only listen, but now I have so many of my own questions to ask her.'

'She may get in touch with you on her own initiative after her sister has brought her up to date.'

'Or she may not,' Rosa said with a despairing sigh. 'One just doesn't know what to believe.'

'I had the feeling that Madame Vitry was giving us straight fact, despite a touch of hyperbole here and there. It's an extraordinary relationship.'

Rosa nodded. 'I don't know why Evelyn Henshaw was so dismissive of her sister when she came to the office. She admitted to her existence, but that was about all.'

'She probably didn't want you getting in touch with her. In fact she wanted to avoid the very thing that's happened.' He paused. 'And what about this illegitimate child she had?'

'I've been thinking,' Rosa said in a reflective tone. 'You don't suppose it could have been Stefan, do you? He was near enough the right age and she could have arranged for Mr and Mrs Michalowski to bring up the child as their own. It would account for his being at Riverview Court. He wasn't her toy boy, but her son visiting his true mamma when she needed support. What do you think, Peter?'

'What I think,' he said firmly, 'is that we should drive back to the hotel and relax on the terrace with a long, cool drink.'

After lunch Peter suggested they should drive up into the mountains.

'We've done enough work for the weekend,' he said. 'It's time to enjoy ourselves.' Rosa gave him a surprised look. 'Well, meeting Madame Vitry can hardly be called fun!' he added.

'You've been very accommodating, my love,' Rosa remarked. 'We'll do whatever you want. You weren't totally bored this morning, were you?'

'I wasn't bored at all, but also it wasn't how I envisaged spending the weekend.'

'How did you envisage spending it?' Rosa enquired lightly.

'Being carefree and making love.'

'We've done that, as well as meeting Madame Vitry,' Rosa pointed out. 'Anyway, you lead and I'll follow. But if we're going to be taking in breathtaking views, make sure I'm not on the side of the precipice. I can just about look out and across, but not down.'

'You miss a lot by suffering from vertigo.'

'So be it!'

Rosa had complete confidence in Peter as a driver, but that didn't mean she wasn't rigid with fear on mountain drives involving spectacular drops. His mistake was in thinking she would still grow out of it, instead of recognising that her phobia grew worse with the passage of years. In Rosa's opinion, men could be exceedingly tiresome in believing they only had to wave a wand to dispel a girlfriend's lifelong fears. She wished she didn't have a phobia about heights, but it was going to take more than Peter to cure her.

By the time they returned to Nice, it was nearly six o'clock and the palms of her hands were indented with nail marks.

'Enjoy it?' Peter asked as he drew up outside the Négresco.

'Blissful,' Rosa said from sheer relief at being safely back.

That evening, which was their last, they dined at the hotel and went up to their room immediately afterwards.

The next morning came all too soon, and it was not long after they had left the hotel that the telephonist explained to a caller they had checked out. The woman at the other end of the line sounded on the verge of panic.

'Are you sure she's not still there?' she asked in English.

'Quite sure, madame.'

'It's terribly urgent that I speak to Miss Epton.'

'I am sorry, madame, but . . .'

'There's a man outside: he has a gun: I can see him from here. I know he's waiting to kill me . . . Please put me through to Miss Epton.'

'I keep on telling you, madame, that she has left the hotel. It was about forty minutes ago. Perhaps you should phone the police, madame . . .'

The line went suddenly dead as if it had been cut.

Evelyn Henshaw was on her own.

Chapter Twenty

The telephonist at the Négresco decided to report what had happened to the duty manager. After all, he was paid to deal with such situations.

Monsieur Seydoux, the duty manager, listened intently and decided he should phone the police. After all, it was what they were paid for. The odds were that it was some sort of hoax, with just the smallest chance that the caller was in genuine trouble.

The police said that without knowing the woman's name or where she was calling from, there was nothing they could do. They would log the matter and keep their ears open, which was as much as any police force anywhere could be expected to do.

Meanwhile, Rosa and Peter had arrived at the airport. They had checked in and gone through passport control and were sitting over cups of coffee in the departure lounge when the tannoy came to life, enquiring after a Miss Epton and requesting her to return to passport control. The message, which had been in rapid French, was then repeated in fractured English.

'What on earth can that be about?' Rosa asked, not without a touch of apprehension.

'We'd better go and find out,' Peter said.

Curious eyes followed them across the lounge.

'Drug smugglers,' one man whispered to his wife. 'You can tell at a glance.'

There were two unmistakable plain-clothes policemen standing by the gate through which they had entered half an hour earlier. They were intently scanning every face in sight and moved forward as Rosa and Peter approached.

'I'm Rosa Epton,' Rosa said before they could speak. 'I've just heard my name called out.'

The taller of the two officers looked relieved.

'Miss Epton, yes? Please come with me.'

They left the lounge and turned into a short corridor guarded by a door marked 'Privée'.

The officer knocked on the second door along and opened it quickly, ushering Rosa in. The second officer tried to block Peter's entry, but it was a half-hearted gesture which Peter brushed aside. A middle-aged man with cropped grey hair and a military moustache was sitting at a cluttered desk. Beside him was an attractive girl with short dark hair and a pair of green eyes as bright as a cat's.

'Monsieur le Commandant Duvalier wishes to ask you some questions, mademoiselle. My name is Sabine. I am an interpreter.'

She turned to Commandant Duvalier and gave him what Rosa took to be the go ahead.

'Is this person your husband?' he asked waving a hand in Peter's direction.

Although Rosa had understood the question, she waited for it to be translated before answering. Let Sabine earn her money! Later on she might be glad of the extra time to think before committing herself to an answer. It was a tactic she always recommended to foreign clients, however competent their use of English. Some were over keen to show off their mastery of the English tongue and this could prove to be their undoing when they landed up in the dock of a criminal court.

'He is a fellow lawyer and a friend and we're in Nice together,' she replied.

Duvalier pursed his lips as if it were an answer that required examination.

'A lawyer and a friend,' he mused. 'Not a lover?'

'Yes, that, too.'

'Ah! And he helps you look for Madame' – he glanced at the piece of paper in front of him – 'for Madame Henshaw?'

'Madame Henshaw is my client in England and I'm trying to get in touch with her.'

'That is why you come to Nice?'

'No. We came to Nice for a weekend break and decided to take the opportunity of making a few enquiries about Madame Henshaw. Her sister, Madame Vitry, lives at St Virgile de Var.'

Commandant Duvalier obviously knew this, but his expression gave nothing away. He was wearing a broad wedding ring which he kept on turning. Perhaps, Rosa thought, despite his middle-aged appearance, he was newly married and hadn't got used to it on his finger.

'And so you managed to run Madame 'Enshaw to earth?' he said, watching Rosa intently.

'We did no such thing. Her sister didn't know where she was staying.'

'But you tried to find her?'

Rosa frowned. 'It might be better, monsieur, if you told me the reason for these questions.'

'It might be better, mademoiselle, if you gave me truthful answers.'

Rosa felt she had been struck a blow in the face. Suddenly mere puzzlement became alarm. Though she had nothing to hide and had told no lies, it was as if the commandant's office had turned into a trap.

'I *have* told you the truth,' she said, trying to keep her voice steady. 'I repeat that Madame Henshaw is my client and I don't deny that I'd like to see her as soon as possible. She disappeared from home several weeks ago after a murder there . . . But I'm sure you know all about that. The English police have been looking for her. As a matter of fact, it was only yesterday when I spoke to Madame Vitry that I knew for certain her sister was still alive.'

'It is perhaps fortunate that she is still alive,' Duvalier observed.

'I'm relieved that she is.'

'And that the person hunting her has not yet found her,' he went on.

'If you're suggesting that I've been hunting her, I've never heard anything so absurd,' Rosa said indignantly.

Commandant Duvalier gave a Gallic shrug. 'Somebody wants to kill her, it seems. It could be you.'

'It could be the man on the moon,' Rosa retorted. 'May I ask where you get your information from about Madame Henshaw?'

'I do not divulge my sources, mademoiselle,' the commandant replied with hauteur. 'I am sure it is the same with the British police.' He paused and went on, 'However, I accept for the time being that you did not come to Nice to kill Madame 'Enshaw. If you hurry, you will be able to catch your plane to London.'

Sabine, who had shown herself to be a perfect interpreter, never butting in or interposing herself between interviewer and interviewee, now stood up.

'I will take you to the departure gate,' she said with a smile. 'Come with me.'

Rosa and Peter followed her from the room. Commandant Duvalier was meanwhile talking rapidly on the phone, having given Rosa a cursory handshake and Peter an even briefer one.

'What did you make of that?' Rosa asked when the plane was airborne and she was beginning to feel more relaxed. Up till that moment, she and Peter had spoken no more than a few monosyllables since leaving Commandant Duvalier's office.

'If Evelyn Henshaw's life is genuinely in danger, it shouldn't be difficult to name the suspects,' Peter said in a thoughtful tone.

'Including me,' Rosa observed wryly. 'But I don't think it's as simple as that, Peter. We know so little about her and what we do know isn't particularly reassuring. At least her husband can be eliminated, he's safely in prison.'

'There are such things as hired killers,' Peter said in a matter-of-fact voice. 'If anyone *is* after her down here, it'll be somebody hired to put the frighteners on her.'

'But for what purpose?'

'Forget frighteners, it'll be somebody hired to kill her,' Peter remarked.

'That could mean her husband, even if he is inside.'

'It could also mean Anthea or Fran Gifford.'

'Or someone out of the past. Someone who knew about the first Mrs Henshaw's death and who sought revenge.' Rosa gripped Peter's arm as the plane hit an air pocket and gave a sideways lurch. 'I wish planes didn't do that,' she said. 'What was I saying?'

'You were speculating over who might have it in for Evelyn Henshaw. If she's still alive, the sooner you run her to earth and interrogate her the better.'

'And if she isn't still alive?'

'You might as well give up. You'll never find out the truth.'

The visit to Nice had convinced her that Evelyn Henshaw was alive and that she, and only she, held the vital clues to everything that had happened. She almost wanted to tell the pilot to turn about and return to Nice, so that she could resume the search.

She was unaware, of course, that events might have been different had she and Peter left the hotel half an hour later . . .

Someone had obviously alerted the authorities as to her and Peter's presence in the area and to their interest in Mrs Henshaw. It was difficult to see who this could have been other than Madame

150

Vitry. Given that she was an obvious eccentric, Rosa couldn't think what motive she could have had for going to the police and telling them a story as perverted as any her sister might have spun.

Despite the odd business of her coming to the villa gate pretending to be a servant, Rosa had been inclined to believe what she told them about her sister.

The only alternative was that both women were completely dotty and lived in a world of fantasy. But there were too many hard facts for that simplistic explanation. Facts such as Stefan's death and the fire at Riverview Court.

Somehow Evelyn Henshaw had to be found . . .

The plane did a few more slides and bumps, through which Peter slept, and then they were making their descent to Heathrow.

'Are we there?' Peter enquired, blinking like a half-awake child, as they touched down. 'Did you sleep, too?'

'I not only didn't sleep but I've decided what to do next.'

'Go back to Nice next weekend and continue the search?' he enquired hopefully, smothering a prodigious yawn.

'Could be,' she said cryptically. 'Anyway, it depends on a preliminary reconnaissance. I'll tell you more when you're awake . . .'

Chapter Twenty-One

It was the following evening that Rosa and Peter drove down to Briar's End.

'It'd be nice to pop in to the Red Squirrel and renew acquaintance with Bob King, but I'd sooner we weren't seen in the village,' Rosa said when they were within a mile of their destination. 'Without being too cloak-and-dagger, let's go to Riverview Court first. Depending on what we discover there, we can decide afterwards whether or not to show ourselves. It's possible we shan't even be able to get inside the house.'

'You're underestimating my non-legal skills,' Peter remarked.

Making a detour to avoid the main village street, he parked beneath some trees near the perimeter fence of Riverview Court.

'There's a gap in the fence a bit further on. How do I know? I discovered it on our previous visit. Costs the earth to maintain the fences round a property this size.'

They arrived at a point where the paling fence looked as if it had been a target for attack. Whoever had been responsible had removed two of the staves of wood and left a gap. Immediately on the other side was a congestion of shrubs which formed a second line of defence. Or would have done had not somebody beaten a path through them to the lawn beyond. They emerged into the open halfway between the lake and the house.

Dusk had fallen, but there was still enough light for them to see where they were going.

'Won't all the furniture have been removed?' Peter asked.

'Mrs Henshaw's family solicitors were supposed to be attending to that,' Rosa replied. 'But we'll find out if we ever get inside.'

'I bet the vandals have got here first. And they don't usually stop to make repairs on their way out.'

They made their way round to the yard at the back and were

rewarded by finding a window flapping forlornly like a bird with a broken wing. Peter stood on tiptoe and peered in.

'A small room with a sink and a washing-machine,' he remarked.

A moment later he had heaved himself through the window and was holding his arms out to aid Rosa's entry.

'Are you all right?' he enquired anxiously, as she bent down to rub a knee.

'I think so,' she said, as she hopped around on one foot. 'Clambering through windows has never been my favourite pastime. It looks easy when others do it, but I know better.'

They walked along a short stone-flagged passage and through a swing-door to emerge in the main hall. The aftermath of the fire still manifested itself in a lingering acrid smell of burning. It was apparent that the fire had been selective in its destruction and that the thousands of gallons of water which had been poured on to it had caused as much damage as the flames.

'It's clear,' Rosa said, glancing about her, 'that someone set fire to the house in order to destroy evidence. It's obvious there was no other motive. It's equally obvious that the person who started it didn't know where the evidence in question was concealed, so he had to destroy the whole house to make sure. It's my guess that the evidence in question touched on the death of the first Mrs Henshaw . . .'

'You mean like a diary?' Peter interjected.

Rosa nodded. 'Ralph Henshaw mentioned that Evelyn used to keep a private journal in which she recorded her thoughts. He said nobody else had ever read it and that Evelyn had never let him see it. Come to that, he didn't seem particularly interested in it.' She paused. 'But where would Evelyn have kept it? It certainly wouldn't have been left lying around to be destroyed by fire or water. So where?'

'In a safe?' Peter said.

'Seems likely. And remember that this was Evelyn's house and that from all accounts Ralph Henshaw didn't spend a great deal of time here. He mayn't even have known of the safe's existence . . .'

'Assuming there is one! Anyway, isn't it likely to have been removed and examined by the police by now?'

'There's a chance they've missed it, Peter. After all, unless their reasoning is the same as mine, they won't have been looking for

it and if it's cunningly concealed, they won't have come across it.'
She gave him a hopeful look. 'So where would you look?'

'In the loo!'

'No, be serious.'

'I am being serious. Where better? Nobody would ever come barging in and surprise you, nor would they question you being there. It's the perfect place.'

'But where in the loo?'

'Beneath the floorboards, of course. She presumably had a bathroom and toilet en suite. And on the rare occasions her husband visited, we know he had a separate bedroom.' He moved toward the staircase. 'We'll never know unless we go and look.'

'Do be careful, Peter, it could collapse.'

'It looks badly scorched, but otherwise intact,' he observed.

Rosa followed him to the foot of the staircase and followed him gingerly, hugging the side that ran against the wall. The banister on the opposite side looked in a perilous state. Peter gazed at it with interest. 'Whoever started this fire didn't make a very good job of it,' he remarked. 'The result has been selective damage, some of the place burnt well, whereas other parts appear relatively undamaged.'

As far as Rosa was concerned, the house was a write-off. She couldn't imagine anyone having the money to restore it, even with an insurance company at its most munificent. Come to that, she wouldn't have wanted to live there before the fire took place, not even in its Victorian prime.

They reached the landing.

'That'll be her bedroom,' Rosa said, pointing at a door to their left, which was ajar. 'It looks out over the main garden.'

Rosa was one of those fortunate people who never lost their bearings. She had an in-built compass that functioned both indoors and out in the open.

Testing the floorboards before putting his weight on them, Peter moved across, then held out a hand for Rosa to join him. Together they entered what was obviously the master bedroom. This side of the house seemed to have got off lightly and the only apparent damage was from water.

Peter shone his torch around the room, carefully avoiding the windows. Focusing the beam on a door in the further wall, he remarked, 'That must be the bathroom.'

Rosa watched him cross the floor and arrive safely at the bathroom door. The air in the room stank from a mixture of stale smoke and dampness. Peter disappeared through the door, while Rosa stood rooted where she was. Though it had been her suggestion to come, she suddenly felt it was a futile quest. A moment later, however, Peter appeared in the bathroom doorway.

'I think I've found something,' he said softly.

Rosa tiptoed uneasily across the room and joined him.

'It isn't exactly a safe,' he said. 'More a carefully prepared cavity beneath the floor with a trap-door.'

He shone the torch into a corner from where he had removed an old-fashioned clothes basket. Beneath where it had stood was a section of floor with hinges at one end and a ring at the other for lifting.

'Don't get too excited,' he said, 'it's empty. I've already looked.'

For Rosa's benefit, he lifted the section of floor to reveal an empty space about twelve inches deep, lined with a plastic material. He played the beam of his torch into the cavity.

'I bet that's where she did keep her journals,' he said. 'It's a perfect hiding-place. I suggest we call on Mrs Santer and see what she knows about it.'

The house and its repellent atmosphere had given Rosa the creeps and she was quite ready to leave.

'I hate it here, Peter,' she whispered, gripping his arm.

'You don't want to see if there are other hiding-places?' he asked.

'No, I just want to get out.'

'Sure. Hang on to my arm and we'll go.'

It wasn't often he had seen Rosa lose her nerve, but now he recognised the signs and carefully steered her back the way they had come. As they stood outside in the yard, breathing the fresh evening air, he gave her a warm hug.

'I'm sorry,' she murmured, 'but I suddenly came over all weak-kneed. I'm all right now.'

'Sure?'

'Yes. It's a good idea to call on Mrs Santer. I think I can remember her address.'

'What about a drink at the Red Squirrel first?'

Rosa hesitated. 'Yes, let's,' she said after a pause.

The saloon bar was fairly empty when they arrived with only a pretty dumpling of a girl serving behind the counter. She greeted them with a friendly smile.

'He's out at the back,' she said, when Peter asked after Bob King. 'He'll be here in a moment.'

She went off to serve another customer, and while she was doing so the landlord came in. His face lit up as soon as he saw Rosa and Peter and he moved along to the end of the bar where they were standing.

'I've been expecting to see you,' he said cheerfully. 'What a time we've had!'

'Why have you been expecting us?' Rosa asked in a puzzled tone.

'Everyone else has been nosing around and I thought you'd be back.'

'Who's everyone else?'

'Apart from the police, Mr Henshaw's son was down one evening and er . . . the lady with whom Mr Henshaw lived.'

'Mrs Gifford?'

'I don't think I ever heard her name, but that's who she was. She just said she was a friend of Mr Henshaw's.'

'What was she doing down here?'

'Said she'd come to see if she could salvage any of Mr Henshaw's things from the house.' He paused. 'And then there was a good-looking young chap, who was trying to get information about the Henshaws. Think his name was William.' Bob King lowered his voice, even though there was nobody at the end of the bar where they were talking.

'Probably shouldn't say this, but he was a half-caste. I'm not a racist, but he was coffee-coloured. He had a bit of a talk with Wanda. That's her serving at the other end of the bar. Would you believe it, she has a university degree, but doesn't have any greater ambition than working in a pub.' He sighed. 'Young people these days! I'd have given my right arm to have gone for higher education. You wouldn't have found me running a pub if I had a degree . . .'

'Would it be possible to have a word with her?' Rosa asked.

'Sure.'

He moved away and spoke to the girl, who at that moment was leaning on the bar and giving desultory attention to a crossword puzzle in the folded newspaper in front of her. She straightened up and came toward them.

'You were enquiring about William?' she said.

'I was wondering if he was the same young man I noticed in court at Utwell when Ralph Henshaw appeared?' Rosa said.

'He probably was. He told me he'd been to court, but had found it pretty uninteresting. He must have looked a fish out of water in a country magistrates' court.'

'He did. I suppose that's why I noticed him,' Rosa said with a smile. 'I vaguely wondered what his interest was. Did you learn anything about him?'

'He asked a lot of questions about the Henshaws, but I had the impression he was only really interested in Mrs Henshaw. The rest was just a smokescreen. He said he was a freelance journalist and was going to write an article about her disappearance.'

'Has he been in again?'

'No, just the once.'

'Was that before or after the court case?'

'A day or two before.'

'Do you remember if he was carrying anything like a shoulder bag?'

Wanda frowned, then slowly shook her head.

'If he was, he didn't put it on the counter.' She grinned, showing a gap in her upper teeth. 'You don't think he was making off with the family silver? He did say he'd been up to Riverview Court.'

'I imagine the family silver would have been salvaged before he ever got there,' Rosa said with a smile. Pillaged if not salvaged, she thought to herself. She wondered if she shouldn't have shown greater initiative in respect of the house's contents, but reminded herself that her only real status was as Ralph Henshaw's solicitor on the criminal charges brought against him.

Bob King came back to their end of the bar and Wanda moved away.

'Learn anything?' he enquired, as he idly polished a mug. 'I doubt whether William was anything more than a ship who passed in the night.'

'Possibly not,' Rosa said. 'I'll ask Ralph Henshaw about him when I visit him in prison next week. What's the current feeling around here?'

'It's divided. There are those who believe Mrs Henshaw engineered the whole thing and has gone to ground and others who are convinced she's lying six feet under. Personally, I'm much more concerned with Stefan than I am with Mrs H. He was a decent young man and didn't deserve to end up in the lake.'

157

'You've no idea who killed him?'

'Oh, I've got an idea all right.'

'Who?'

'Your client.'

'Ralph Henshaw, you mean?'

He nodded. 'I think that's the police view, too.'

'He has an alibi,' Rosa replied.

'Alibis are not too difficult to concoct. Not for a man of his intelligence. I'm sorry, I probably shouldn't have said that to you.'

'That's all right, provided you don't expect me to agree,' she said with a small smile. 'After all, I did ask you the question.'

He looked relieved, as if he had thought Rosa might blow up in his face.

'One thing for sure, nobody's going to want to live in that house again. Not after all that's happened. Anyway it'd cost more to restore it than build a new one.'

A middle-aged woman came in, and after giving Bob a nod went and sat in a corner.

'You know who that is?' he said and when Rosa shook her head, added, 'Mrs Santer. She's had more free drinks since all this happened than she ever cooked hot dinners for her husband. She doesn't do so well now, but in the early days the media fell over themselves to buy her drinks.'

'Thanks for telling me,' Rosa said as she put down her glass and walked across to where Mrs Santer had sat down.

Peter turned back to the landlord and ordered himself another drink. Rosa seemed to have recovered her spirit and that was all that mattered.

Mrs Santer was sitting with a prim, but relaxed air as she surveyed those in the bar, presumably with an eye for somebody eager to offer her a drink. She obviously didn't regard Rosa as a promising candidate for she awarded her a stony look as she came up.

'Mrs Santer? My name's Rosa Epton. We've spoken on the telephone.'

For a moment or two, Mrs Santer frowned in uncertainty, then her brow cleared.

'Yes, of course, you're the solicitor. I knew your name at once, but couldn't place you.'

'May I get you a drink and then perhaps we could have a talk. What would you like?'

158

'A spritzer,' she said, as if it were the only possible drink for ladies.

Rosa decided it was rather a good choice for a warm evening and ordered one for herself as well. It might also prove to be a short-cut to establishing a rapport.

'Have you been doing some cleaning-up at Riverview Court since the fire?' Rosa asked as she rejoined her companion.

'Not since the fire. I went in once or twice before at the request of Mr Bacon. He was something to do with the insurance people and used to visit on business from time to time.'

'I seem to remember your telling me that Mrs Henshaw used to look after her own bedroom and you didn't go in there?'

'Yes. She had funny ways.'

'Used you to clean her bathroom?'

'No. Not that I minded, there was enough to do without taking on an extra bedroom or bathroom.'

'Did you ever see Mrs Henshaw writing in a diary she kept? Or reading one?'

'She did all her writing upstairs in her bedroom, so I wouldn't have.'

'And this young man, Stefan, what was his relationship with Mrs Henshaw?'

'She was old enough to be his mother,' Mrs Santer observed, as though that answered the question. 'All these journalists who have been buzzing around like hornets tried to get me to say he was her lover, but I never saw anything to suggest it.'

'But one still wonders where they met and why she offered him a home? It wasn't as if she needed his rent to keep the place going.'

'I've known stranger things,' Mrs Santer observed, darkly. Rosa supposed that so had she, though she couldn't readily call anything to mind.

'I gather there's been another young man asking questions about Mrs Henshaw?' Rosa said, setting off on a fresh tack.

'You mean William? He's like one of those TV adverts for a tropical drink. Good looking and all charm.'

'What exactly did he want to know?'

'He wanted me to tell him everything I could about Mrs Henshaw.'

'For what purpose?'

'For this article he was writing.'

'Did he say why he was doing a piece on Mrs Henshaw?'

'Because he thought she sounded an interesting woman.'

'Did he tell you much about himself?'

'Only that he lived in Greenwich, but was thinking of moving to the Crystal Palace area.'

'What was his surname?'

'Smith. At least, that's what he said.'

'But you obviously didn't believe him?'

Mrs Santer shrugged. 'Maybe I did. Maybe I didn't. I don't really know.'

'If you see him again, will you ask him to get in touch with me?'

'You'll probably see him next time you go to court.'

'I'd like to meet him sooner than that if possible,' Rosa said.

A man loomed over them, precariously holding three glasses.

'I've got you a drink, Nellie,' he said, sitting down next to Mrs Santer. 'One for you, too, Miss Epton . . . No, don't move, I'm Trevor Cookson from the *Journal* . . . I saw you in court the other day . . . You don't mind me joining you, do you?'

He clearly didn't expect an answer, let alone a rebuff, for he pushed the drinks around the table and raised his glass.

'Cheers to one and all.' He turned to Rosa. 'How's the defence coming along? Still no sign of Mrs Henshaw, I gather? She's the crucial factor in the whole saga. And I use the word deliberately. I'm convinced, you see, that everything goes back to the death of the first Mrs Henshaw. For some reason the police never dug into that as thoroughly as they should. I'm not suggesting there was corruption or anything like that, I think it was just laziness. Detective Inspector Jarvis, the officer in charge, was nearing retirement and it was easier to accept what he was told than to test the story told him by Ralph and Evelyn Henshaw. Of course, now they've split and are giving diametrically opposite stories, it's much too late to hope to find any evidence worth the name. It's my bet that even Evelyn Henshaw's guilty conscience has become blunted by now.' He glanced from Mrs Santer to Rosa. 'That's my view. What's yours, Miss Epton?'

Rosa gave him a fleeting smile.

'I'm still in the business of listening to other people's,' she said.

'I always knew there was something funny about her,' Mrs Santer remarked. 'Still waters run deep, isn't that how the saying goes? She was a bit of still water all right.'

160

Trevor Cookson nodded encouragingly. 'Let me get you another drink, Nellie. You can tell us more than anyone. And I want to hear more about this coffee-coloured young chap. I think there could be a link between him and Stefan.' He jumped up and crossed over to the bar.

'I was going to have a rum and blackcurrant juice this time, but he never asked. Oh well . . .' Mrs Santer's tone was faintly aggrieved as she sat back and blinked. 'I didn't really know Mrs H. as well as people might think,' she said, suddenly. 'And I didn't like her either. I only stayed there because I needed the money, but, between you and me, she used to give me the creeps.'

Rosa had no difficulty in understanding Mrs Santer's judgment of her employer. She, too, had decided she was a creepy person. She wished she had never taken on the case. And yet . . .

Trevor Cookson returned with their drinks and sat down. After a quick glance around the now busy saloon bar, Rosa spotted Peter talking to a couple of elderly locals in a farther corner. They looked as if they'd known each other all their lives. He had a knack, she reflected, of making himself at home in any company from yacht-owning millionaires to locals in a village pub.

Trevor Cookson raised his own glass and said 'Cheers,' followed by, 'I want to hear more about this William fellow. As I was saying, I believe there may have been a link between him and Stefan. It's Stefan's death that's brought him here. Did he mention Stefan?'

Mrs Santer shook her head. 'As far as I know he was only interested in Mrs Henshaw,' she said.

'I wish I could find out what had brought him to the scene,' Cookson said thoughtfully. He glanced quickly at Rosa. 'Come on, Miss Epton. You're amongst friends, tell us what *you* think.'

'I'm as interested in William Smith as you are, but I've no idea where he's sprung from or what he's doing. The odds are he'll prove to be a complete red herring.'

'You don't really believe that,' Cookson said, 'and nor do I.' He sighed. 'It's a pity you lawyers don't put more trust in the press. We can help you; provide information you wouldn't get from any other source. Our resources are greater than those of prosecution and defence put together.'

His tone was a mixture of bombast and irritation, but Rosa accepted that what he said was largely true, for when they put their mind to it, the press was able to outstrip all others in digging into the background of a case.

She saw Peter coming over to where they were sitting and felt relieved. She was ready to be rescued. The landlord insisted that they had a final drink on the house and after that they departed.

Rosa suddenly felt very tired, a reaction to their visit to the house with its spooky atmosphere and cloying smell of destruction.

They didn't talk much on the drive home, though Rosa told Peter of Trevor Cookson's theories and of Mrs Santer's capacity for alcohol.

'Good luck to her,' he observed. 'It won't go on for ever.'

Rosa thought Nellie Santer would probably be able to free-load for quite some time yet. Obviously somebody had found Evelyn Henshaw's hiding place in the bathroom and had removed the journals. Admittedly it was no more than supposition, but she was sure she was right. The question was who, and the answer seemed to be Fran Gifford, acting on her lover's behalf. She had motive, and opportunities abounded. Perhaps she had returned to the scene of the arson attack to make sure the fire had done its job, which it hadn't. But if she knew where to look, why had she not been there sooner? Why set the house on fire in order to destroy the journals – Rosa was now satisfied that was the purpose of the arson – if she knew where they were hidden? The answer had to be that she hadn't known earlier, but if so, how had she found out? Rosa pondered this for a while and decided that if Peter could work out where the hiding-place was, somebody else could do so as well. And there were certainly no flies on Fran . . .

They arrived outside the Victorian mansion block in Notting Hill where Rosa lived and Peter came round to open the passenger door.

'You've been very quiet,' he said. 'Feeling OK?'

'Apart from a headache, yes.'

'I'll soon massage that away,' he remarked keenly. 'Give yourself a break from the Henshaw saga,' he went on as they began to climb the stairs to Rosa's top-floor flat. 'There's no urgency about it. Ralph's trial won't be for several months and for the moment, there's nothing further to be done. Put the case on a back burner.'

Rosa gave him a seraphic smile. 'You're absolutely right, Peter love,' she said.

'So?'

'I shall go and visit Ralph Henshaw in prison tomorrow.'

Chapter Twenty-Two

In Rosa's experience, alibis came in two varieties. There were those that were suspiciously watertight and those which were transparently flawed. Occasionally there was a third, the genuine article, which shone like a small bright light in a wicked world.

Ralph Henshaw's alibi for the night that Riverview Court was set on fire fell into the second category. Rosa had lost no time in obtaining statements from the barman where he said he had spent the evening drinking and from the owner of the hotel where he had spent the night. Both supported what he had told Rosa about his movements so far, but not far enough. They were hazy about exact times, having had no reason to note precisely his comings and goings. The result was there were a vital two hours when he might have been drinking the evening away in London or dashing down to Briar's End and back.

A capable advocate could advance the alibi, skating rapidly over the thinner ice; on the other hand an experienced prosecutor could leave it looking distinctly tattered after some adroit cross-examination.

As he was being held on remand in Oxford prison while he awaited trial, Rosa decided to go by train, rather than grapple with traffic at either end of her journey.

She walked from the railway station to the prison and hadn't long been in the lawyer's interview room when Ralph Henshaw came in. He looked sprucer than she had expected, as if the regime suited him. Being on remand he was wearing his own clothes, which helped his appearance, but he looked in good shape and had had a recent hair-cut. It was Rosa's guess that he was sleeping well.

'If you bring good news, let's hear it,' he said with a small, twisted smile as he sat down opposite her.

She wondered what good news he might have expected.

'I'm pretty sure your wife's alive and hiding in the south of France,' Rosa said. 'I hope you'll think that's good news.'

'You mean, I'm not likely to be charged with her murder?' he enquired sardonically. After a pause, he went on, 'I suppose it is good news, not that I've ever thought she was dead. But I'm glad you've reached the same conclusion.' His eyes met Rosa's in a hard stare. 'What's convinced you?'

Rosa told him of her and Peter's long weekend in Nice and of their encounter with Zena Vitry. She also mentioned, without going into detail, what had happened at the airport on their way home.

A frown grew on his face as he listened.

'It sounds as if Evelyn is still determined to make as much mileage as she can,' he said in a harsh voice when she finished.

Rosa ignored the observation. 'You remember,' she said, 'telling me that she kept a private journal?'

His expression became suddenly wary. 'Yes, what of it?'

'Have you any idea what happened to it?'

'Presumably it was destroyed with the house.'

'Unless, of course, she took it with her when she fled?'

'I don't know how many notebooks there were, but too many to lug around if you were in flight.'

'You said you had no idea where she kept them?'

'That's right. They were none of my business and I didn't care.'

'Not even when you must have known she had recorded her thoughts about your first wife's death?' When he didn't reply, Rosa went on, 'Unless, of course, you knew what had happened to her?'

'Are you suggesting I was responsible for Jean's death? If so, it's rubbish. Evelyn's the only person who knows the truth and whether she recorded it in her journal or not, I don't give a damn. Anyway, Miss Epton, whose side are you on?'

'Oh, don't worry, I'm on yours. But I still like to look all round the facts of a case in which I'm involved. It's like poking into every corner of a house before you make an offer.'

'I'll give you the benefit of the doubt, though it doesn't seem a particularly apt analogy,' he said grudgingly. 'Anyway, how are you getting on in preparing my defence? That's much more important to me than all this probing into the past. Fran Gifford says you haven't yet been in touch with her about her evidence.'

Rosa was doubtful whether Mrs Gifford had any worthwhile

evidence to give and in any event she knew the police had already interviewed her and taken a statement and might, indeed, be proposing to call her on some small detail or other.

'I'm still waiting for the Crown Prosecution Service to serve the statements on me,' she remarked patiently. 'Only then shall we know the strength of their case and the names of the witnesses. We'll then have to decide whether to accept a paper committal or go for a full hearing before the magistrates. When I do receive the prosecution statements, I'll bring you a set and shall want you to go through them and add your comments.' Rosa gave him a rueful smile. 'I'm afraid there aren't many short cuts in the law and that criminal justice winds along at its own unhurried pace.'

'Without any guarantee of achieving justice at the end,' he remarked sourly.

'Human beings are all fallible.' Rosa spoke patiently. 'And for the most part those involved in the administration of criminal justice do their best to reach a proper result, but I'm afraid it doesn't always work out that way.'

'Like if I'm found guilty of crimes I've never committed,' he said grimly.

Someone committed them all right, Rosa thought to herself, and I'm darned sure you could tell me a great deal more if you wanted. But it had been so ever since he first appeared in her office, hard on the heels of his wife. Over the weeks that had passed Rosa had formed and discarded various views without coming to any satisfactory conclusion. Except one. She had to find and confront Evelyn Henshaw. She had been closer to it than she was aware when she was in Nice. As it was there had been the whole mysterious and unexplained business at the airport which had suggested she had been threatened and was still fearful for her life.

She gave Ralph Henshaw a covert glance. He had received her news about his wife still being alive with a strange lack of curiosity. Certainly without any sign of joy, let alone of relief.

'Is there anything you want to tell me before I go?' she said, shuffling together the sheets of paper on which she might have made notes, but which, in fact, remained blank.

'Has my daughter been in touch with you?' he enquired.

There was something in his tone that told Rosa the question wasn't as casual as it pretended to be.

'No, why do you ask?'

'I just wondered, that's all.'

But it wasn't all, though there was nothing Rosa could do about it.

'Has she been to see you?' she asked.

He nodded. 'I rather wish she wouldn't come so often. Family visits are a bit of a strain.' He gave a shrug to register distaste. 'And they couldn't be less private.' He pushed his chair back. 'Anyway, thank you for coming and I hope it won't be long before we get the prosecution statements.' He looked about him with an expression of distaste. 'What could be more barbaric than keeping innocent persons in an overcrowded Victorian jail, as if they were cattle awaiting export?'

Used as she was to visiting clients in prison, both before and after conviction, Rosa never ceased to feel for them. For most it was a degrading experience with all its attendant suffering. For the likes of Ralph Henshaw, who were accustomed to travelling the world, the total lack of liberty was in itself a hideous deprivation.

Though he had made it clear that he was ready to bring the interview to an end, Rosa had one more question she wanted to ask him.

'Did you know that your wife had a grown-up son?' she asked.

He stared at her in astonishment. 'Evelyn?' he asked, disbelievingly.

Rosa nodded. 'Her sister told me. I gather it wasn't her then husband's son.'

'And what happened to him?'

'He was adopted.'

For a time he stood in thoughtful silence.

'Who was the father?'

'I don't know. Madame Vitry professed ignorance. She was prepared to believe the man was a ship that passed in the night.'

'Evelyn was a beckoning light to quite a few of those,' he remarked grimly. After a further pause, he went on, 'Does it in any way affect your view of the case?'

'As far as I know,' Rosa said carefully, 'it has no relevance at all to what has happened.'

'I wonder if old Johnson knows?' he said in a musing tone. 'Arthur Johnson, who was Evelyn's family solicitor. I imagine she put you in touch with him?'

'Not exactly. She did mention his name and said why she had

come to see me rather than bare her soul to him. I got in touch with him after her disappearance and told him of my involvement. He seemed relieved not to be involved himself. I had the impression he regarded any contact with the criminal law as being worse than cleaning out the drains.'

'He was a friend of Edward, her first husband. A legal fusspot, if ever there was one. Did Zena Vitry say what Edward's reaction was to this baby?'

'I gather he was very understanding as long as she agreed to have it quickly adopted and, I presume, never referred to again.'

'Edward wouldn't have told Arthur Johnson,' Henshaw remarked. 'He didn't believe in washing his dirty linen in public, *or* in letting his wife do so.'

Rosa would have to decide whether to test the truth of this.

First, however, she must give further thought to her own position in the case. It seemed that the conflict of interest between her clients, which had loomed from the outset, was now confronting her whichever way she faced.

Peter came round that evening and she made a huge cheese omelette and sliced a pineapple she had bought on her way back.

'It's not really any different now from what it was,' he said, after listening to her. 'Evelyn Henshaw's alive and there's no crime her husband can be charged with in respect of her. And if she isn't alive,' he went on before Rosa could speak, 'it can't have been her husband who killed her as he was inside.'

'That doesn't mean somebody mayn't be acting under his instructions,' Rosa replied.

'You're not being realistic,' he said firmly.

'And anyway she mayn't be still alive. There was something very ominous about the goings-on at Nice airport.'

'The trouble is you've become too embroiled. It's unlike you to fret in this way. You must regain your sense of objectivity. Come to New York with me at the weekend, that'll restore your sense of perspective.' He paused. 'It'll be good for mine, too.'

Rosa laughed. 'Do you never fret and brood over any of your clients?'

'No, only over you and yours! The last time I brooded over one of mine was when I thought he was going down the drain before he'd paid my bill.'

It was half-past midnight when Peter departed and Rosa stacked the dish-washer and turned her back on the kitchen. Twenty minutes later she was in bed and asleep. Peter seemed to know instinctively when not to stay the night and this was one of them. Solitude was an element of Rosa's therapy.

She arrived in the office at eight thirty the next morning to find that not only Robin, but Stephanie, too, had preceded her. It was not unusual for Robin to get in early. He often left home soon after six to avoid the build-up of traffic on the M4.

'What on earth are you doing here this early, Steph?' she enquired.

'Bruce offered me a lift and, God knows why, I accepted,' she said in her cool, detached voice.

'How is Bruce?' Rosa asked.

'I think we're probably nearing the end of the line. I do like him, but . . .' She let out a heavy sigh. 'It seems to me that blokes either take you out, then ignore you for other blokes, or they can't keep their hands off you, so that you feel like a piece of fruit that everyone picks up, squeezes and puts down again as they enter the shop. I'm sure your Peter is neither. Incidentally, in case you hadn't guessed, R.S. is in. I think he wants to have a word with you.'

Rosa frowned. 'Did he say so?' she asked.

'More or less,' Steph said, shifting uncomfortably.

'What's happened?' Rosa said, sharply.

'I shouldn't be saying this,' Stephanie said, biting her lip. 'Why don't you go in and see R.S.?'

'What shouldn't you be saying?' Rosa asked.

'I think one of your clients has complained that you never seem to be in and you've been neglecting his case. He came shouting down the line a couple of days ago and demanded to speak to a partner. I put him through to Mr Snaith.'

'Would that have been the unfavourite Luke Alsop? Don't answer that, Steph, and accept my apologies for putting pressure on you. It was unfair of me and I had no right to do it.'

'As a matter of fact, it was Mr Thomas Jackson of Rotherhithe,' Stephanie remarked with a smirk. 'Just as objectionable as your Mr Alsop, but where one is a viper, the other's a crocodile.'

Before Rosa could say anything, Robin Snaith's door opened. 'Ah, Rosa!' he exclaimed. 'Can you spare me a moment? We seem to have been boxing and coxing of late.'

Rosa followed him into his room feeling as if she were entering

169

the headmaster's study for an uncertain reception. She and Robin had always got on well and she knew she had his respect as well as a large measure of paternal affection despite his being a mere twelve years her senior. She owed her career to him and regarded him as both friend and protector. There were times, however, when he felt it necessary to dress down his junior partner, something he did in the nicest possible way, making his point without humiliating her.

As Rosa closed the door behind her, she felt she was in for one of these occasions.

'I had a call from one of your clients a few days ago, one Thomas Jackson of Rotherhithe,' Robin said. 'I found him thoroughly objectionable and ended up by telling him so.'

He looked at Rosa with a raised eyebrow as if half-expecting her to rush to her client's defence.

'He's one of my more obnoxious clients,' Rosa remarked.

'*Was*,' Robin said. 'I'm afraid I told him to go elsewhere and that we'd let the clerk of the court know we were no longer acting for him. He was your client and I shouldn't have acted the way I did. I'm sorry.'

Rosa's face broke into a broad smile. She'd entered his office expecting a rebuke and instead was receiving an apology.

'I'm delighted,' Rosa said. 'I've got a few more I'd gladly be rid of. What was he calling about?'

'That you seemed to be more interested in other clients and were never in the office to attend to his case . . .'

'I got him out on bail!' Rosa expostulated. 'What's more his case isn't due to be heard until next month and I doubt whether the CPS will be ready then.'

'Say no more. I listened to all he had to say, before telling him to find another solicitor. Some of these people on legal aid seem to think one's at their beck and call and they can bully their lawyer the same way they bully everyone else in their sights.' He gave Rosa a quizzical smile. 'Anyway, I'm glad you're not cross with me for being high-handed.'

'If it weren't so early in the morning, I'd give you a hug,' Rosa said.

'And now before you disappear again, tell me about l'affaire Henshaw,' he said, sitting comfortably back in his chair.

He listened attentively while Rosa gave him a run-down of events. When she finished he said, 'You're never going to get to the bottom of events until you run Evelyn Henshaw to ground and squeeze the truth out of her.'

'But will I recognise the truth when I find it?'

'I'd put my money on your doing so,' Robin said with a faint smile, 'though I'm bound to say it sounds the most unprofitable case you've handled.'

'Don't worry,' Rosa remarked grimly, 'there's money around and I'll make sure that Snaith and Epton are not out of pocket at the end of the day.'

'And what about a possible conflict of interest between your two clients?'

'I'm less worried about that now than I was at the outset. Neither is likely to have to give evidence against the other. In a way they're on parallel lines.'

'Nevertheless, watch out . . .' His voice tailed off. 'One would very much like to know what she makes of events back here. The burning down of her house and her husband's arrest . . . One imagines she has her sources of information and keeps in touch.'

'If so, I don't know who they are.'

'What about the old girl in Bromley?'

'Mrs Upjohn?' Rosa was suddenly thoughtful. 'I wonder . . . I must say she never occurred to me as Evelyn Henshaw's English contact, but she could be. In fact she's rather obvious in one way, but she's always affected anxiety when I've spoken to her and pretended not to have heard anything. She's always adopted the pose of the anxious friend without news, which could, of course, have been a front to put one off . . . I wonder . . . ?'

'Glad to have struck the right button,' Robin said. 'At least, what may prove to be the right button.'

'It's certainly worth further investigation. If Vera Upjohn *is* Evelyn Henshaw's contact, she can operate under excellent cover. I'll go and visit her this evening.'

'Don't get too excited. She may yet prove to be a harmless old soothsayer.'

'Old soothsayer, yes. Harmless, I'm not so sure. I've always thought that once she got her claws round a client's moneybag she wouldn't easily let go. And if Evelyn Henshaw was constantly running up to town to be straightened out by Mrs Upjohn, the need would have been even greater after Stefan's death and the build-up of threats, real or imagined, against herself. Mrs Upjohn wasn't letting on because it would have been against her financial interest to do so.'

'Good luck,' Robin said, 'and don't let her turn you into a cat!' He glanced at his watch. 'I must away to the Mansion House for what will be a wasted, but well-paid morning.' He gave Rosa a sly smile. 'We can't all have your sort of fun.'

Rosa spent the morning at her desk and the afternoon in court defending a benign-looking, silvery-haired old man who ingratiated himself with ladies of similar age until invited to their homes when he would do a quick job of nicking anything that looked valuable and which was small enough to be pocketed. Woe betide any of his selected victims who left him alone with their handbag when they went to put on the kettle. He had an old-world courtly charm, which he would use on Rosa if given the chance.

It was six thirty when she pulled up outside Mrs Upjohn's large Victorian villa in Bromley. She didn't know whether the palmist kept regular hours for seeing clients, but imagined she would be ready to see them at any hour of the day or night if the money was right. She thought it likely there were days when she did no business at all. She rang the bell and waited.

'Who is it?' a voice enquired peremptorily. It came from a grille just above the bellpush.

'It's Rosa Epton, Mrs Upjohn. May I come in? I need to see you.'

'Do I know you?' the voice asked with a continuing note of hostility. 'Why don't you ring and make an appointment?'

'I'm Mrs Henshaw's solicitor. We've met and spoken on the phone.'

'Rosa Epton, did you say?'

'Yes.'

A moment later the door was opened and Mrs Upjohn's face peered out suspiciously. 'Oh, it *is* you!' she exclaimed. 'The answering device isn't working properly. I thought you said Boozy from Devon. What do you want, dear? I've had a very exhausting day. In fact, I'm about to have a bath.'

'May I come in and wait?'

'Why didn't you ring and say you were coming, dear? That would have been the normal thing to do, wouldn't it?'

Rosa hadn't expected to be greeted with any display of hostility, but rallied quickly.

'I'm sorry for the discourtesy, Mrs Upjohn, but I've been busy all day and only decided this evening that I'd seize a sudden opportunity and visit.'

Mrs Upjohn opened the door wider. 'You'd better come in, dear.'

As Rosa entered the hall, which smelt pungently of yesterday's cooking, and this day's incense, she noticed that Mrs Upjohn had a somewhat worn, even bedraggled, look. Her hair, which was kept uncertainly in place by a great number of slides and pins, was tumbling down all round.

'You'd better wait in here,' she said, ushering Rosa into the front room.

She picked up a handful of paper from a side table and gave two cushions a feeble pummelling.

'You'll be all right here, dear,' she remarked. 'I'll be back soon. If the telephone rings, ignore it.'

She shuffled out of the room. Rosa glanced about her. An enormous tree immediately outside the window blotted out most of the light. The furniture was dark oak, with chairs as uncomfortable as they looked. She was about to perch herself on the edge of a chaise-longue upholstered in ruby red when she noticed something lying on the floor. One of the bits of paper Mrs Upjohn had gathered up and must have subsequently dropped as she was leaving. Rosa moved across to pick it up, and saw that it was an envelope.

She turned it over and recognised Evelyn Henshaw's handwriting. It was addressed to Mrs Upjohn and the postmark, 'Alpes Maritimes', was but three days old.

So the two ladies were in contact, she reflected.

Replacing the envelope with care so that Mrs Upjohn was bound to notice it when she returned to the room, Rosa went and sat down on the chaise-longue to await events.

The house was in silence. If Vera Upjohn was indeed taking a bath, there was neither sound of running water nor of a gurgling tank. She picked up a newspaper from the table behind the chaise-longue and put it down again when she observed it was two days old. She never heard the door open and started when she heard Mrs Upjohn's voice.

'I didn't startle you, did I, dear?' the now familiar voice enquired with a touch of complacence.

She was standing just inside the door wearing a dark brown

kaftan that made her almost invisible against the wall. Her hair was loose around her shoulders so that she resembled a Wagnerian heroine about to give voice.

The envelope suddenly caught her eye and she stooped quickly to pick it up, slipping it into a capacious pocket of her garment. She made no comment as she did so; indeed, she made it look like a fumbled sleight of hand.

She was about to join Rosa on the chaise-longue, when she said, 'Would you like a glass of elderberry wine, dear? It's home-made and very refreshing.'

'No, I won't have anything, thank you very much. I make a point never to drink when I have the car.'

'A cup of camomile tea, then?'

There was obviously no easy escaping Mrs Upjohn's range of herbal offerings. While Rosa made a demurring sound, her hostess walked across the corner of the room and returned with a tray on which there was a flask and two plastic mugs.

'I couldn't get through the day without my camomile tea.' She removed the stopper and gave the contents a good sniff. 'It calms the nerves better than anything.' She poured some into one of the beakers and handed it to Rosa. She filled the second mug and sipped it with obvious appreciation. 'Now you can tell me why you've come? You've heard from Evie, perhaps?'

'No, but I'm hoping you have, Mrs Upjohn.'

The palmist gave her head a sorrowful shake.

'I try to get in touch with her every day, but I can't get through.' She made it sound as if she operated an old-fashioned crystal set without success. 'It's very worrying. I'm sure Evie needs me and that I could help her . . .'

'Have you tried calling her sister at St Virgile de Var?' Rosa asked.

Something in her tone caused Mrs Upjohn to pause in her tracks. When she spoke it was with a note of severity.

'I'm sure you mean well, dear, but my relationships with my clients are confidential, just as yours are.'

'But where crime is involved, circumstances change,' Rosa said. She hoped she wouldn't be asked to explain in what way and was fortunately saved any such embarrassment. While Mrs Upjohn was blinking, clearly uncertain how to reply, Rosa went on, 'You've had letters from Mrs Henshaw, haven't you?'

'I'm not prepared to discuss my private affairs with an outsider,' she replied stiffly.

'The envelope you dropped and picked up when you came back into the room bore Mrs Henshaw's handwriting. It was postmarked only a few days ago.'

Mrs Upjohn gave her a look that one snake in the grass might exchange with another.

'What of it?' she said in a stubborn tone.

'I imagine you've been keeping her informed of what's going on at this end. Incidentally, does the name William Smith mean anything to you?'

'Never heard of him,' Mrs Upjohn said quickly.

'Has he phoned you or even been to see you?'

'Look, dear, I've had an exhausting day, I need to lie down and recharge my batteries.'

'Does that envelope you have in your pocket bear a return address?'

'I've no idea.'

'Perhaps you'd take it out and have a look. Or let me see.' When Mrs Upjohn made no move, Rosa went on, 'If you're not prepared to help me, I shall tell the police you've been in secret touch with Mrs Henshaw all the time they've been looking for her.'

Mrs Upjohn gave her a malevolent look. 'She's afraid for her life,' she said explosively. 'She's even being hunted down in France.'

'Yes, but who by?'

'Her family, of course! Who else?'

'Which particular member of her family?' Rosa asked.

'They're all down on her,' Mrs Upjohn went on, ignoring the question. 'I'm the only person she can turn to. Poor Evie is defenceless against so much wickedness when the forces of evil are ranged against her.'

'I wish you'd be specific,' Rosa said, reflecting that camomile tea was for once failing in its calming effect. 'I'm sorry,' she went on rapidly, 'I didn't mean to sound critical, but as a lawyer I'm used to dealing with facts. Tell me just one fact relating to Mrs Henshaw's position at this moment.'

All she got, however, was a tirade of scorn and denunciation. 'Facts, facts! How can you hope to solve your silly cases if you won't let the spirits guide you?' She rose to her feet. 'I'm far too

175

upset to continue this conversation and I must ask you to leave.' She pointed dramatically at the door and Rosa decided that retreat was the only option.

'I'm sorry if I've offended you,' she said, 'it's the last thing I wished to do.'

But Mrs Upjohn had turned her back on her retiring visitor and sat slumped on the chaise-longue.

Rosa let herself out of the house and walked down the short path to the pavement. There was a half-open gate which she tried to close behind her, but it didn't appear to wish to move in either direction. It had been the same when she arrived.

It was a pleasant tree-lined street and Rosa wondered how Mrs Upjohn came to live there. It must surely be above her means. Maybe it was a family property which she had inherited and hung on to. Other similar houses in the street had mostly been converted into flats, but Mrs Upjohn appeared to have the whole property to herself. Perhaps she took in a lodger, who was conveniently out all day?

The thought had just entered her head when she observed a young man approaching on the opposite pavement. She wouldn't have given him a second look, but for the fact he was obviously in a cheerful mood, skipping along like a child and kicking bits and pieces that lay in his path. He was about level with Rosa when he suddenly ran across the road to her side and joined the pavement behind her. She paused beside a chestnut tree and glanced back.

It was the young man she had immediately recognised as the mysterious William Smith, who was suddenly showing an unusual interest in her case. As she watched, he stepped over Mrs Upjohn's garden gate in one balletic movement and took the path in three comfortable strides. He obviously had his own door key from the speed with which he disappeared inside.

Rosa continued slowly and thoughtfully on her way. She was glad they hadn't come face to face, as she wouldn't have known what to say to him. As it was she felt one up. Much good that it did her!

Chapter Twenty-Three

Fran Gifford had not been idle since Ralph Henshaw had been held in custody.

She kept the business running with her customary efficiency, visited him once a week in prison, and busied herself with thoughts of the future.

She had just got home that evening, kicked off her shoes, and poured herself a strong vodka and tonic when the phone rang.

'Oh, hello,' she said warily, immediately recognising the voice at the other end. 'I've been meaning to ring you.'

This was quite untrue, but her caller seemed to accept it at face value.

'I gather from Father that you visit him regularly,' the voice went on. 'I try to get to the prison at least twice a week. Thank goodness there are no restrictions on the number of visits a remand prisoner can have. I'm calling you because I think it's time we had a meeting. Anyway, it's my duty to keep in touch with the preparation of his defence.' Fran Gifford remained silent and waited for Anthea to continue. This she did, though clearly nonplussed by the silence at the other end of the line. 'So when shall we meet and compare notes?'

'I really don't think I have any notes to compare,' Fran replied coolly.

'I'm quite sure you have. Anyway, I want to talk to you.'

'About anything in particular?'

'Why are you being like this?' Anthea asked crossly. 'Don't tell me you can't spare the time!'

'I wasn't going to.'

'It looks certain that we'll both be called to give evidence, not that I've told the police anything to damage Father's chances. But I'd like to hear what you've said to them. She paused. 'Father doesn't wish me to become involved . . .'

'I know. He's told me so.'

'What else has he told you?' Anthea asked quickly. 'I really do think we ought to meet. What about Thursday evening? I'll try and get away from the office a bit early. I imagine you're your own mistress when it comes to hours?'

As things were, Anthea Henshaw was the last person Fran Gifford wanted to see. She was about to make a generalised excuse, when Anthea went on, 'If Thursday's not convenient, it'll have to be one day next week.'

'The weekend wouldn't suit you?' Fran enquired with a touch of malice.

'No, I shall be away,' Anthea said briskly.

'Oh, well, we'd better leave it for the moment. There's no urgency as far as your father's trial is concerned.' Fran kept her tone deliberately casual, though it far from reflected her mood.

As soon as Anthea had rung off, she went across to the desk by the window and pulled open the bottom drawer. It was here she had hidden those of Evelyn Henshaw's journals she had removed from Riverview Court.

She was reading them for the second time in the hope of finding something she had missed before. What exactly, she wasn't too sure, for she already knew that the vital one covering Jean Henshaw's death was missing. Somebody had got there before her. Somebody who knew precisely what to look for.

As for the other volumes, they were not easy to read. First, Evelyn Henshaw's handwriting was ornate and frequently difficult to decipher. Secondly her prose style swung from the platitudinous to the arcane, particularly when she was stretching her descriptive powers to their limits. The polysyllables tumbled out on to the page and congealed in indigestible sentences.

She reckoned that the final two, possibly three, journals were also missing, for the last one in her possession ended six months previously. It had been interesting to read Evelyn's opinion of herself. She was usually referred to as 'the Gifford woman' and given dismissive treatment, as if the rightful Mrs Henshaw was writing on a superior plane.

She put the pile of notebooks back in the drawer and closed it.

Chapter Twenty-Four

Rosa had made up her mind to return to Nice at the weekend. If she didn't waste time eating and drinking and gazing at scenery, forty-eight hours should be sufficient. She was quite certain that Zena Vitry knew her sister's whereabouts and could be persuaded by means fair or foul to divulge them.

The immediate problem was persuading Peter that she would be all right travelling alone. He couldn't put off the weekend meeting in New York and he fretted and fussed about her going alone.

'Surely it wouldn't hurt to put it off till the following weekend and then I can come with you?'

'I can't manage the following weekend, it's my godson's birthday party and I've promised I'll be there. It's very important not to let down four-year-olds. Besides it's a long-standing engagement and I haven't seen Becky for ages.'

She had been at school with Rebecca Ross and they had remained friends ever since. A girls' gossip with her friend was one of the truly relaxing pleasures in her life, Peter notwithstanding.

'Adam's too young to miss you,' Peter countered. 'Anyway there are going to be thousands of other children there, all yelling and throwing jelly at each other and you certainly aren't going to have an opportunity of talking to Becky. By the time it's over, they'll be carting her off to a padded cell.'

Peter, who was extremely good with children and had spent hours playing on the floor with Adam, still pretended they were all unspeakable little horrors.

'Adam's very fond of me and I of him,' Rosa said firmly, and Peter fell silent for a few thoughtful moments.

'I'd better call the Négresco and book you a room,' he said grudgingly at last.

'Good gracious, this won't be a luxury weekend like the one

we had together. I'll stay at a pension near the airport and live on black coffee and liver sausage.'

'Don't be disgusting!'

'I shall, Peter, I'll hire a small car for getting around, but that'll be my only extravagance. From time to time I'll think of you living it up at the Ritz in New York. If you give me the telephone number, I might even call you.'

Peter sighed. 'You can be very stubborn at times.'

'Look who's talking!'

'I'm a man,' he said with quiet dignity, and after a pause burst out laughing.

Now for the easy part, Rosa thought as she boarded her plane two days later. Two days during which Peter had waged a continuing war of quiet oriental attrition.

She arrived at Nice airport after an entirely uneventful journey. After officialdom had barely given her or her passport a second glance she emerged into the usual seething mass of passengers and those awaiting them or seeing them off. There was a slight hitch when the hire car she had ordered wasn't ready. The company made it sound as if it were being vacuumed and fine tuned, but Rosa guessed they were making a frantic search for something with four wheels to meet her requirements. After thirty minutes they came up with a white Ford Escort and she drove away.

She had noticed on her previous visit a modest-looking hotel on the drive into the city, but nearer to the airport than the start of the suburbs. It stood on an isolated plot of land and was covered with bougainvillaea and oleander. Its verandah looked cool and inviting. That's the place if I come again, she had thought when Peter drove past it on a number of occasions.

The name 'Mimosa' mightn't be exactly original for a hotel on the Côte d'Azur, but who cared about a name?

She parked outside, locked the car and walked up the short, uneven path to the half a dozen steps that led to the entrance. A young lad sprang from nowhere when she reached the top, only to be pushed roughly out of the way by an old man with several days' growth of beard and an overpowering smell of garlic in his wake. He led the way over to the small reception desk where a stern young woman greeted their arrival without any sign of pleasure.

Had Rosa reserved? the receptionist asked. No, she hadn't.

How long did she wish to stay? Two or three nights, came the reply.

There followed much turning back and forth of the huge pages of a register, with the young woman eventually saying, yes, it could be managed and handing her a form to fill in and relieving her of her passport.

The room to which the old man led her up a staircase, whose every stair provided its own unmusical contribution to their ascent, looked out at the side of the house. In one corner were a shower, a bidet and a toilet, discreetly curtained off. The bed looked comfortable enough, not that Rosa ever had much of a problem sleeping, and there was a telephone on the table in the window.

She was aware that the old boy was hovering by the door waiting for his tip. Rosa gave him one which he accepted as if doing her a favour.

It was six thirty and she decided to call Zena Vitry and announce her presence. She had contemplated turning up at the daunting iron gate to the house in St Virgile de Var without warning, but decided against such shock tactics. After all, she still needed Madame Vitry's cooperation.

The phone was answered by somebody who was clearly not Zena Vitry. Her comprehension of English was negligible and Rosa's French fared no better in bridging the language gap. Suddenly a child's voice came on the line.

'This is the home of Madame Vitry,' it said in a crystal-clear voice. 'Who are you?'

Rosa told her and was relieved when the child responded.

'I am Chantal,' she said. 'My maman works here. Madame Vitry is away. I will give her message on her return. Where are you?'

'I'm at the Hotel Mimosa near Nice airport. Shall I give you the number?'

'Slowly please,' Chantal said severely.

As Rosa replaced the handset, she felt as if she had just climbed Everest, when in fact Chantal's school English was infinitely better than her school French had ever been.

All she could do now was wait. If she didn't hear anything by bed-time, she would phone again first thing in the morning.

She was sitting down to an evening meal in an empty dining-room when she was summoned to the telephone.

'Is everything all right?' Peter asked in an anxious voice.

'Of course, but how did you find out where I was staying?'

'Every time we drove past the Mimosa you said it looked a nice place to stay. Is it?'

'Perfect for my needs.'

'Have you seen Madame Vitry yet?'

'No, but I'm awaiting a call from her now.'

'Take care, little Rosa, she's another screwball.'

'Even if she is, she's a harmless one.'

'So far,' Peter observed. 'Take care, little Rosa,' he said again. 'Now I have to go to lunch with a lot of dreary people and make boring conversation.'

'Give my love to the prince or whoever it is this time,' Rosa said in a flippant tone.

'I once showed him your photograph and that was like feeding an orang-utan a stick of aphrodisiac. If he ever comes anywhere near you, I'll lock you up and swallow the key.'

'I don't think anything like that ever happens in the Hotel Mimosa,' Rosa said.

'Just take care,' Peter said solemnly and rang off.

She had just finished her meal when she was again summoned to the telephone. This time it was Zena Vitry. She sounded wary and distant, but she had at least called back.

'May I drive out and see you?' Rosa said. 'It is important that we have a talk.'

'How long are you staying?' Madame Vitry enquired.

Rosa bit her lip. She felt that if she said Sunday evening, Madame Vitry would say too bad as she was going away for the weekend.

'Only a few days,' she said, 'but I do need to see you very urgently. I could come this evening . . .'

'Impossible! I am very busy this evening.'

'May I ask if your sister has been in touch with you recently?' Before Madame Vitry could answer, she went on, 'I was worried because we were held up at the airport on our way home and questioned by the police. Is she all right?'

'She tried to phone you at the Négresco before you left, but you'd already gone,' Madame Vitry said and let the sentence hang in the air.

'I wish I'd spoken to her. Do you know what she wanted? More important, do you know where I can reach her now?'

'Somebody has been trying to kill her. She was shot at and the bullet only just missed her. The police are still looking for the person.'

'Have there been any further attempts on her life?'

'Someone is determined to kill her, Miss Epton.'

'It's all the more important I speak to her. Can you give me her number?'

'It is not safe on the telephone.'

'Then let me visit you . . .'

There was a pause before Zena Vitry replied. There were no background voices or sounds to indicate communication with another. For a moment, Rosa had wondered if Evelyn Henshaw might actually be at her sister's house.

'It must be early,' she said at length. 'Nine o'clock tomorrow morning.'

'I promise I won't be late,' Rosa reassured her.

Heartened by her phone call, she went out on to the verandah and ordered coffee and a crème de menthe frappé as a welcome nightcap.

Rosa was up early the next morning, having slept through, and after a modest breakfast of croissants and coffee set off for St Virgile de Var.

She parked just beyond the main gate and walked back. The house was below the level of the entrance and the road had a stiff gradient at that point.

The iron gate guarding the entrance looked unwelcoming and parts of the house peeked at her through the trees.

It was five minutes before nine when she pressed the bell which was set in the gate-post. She was about to repeat the procedure when the gate gave a buzz and sprang open.

Closing it behind her she set off down the drive toward the front door. There was a huge porch with an outer and an inner door.

She rang another bell and waited. Eventually a mournful-looking female arrived and opened each door, standing aside for Rosa to enter.

'Madame Vitry is expecting me,' Rosa said in a well-rehearsed sentence.

The woman turned and led the way into the gloomy interior of the house.

It was several seconds before Rosa could get her bearings. The blinds were drawn and the room had a musty smell. The maid, or whoever she was, had meanwhile closed the door and disappeared. She moved across to the window and peered round the edge of the blind. She found herself staring at a scene of overgrown desolation. It was plain that Madame Vitry was no gardener and didn't employ one either.

The house was totally silent and Rosa shivered at the eerie atmosphere in the room. She had not heard anyone enter and started when a voice suddenly spoke.

'I wonder why exactly you have come looking for me?' Evelyn Henshaw said.

She was standing just inside the door, staring at Rosa with a feverish expression.

'You haven't come to kill me, have you?' she asked, as if it were a perfectly natural question.

'Of course not . . .'

'Somebody wants to kill me,' Mrs Henshaw broke in harshly. 'It could be you.'

'That's absurd. If it were me, I'd hardly be standing here like this. I need to talk to you and this time I need the truth, which is not what you told me when you came to my office the one and only time and asked for my help.' When she didn't move, but remained standing irresolutely by the door, Rosa went on, 'Where can we talk? In here? If so I'd like to draw the blinds and let in some daylight.'

Evelyn Henshaw walked across to the window and pulled a cord which partially opened the slats of the blind. 'My sister doesn't like too much sun in this room. It damages the fabrics.' She then came and sat down on a small upholstered chair that kept her a safe distance from Rosa.

She was wearing a deep purple trouser suit and her hair was pulled back into a large bun at the back. She could have stepped out of a Charles Addams cartoon, resembling as she did one of his doom-laden females.

'Who was Stefan Michalowski?' Rosa asked.

'Poor unfortunate boy!'

'But who was he?'

'He loved me very much and it cost him his life.'

'Yes, but where did he come from?' Rosa asked with a trace of impatience.

'He was studying in London and I offered him a refuge.'

'Where did you meet him?'

'I think it could have been at some club or other,' she said vaguely.

'I'm sure you must remember,' Rosa urged her, wondering what sort of club it was that catered for the tastes of Stefan and Evelyn. Her imagination failed, but that could have been because she knew so little about her client.

But no answer came and she moved on to her next question.

'Did you kill him?' she asked.

Mrs Henshaw threw up her hands in a dramatic gesture.

'You can't think that!' she exclaimed. 'Me kill Stefan . . . ?'

'He was found dead in the lake and you had disappeared.'

'I fled for my life.'

'From whom?'

'From my husband, of course.'

'You know that he's being held in custody, charged with arson and murder?'

Evelyn made no response.

'Why did your husband murder Stefan?' Rosa prompted.

'Because he was jealous.'

'Did you witness the murder?'

'I came home from a shopping expedition and found him dead.'

'How do you know it was your husband who did it?'

She gave an impatient shrug. 'You've just said so.'

'I was arguing your case, I hoped you'd tell me more. Your husband flatly denies killing him.'

'He would, wouldn't he?' she said disdainfully.

'Well, I don't believe he did,' Rosa remarked.

'I'm not surprised he's won you over. He can be very persuasive.'

Rosa let the comment go. She decided to keep her deductions to herself for the time being, for it was these rather than Ralph Henshaw's persuasion that had led her to reach her present conclusion.

'Was Stefan your natural son?' she said.

If she had hoped to throw Evelyn Henshaw off balance, she seemed to have succeeded, for her client's jaw dropped as if a button had been pressed in her back and she stared at Rosa apparently searching for words.

'I suppose Zena told you,' she said at last. 'No, he wasn't

Stefan.' She gave a little laugh. 'Funny, but it never occurred to me that anyone might think that. But then it wouldn't have . . .'

'Why not?'

'Because the child I gave birth to died when he was only a few months old. Don't look so sceptical, Miss Epton, because it's the truth. The only people who knew were the couple who were looking after it and myself. I saw no reason to tell anyone else. My sister had been very helpful over the birth, but I saw no reason to burden her with the information. He died out here in France during a measles epidemic.' She paused and let out a short mirthless laugh. 'I suppose he'd have been about the same age as Stefan if he had lived, but he didn't and that's that.'

'Do you know who the father was?'

'That's an extremely insulting question,' Mrs Henshaw remarked with a sudden spurt of indignation.

'I'm sorry, it wasn't intended to be.'

'I didn't go around offering myself to all and sundry. As a matter of fact, it was all rather romantic. He was a hot-blooded Hungarian whom I met at a reception in London. Edward was away on business and we spent a passionate weekend together in Maidenhead. Of all the corny places to go.'

'After which he disappeared out of your life?'

'Completely. He never knew he had fathered a child, though I like to think he must sometimes have wondered,' she observed wistfully.

So Stefan's identity and role remained a mystery. Rosa was certain that Evelyn Henshaw could have told her more if she had wanted. She mustn't, however, expect everything to fall into her lap just because she had finally caught up with her enigmatic client.

'I've been in touch with Mrs Upjohn a few times,' Rosa said, hoping for a reaction.

'Poor Vera, I'm afraid I haven't treated her very well, but she's had her uses. I visited her on a regular basis when I was in England. She's not just a charlatan, as you probably think. She's helped me a lot.'

'After the death of Ralph Henshaw's first wife, for example?' Rosa said.

Mrs Henshaw gave her a long, hard stare, then said in a ruminative tone, 'I wonder what Ralph has told you about that.'

'And what you wrote about it in your journal?' Rosa said, hoping to goad her into a reaction she might subsequently regret.

Instead, she smiled. 'You're just fishing, Miss Epton. I couldn't bring all my journals with me, but there were one or two volumes I had no intention of leaving to the mercy of hostile eyes.'

'Would they have been notebooks relating to the more discreditable events in your life?'

'You really can be extremely impertinent,' Evelyn Henshaw remarked. 'I can't think why anyone should employ you to be insulting.'

'I'm afraid you can't get rid of me as easily as that,' Rosa said in an unruffled tone.

'What exactly is it you're after? As I recall, I employed you to guard my interests should anything happen to me, not to go digging into my past.'

'Quite true, but then you vanished off the face of the earth, leaving a dead body in your lake. Did you expect me to do nothing?'

'Look, Miss Epton, I think it'd be better if I withdrew my instructions and you bowed out of my life.'

'It's not as simple as that.'

'What do you mean?'

'I'm far too involved, I can't just walk out,' Rosa said boldly, and went on, 'You're doubtless aware that your husband has also been charged in respect of the death of the unfortunate vagrant who was caught in the fire while sheltering in the paraffin shed?'

She hoped that Evelyn Henshaw wouldn't call her bluff for she was aware she didn't have a professional leg to stand on. She reckoned, however, that her client wouldn't dare cast her adrift without knowing exactly how much she had found out.

'I could report you to the Law Society,' Mrs Henshaw said, in what amounted to a last flicker of resistance.

Rosa nodded. 'I think that would bring you short-lived satisfaction,' she said. 'Now, let's talk about the day – years ago – when you set off with the first Mrs Henshaw and returned home without her. What happened to her?'

Rosa could have frozen from the look Evelyn Henshaw gave her.

'She obviously drove to the beach, went for a swim and drowned. As I told you, her body wasn't found for several weeks.'

'Why should she have suddenly gone off to the beach on her

187

own without telling anybody? After all, it was a sixty-mile drive to the coast.'

'Whoever said she went on her own? She didn't, of course; Ralph was with her.'

'Was it a plan you concocted between you, to kill her and make it seem an accident?' When there was no answer, Rosa went on, 'It's my belief that it was you who accompanied her. I don't think you killed her deliberately, but that you let her drown when you could have saved her. Hence the guilty conscience from which you've been suffering ever since. At first Ralph supported you, but then you fell out when Fran Gifford entered his life and you decided to get your own back by pretending he had killed his first wife and was about to do away with you as his second victim. It was at that juncture you came to my office and told me your story of being a threatened wife. It was difficult to know how much to believe; how much was truth, how much fantasy and how much deliberate falsehood. But then with Stefan's murder, events moved dramatically out of your control. You fled for your life, or so you say, and I think that perhaps you were in danger . . .'

'I still am,' she burst out. 'I'm being hunted like an animal.'

'If somebody really wanted to kill you, I'm sure they could have done so by now,' Rosa observed.

Evelyn Henshaw winced, but Rosa was not concerned with her feelings. She went on, 'Presumably you have some idea who's after you?'

'Perhaps I have.'

'Have you told the police?'

'I don't wish to say anything further,' she said loftily.

'The only reason for not going to the police is for fear of opening a can of worms you wouldn't be able to close again. In other words, you're frightened of what an investigation might bring to light.'

Evelyn Henshaw sprang up from her chair, and began pacing around the room. She paused abruptly and said, 'When is Ralph's trial?'

'Some time this autumn. Possibly in November, provided everyone's ready.'

'That's still several months ahead, so there's lots of time.'

'Time to do what?' When Mrs Henshaw made no reply, Rosa went on, 'You needn't think I shall just fly home and forget we ever met.'

Her client looked at her sharply.

'I'm beginning to regret the day I ever came to your office,' she remarked coldly.

'I thought you probably did that a long time ago,' Rosa said in a tone without rancour.

Evelyn Henshaw walked over to the window and stood staring out. Suddenly there was a sharp crack and almost simultaneously a sound of splintering glass. Mrs Henshaw staggered back clutching her left shoulder.

'Keep out of sight,' she said, flopping down on the settee. Her face was ashen as she sat holding a small cushion against her wound.

Rosa, meanwhile, had opened the door and was calling for help. When nobody came, she returned to the settee.

'Where's your sister?'

Mrs Henshaw shook her head vaguely and held on to Rosa's hand.

'I'll call a doctor,' Rosa said. 'You need medical attention.'

'No, no. No doctor,' Mrs Henshaw murmured and closed her eyes.

Making her as comfortable as she could she went off in search of the kitchen and returned with a glass of water. Noticing the dining-room on her journey, she popped back there to look for something stronger in the cupboard, which formed part of the massive mahogany sideboard. It seemed to be full of empty and half-empty bottles, among them one of cognac. She seized it and dashed back to the room in which she had left her client, pausing only to wonder why the house was suddenly deserted. Perhaps everyone had gone out to look for the intruder, though a further moment of thought persuaded her that this was unlikely. It seemed more probable that the woman who had admitted her to the house had been the sole occupant apart from Evelyn Henshaw and that she had taken off.

As she re-entered the room she started in surprise, for the settee on which her client had been slumped was now unoccupied. She glanced quickly around before becoming aware of the lumpy shape of a body on the floor behind it.

She bent over the body and put the bottle of cognac to her lips. Mrs Henshaw opened her eyes and spluttered and Rosa cradled her head to give her a further drop. Her reaction was to seize the bottle and take a lengthy gulp, after which she leaned her head back on Rosa's lap.

'I can't find anyone,' Rosa said. 'I ought to call the doctor, do you know his number?'

'I don't want a doctor,' Mrs Henshaw said vigorously.

Rosa decided that perhaps she ought to look at the wound. Gently she lifted the small cushion that Mrs Henshaw was still holding to her shoulder. She had quite a tussle to separate the two, but inspection satisfied her that her client had suffered no more than a flesh wound from a small-calibre bullet.

Whoever it was that had fired the shot was either no marksman or hadn't tried very hard. In which case why try at all?

'Have you any idea who shot at you?' she asked.

Mrs Henshaw gave her a suspicious look.

'One of my husband's hired killers,' she said, as though the question was unnecessary. 'I can see you don't believe me, but that's because you don't know as much as I do.'

That's for sure, Rosa thought; even so I don't believe Ralph Henshaw is involved, pulling strings from his prison cell.

'Have you thought who else it might be?' she asked.

Instead of answering, Evelyn Henshaw clambered to her feet, holding on to the back of the settee for support.

'I'm going to the bathroom,' she announced as she tottered toward the door. She departed from the room leaving Rosa feeling as if she had strayed into someone else's dream. The house was once more completely silent. She walked across to the window and looked out without detecting any sign of life apart from a lean cat that slunk into the bushes and was swallowed up in the silence.

When after five minutes Evelyn Henshaw had not returned, Rosa decided to go and look for her. After all, she might have fainted somewhere inside the house and be in need of help. She went out into the gloomy hall and began trying doors, all of which opened at her touch only to reveal signs of mustiness and disuse. There was a downstairs lavatory. Its door was unlocked and it was empty. She went down a short stone passage which led to the kitchen. The door was ajar and she pushed it open, feeling like a trespasser. Not only was the kitchen empty, but the top of the cooker was bare of any of the usual utensils. Nothing was on the boil or even off it. The next meal, whenever and whatever, was not in course of preparation. There was a tin of small green peppers on the solid kitchen table and a bottle of olive oil. Hardly enough for a nourishing meal.

There was still no sign of her client and she decided to look upstairs. At the top of the stairs she paused and called out 'Mrs Henshaw' a couple of times without getting any response. It was a question of trying the doors in turn. There were five, all of them shut: in addition a narrow staircase which led to the top of the house and to what were once the servants' bedrooms, if no longer put to that use. It seemed more likely that Evelyn Henshaw had been relegated to the top of the house for her supposed safety: though even that made it seem as if somebody's imagination had run wild.

She turned to the nearest door on her right and cautiously opened it. The room was dominated by a large four-poster bed. She walked across to a door in the corner and found herself looking into a modern bathroom. This had to be Zena Vitry's own room. The next one to it was another bedroom, infrequently used from the smell of musty air and its neat, tidy appearance. And so on to the other rooms on the floor.

Retreating once more on to the landing, Rosa decided she must explore the top floor. After all, Evelyn Henshaw had to sleep somewhere. She mounted the narrow staircase. Cracked linoleum reminded her of the country vicarage in which she had grown up and whose linoleum-covered floors were more cracked than the Kalahari Desert.

She reached the top of the stairs and opened the first door she came to, letting out a quiet sigh as she surveyed the signs of habitation within. There might not be any sign of Evelyn Henshaw herself, but it was clearly the bedroom she was using. A duvet lay folded back and two large square pillows looked as if they had been thrown down in a hurry. Beneath the bed was a large suit-case, its top resting unfastened. Rosa bent down and pulled it out into the middle of the floor. With luck the missing notebooks of Evelyn's journal might be lurking inside.

Kneeling in front of the case she raised the top and began feeling round the edges with the care of a customs officer searching for contraband. From beneath a pile of underwear she struck lucky: carefully, heart pounding, Rosa pulled out two red-covered notebooks. Each had a small label stuck on its front. She sat back on her heels and opened the one labelled 'July 198–'. It fell open at a page marked 'Friday, 24 July'. Rosa got herself into a more comfortable position and began to read.

A week has gone by and I've not been able to write a word since that terrible day, the day when Jean met her death. Out of a clear blue sky, disaster struck. We had had our picnic and were packing away the things when she said, quite suddenly and without warning, 'Of course I know about you and Ralph, I have done for some time.' 'What on earth are you talking about?' I asked with an innocent smile. 'About you and Ralph behaving like a couple of alley cats. But I'm afraid it's got to stop. It'll be best if we don't come for any more weekends.' I suggested she should sit down and tell me what she was trying to say, though naturally I was only too well aware. My mind was racing, my one thought being to gain time until I could compose myself and decide how to play things. At that point she stood up abruptly and stared down at me as if I were an unpleasant insect. 'Oh for heaven's sake, Evelyn,' she said. 'Try and behave like an adult.' That really stung me. I'm afraid I blustered, and the more I did the greater became her disdain. The greater, too (I can write this now), became my sense of shame. I hadn't intended seducing Ralph, indeed it was more the other way round. I'd been a lonely widow for years and I found Ralph attractive. Our falling in love was just one of those things. It wasn't meant to hurt anyone. Anyway after we'd packed the picnic things into the car, in silence, Jean said she was going for a walk along the beach and if I didn't want to wait for her, I needn't. Heaven knows how she thought I'd get home without her. We'd come in her car, though I'd done the driving and given her back the keys when we arrived at the beach. She disappeared behind an outcrop of rocks, leaving me to ponder the situation. It's difficult to describe my emotions. I was angry with her and indignant at the way she was treating me. After all, she and Ralph were my guests for the weekend, as they had been many times before. I'd shown them great kindness and here she was throwing it back in my face, saying that in future they'd stay away. What made her think she'd be asked again! I just stood there trying to compose my thoughts, expecting she would reappear and apologise for her behaviour. But she didn't and I began to get cold. I supposed

I'd better go and look for her. I walked to where she had disappeared behind the rocks and looked down into the cove on the further side. Jean was sitting on the sand with her back against a rock, her arms laced round her knees. I called out her name and she glanced up. I gave her a wave, a friendly sort of wave, but all she did was turn away. I clambered down beside her, ready to make my peace, but she ignored me. I was getting annoyed being treated as if I were a tiresome child, and said, 'Oh, for heaven's sake, Jean, pull yourself together. It's time we went back. Perhaps we can discuss what we're going to say to Ralph . . .' 'You mean, tell him you're a whore?' she said with a sneer. How dared she speak to me like that after all I'd done for them! I began to remonstrate and she picked up a handful of sand and threw it at me. Some of it fell down inside my dress. She got up and ran toward the water's edge. I followed her. 'I warn you not to come any closer,' she called out defiantly. While I was trying to decide what to do she picked up another handful of sand, wet this time, and splattered my head with it. I told her she was mad and she shouted back that I was a husband-stealing whoremonger. 'That's what I'll tell the world about you,' she added. She started to run away when she stumbled and fell face down in shallow water. I suppose that should have brought me to my senses. Instead I found myself staring at her prone form, thinking that'll serve her right. But she didn't move and I suddenly realised she wasn't going to. She was dead. I knew the tide was on the turn and there was a strong under-current along that particular stretch. I realised there'd be endless questions to answer with no guarantee I'd be believed, so I decided to pull her body further out, where the current could take it, though not before I'd removed her car keys from a pocket in her dress. I was surprisingly calm and when I got back to Riverview Court and Ralph came in, I told him what had happened. 'Leave everything to me,' he said.

I was on the edge of panic for the next few days, but Ralph told me not to worry and that everything would be all right. He gave me the strength to carry on. When Jean's body was found, he attended to all the formalities and I did as he said . . .

The journal went on to describe an idyllic trip to the Caribbean, with Ralph as perfect as everything else on the cruise.

Rosa turned the pages quickly and reached a more recent part where one particular sentence jumped off the page.

I now realise that Ralph is a crude gold-digger and wom-aniser. I should have recognised the signs before. He has a mistress in London who is quite prepared to help him get rid of me. I don't trust her an inch, she belongs to the jungle . . . I don't know why Anthea (his daughter) hates me so much, but she does. I tried to be nice to her when Ralph and I were first married, but she was cold and disdainful. I know she was very fond of her mother, but I've never done anything to hurt the girl. Indeed, I've gone out of my way to make friends with her . . . I think Ralph could do more and told him so . . . Ralph takes Anthea's side on every occasion . . . I know Ralph would like to know if I've changed my will. As far as he is concerned, it's become a race against time! . . . I wouldn't put any chicanery beyond him.

Rosa had become so absorbed that she failed to hear a move-ment behind her. She was about to turn the page when the journal was snatched from her grasp. She toppled sideways with surprise and looked up, ready to defend herself.

Evelyn Henshaw stood over her like an avenging angel, clutch-ing her journal to her bosom. Rosa knew she should say some-thing, but found herself bereft of speech. It wasn't often that words failed her, but on this occasion she decided it was better to remain silent than to say anything inane. And she couldn't think of anything that wouldn't sound inane. Silence would at least oblige Evelyn Henshaw to do the talking.

'To think I ever trusted you!' she said coldly. 'You're lower than a snake in the grass. Get out of my sister's house and don't interfere in my affairs again.'

Rosa reckoned she had little choice but to get off her knees and depart. She might have got the sack as Mrs Henshaw's solici-tor, but that didn't mean she was going to turn her back on the case. She even contemplated putting her head down and charging across the floor to wrest the journal her client (or ex-client) had grabbed from her, certain as she was that it contained the final elements of a solution.

But even as the thought entered her head, the target turned abruptly and vanished from the room. This time Rosa lost no time and shot after her. But the house was again as quiet as a tomb. Wherever Evelyn Henshaw had disappeared to, there was no sound of her hurrying downstairs. She must have slipped into one of the other rooms on the top landing. Reckoning that discretion was the better part of valour, Rosa made her way down. Opening doors of strange rooms held no appeal, particularly as Mrs Henshaw might be behind one of them with an axe in her hand.

There was no doubt in Rosa's mind that Evelyn Henshaw was a killer.

Chapter Twenty-Five

Rosa reached the ground floor in less time than an agile monkey would have taken. To her enormous relief she found the front door unlocked and made her exit. It wasn't until she was standing in the shadow of a large hibiscus that she paused and drew breath. She looked back at the house, which was silent and menacing. Presumably Evelyn Henshaw was still somewhere inside, but was she alone?

Using all available cover, she flitted across to the further side of the drive and began moving up behind the bushes that lined it on both sides. Each step that took her further from the house brought her relief until she wondered what she would do if the iron street gate were solidly closed. Surely it must be possible to open it on the inside? If not she would find somewhere to clamber over the surrounding fence which was a mixture of paling fence and hawthorn or its French equivalent.

She hadn't gone far when she became aware of somebody moving with equal stealth through the bushes on the opposite side of the drive. She paused and strained her ears. She had almost forgotten the person who had shot Evelyn Henshaw through the window. That had been less than half an hour previously and she had overlooked the possibility that he was still on the prowl.

Well, too bad for her ex-client! Self-preservation was now uppermost in her mind and she must concentrate on her own escape.

The person on the other side was now on the move again approaching the house. Rosa lingered, hoping to catch a glimpse of whoever it was when they reached the point where the drive opened out at the front of the house. But either they were not in any hurry to expose themselves or the front door was not their target.

Rosa bit her lip in indecision for a second, but only for a second, before heading for the gate and freedom on its further side. A reassuring glimpse of her car through the bars made her feel the worst was over.

A few minutes later, however, she was experiencing a mixture of renewed fright and anger, for whatever she did the gate remained firmly closed. There had to be a way of opening it . . . Unless, of course, it could be completely controlled from the house and somebody was deliberately preventing her from leaving.

She was pondering this suddenly alarming possibility when the entryphone crackled into life and Evelyn Henshaw's disembodied voice spoke to her.

'Come back to the house, Miss Epton. You can't get away until I'm ready. Do you hear me?'

Rosa held her breath and moved back from the grille through which the metallic sounds came. After a pause it went on.

'I know you're there, so do as I say and return. I'm not going to harm you. I'd have done that before now if it had been my intention. In fact I want you to do me a final service when you get back to England. I suggest you walk down the centre of the drive, so that I can see you approach . . .'

There was a jumble of sounds and Rosa heard her call out, 'Who?' followed by 'How dare you come breaking in?' This was followed by an angry screech and abrupt silence.

Rosa stared at the entryphone which had sprung into life and as quickly fallen silent again.

This time she decided that even if discretion was still the better part of valour the equation had altered. Turning her back on the gate, she once more faced the house that squatted ominously at the end of the drive. She had no intention of walking down its centre, as Evelyn Henshaw had so coolly suggested. Retracing her steps, she flitted from shrub to bush until she reached the point where the drive opened out. Here she paused and listened intently, but all was silent again. It seemed safe to assume that the prowler she had passed like a ship in the night had got into the house and been the cause of the angry snatch of conversation, ending abruptly in an animal like screech.

Rosa edged her way round to the further side, using as much cover as she could and pausing from time to time to listen with such intensity that her ears ached.

The room in which she and Mrs Henshaw had spoken was

identifiable by the shattered glass in its french window. She sidled up to it and cautiously peered in. Her one-time client was pacing up and down like an angry cat, save that instead of swishing her tail she waved a revolver which she held in her right hand. Every so often she pointed it at someone who was sitting in a wing chair with her back to the window. Rosa felt certain it was a 'she' from the shape of the ankle which occasionally came into view when she changed her position. She didn't give the impression of someone in fear of her life. Perhaps she knew that Evelyn Henshaw wouldn't actually pull the trigger or that the weapon she held was only a replica. Whatever the explanation it gave the scene an aura of unreality. The woman in the chair was now talking while Mrs Henshaw listened with an intent expression. She occasionally intervened, only to fall silent at a gesture from the woman whose face Rosa yearned to see. She had just concluded it must be Anthea Henshaw when the woman jumped to her feet and Rosa found herself staring at Fran Gifford. It was difficult to know which of them was the more surprised. Meanwhile Evelyn Henshaw fled from the room.

Rosa dashed round to the front door in the hope that one of the two women would come flying out. Armed with a stick, she stood poised to trip up anyone emerging. She almost jumped out of her skin when a voice spoke from immediately behind.

'I'm here, Miss Epton,' Fran Gifford said.

Rosa swung round, at the same time raising the stick to attack.

'Let's see if we can't sort this out in a civilised way. Why don't we go back inside, though I don't expect Mrs Henshaw is still hanging around.'

Rosa was too stunned to do other than follow Mrs Gifford round to a side door and into the house.

'I suggest we go into the kitchen. I doubt whether anyone will be cooking lunch today. They all seem to have jumped ship. Whoever "they" are!' She pulled out a hard chair from a stout wooden table and sat down and waited for Rosa to follow suit. 'I suggest we pool our information,' she went on. 'I take it you know that Anthea is also prowling around. That's why I'm here. To save her from herself. I felt I owed it to her father. I don't know how well you know her, but the truth is she's dangerously mad. Not all the time and obviously so, but mad all the same, which makes her more difficult to deal with. She's devoted to her father and obsessively jealous of him, that's why she couldn't bear his remarrying and why she put all the blame on Evelyn for stealing him. To people who meet her casually, she's just a bit off-beam, but she's a good example of still waters running deep.' She paused and fixed Rosa with a sardonic glance. 'Don't tell me you've not noticed her marbles are an unusual shape.'

'How do you know Anthea's out here?' Rosa asked.

For a moment or two, Fran Gifford frowned in annoyance. Then with a long-suffering shrug, she said: 'I can see you have your doubts about my credibility. Which means you believe I could be your target.'

It was Rosa's turn to shrug. 'I'm a lawyer,' she said, 'and lawyers are a cautious breed.'

'I'd have thought that by now you'd have made up your mind whose story you believed concerning Jean Henshaw's death. Admittedly I don't know exactly what Evelyn has told you, but I know Ralph's side.' She paused. 'Surely you realise he's acting to protect Anthea? A worthy motive, in this instance wasted on an unworthy object.'

'If you're suggesting Anthea is a murderess, I'd need proof. I may not like her, but that doesn't mean she goes about killing people. She may be unhinged, but not that unhinged.'

'Oh, she had a motive all right. A very good motive, in fact. One of the most popular motives in crimes of passion.'

She threw Rosa a challenging look, as if they were playing an intellectual game in which she was in the lead. But there were still questions to which Rosa required answers before she would be satisfied she was not being strung along. She had her own theory about Anthea, but it could just as easily apply to Fran Gifford herself. All she needed was an item of evidence which would give the scales an unequivocal tilt.

'You haven't told me,' she said, 'what exactly you're doing out here?'

'Talk about being able to take a horse to the water without being able to make it drink! Lawyers would ask for an analysis of the water before they'd agree to leave the house.' She gave Rosa a long-suffering look. 'I came out here in the hope of preventing further mayhem. For Ralph's sake, certainly not my own. You see, I found out that Anthea was coming and I knew that didn't bode well for anyone. When I say I found out, I made an intelligent guess when she told me she was going to be away this weekend. A few devious enquiries confirmed she was flying to

Nice.' She gave Rosa a weary smile. 'She uses the same travel agent as her father. Anyway, she'd only be coming for one reason. To settle accounts with her stepmother. She'd been paying someone to track her down and keep her under surveillance and decided that the Villa Montmorency would be the best venue for a showdown. Whether she's succeeded or not, I don't know. Your unexpected arrival hasn't helped.'

'Have you any evidence that Anthea is actually out here?'

'Only that we came on the same plane, thanks to the friendly travel agent.'

'Does she know that you're here?'

'I made sure she saw me. I hoped that would be sufficient to deter her from whatever she had in mind.' She paused. 'She may, however, be committing further mayhem even as we talk. But that won't be my fault.'

Rosa knew she was being taunted, but couldn't decide how to react. She was so bewildered by events that rational thought seemed impossible. She got up from the kitchen chair and moved toward the door where she paused and looked back. Fran Gifford was observing her with a sardonic expression.

'Go ahead, I'm not stopping you. But take care. Anthea knows she's near the end of the line and another death isn't going to bother her. Nor me, provided I'm not the victim!' She waved a dismissive hand. 'I'm not trying to frighten you, merely give you a warning. She may have left, but she could still be on the prowl, so don't stick your head over the parapet.'

Rosa turned and left the kitchen and crept into the hall, where absolute silence prevailed. The salon was exactly as she had left it, broken window and all.

She stood for a moment at the bottom of the staircase, pressed against the wall, her ears aching to pick up human sounds. But there were none. Slowly she mounted the stairs to the first landing, where she paused and listened again. A minute later, she reached the top floor and stood outside the room where Evelyn Henshaw had found her kneeling on the floor reading the journal. The door was ajar, but not sufficiently for her to see inside. Nervously she gave it a gentle push and stood back.

The first thing that met her gaze was a pair of legs dangling over the side of the bed. The legs of a very dead Evelyn Henshaw. She had been shot in the head at close range and the person firing the gun could have had only one purpose in mind. Of the gun itself, there was no sign.

Rosa stood back and closed her eyes. Slowly she opened them again. The scene was unchanged. The murderer had come, done the deed and retired again.

She made her way downstairs, numbed by her discovery. Presumably she would have to notify officialdom, but felt she didn't have the strength to do so yet. English officialdom was bad enough, but French was going to be many times worse.

She reached the ground floor and made for the kitchen. It was deserted. The chair where Fran Gifford had been sitting was empty and there was no sign of her. Rosa's heart sank. She had longed to find her still there, a comrade in arms. Instead, she had silently disappeared, doubling Rosa's doubts. She called out Fran's name in an urgent sotto voce, but to no effect. Where was she and why had she chosen that moment to vanish? Was she lying in wait to ambush Rosa? It wasn't difficult to envisage a scenario in which Fran could point an accusing finger in Rosa's direction when the police arrived. They might turn up at any minute. Determination not to be found on the premises suddenly became Rosa's overriding thought.

She left the house by the side door and headed for the front gate, dodging behind the shrubs that lined the drive. It would be time enough to decide how to scale the fence when she got to it.

'Come over here,' a voice called out from a clump of bushes to her left.

Rosa automatically fell to her knees behind a stout oak and peered cautiously round it. As she did so, Fran Gifford stood up and looked in her direction.

She could have picked me off like a crow on a telephone wire if she had wanted, Rosa thought, as she straightened up and stumbled across to where Fran was standing.

'I guess this really is the end,' Fran observed dispassionately.

Rosa followed the line of her gaze.

Slouched against a tree with a somewhat surprised expression on her face was Anthea Henshaw. She might have been drunk but for the glassy look in her eyes. Her right hand rested untidily at her side as if she had got tired of groping for the small revolver that lay on the ground a yard away.

'Trust Anthea to do it the difficult way. Most people shoot themselves in the head, but she does it through the heart. She could easily have maimed herself and watched her life-blood ooze slowly away. Messy and probably painful. Perhaps she couldn't bear the thought of disfiguring herself. She was always vain about her personal appearance.' She turned away. 'We'd better go back to the house and call the gendarmerie.'

By the time they reached the house, the remaining pieces of the puzzle had fallen into place. It was her sudden recollection of being told that Anthea Henshaw had had a boyfriend called Mike that jerked everything into perspective for her. She quickened her pace to catch up Fran.

'It was you who told me that Anthea had a boyfriend called Mike,' she said a trifle breathlessly.

Fran Gifford stopped and turned.

'Did I?' she asked with a slight catch in her voice.

'Yes,' Rosa said firmly. She fixed her with an unblinking look. 'Was Stefan Michalowski known as Mike to his friends?'

'Only to one friend as far as I know,' Fran said heavily. 'To the girl who was completely besotted with him and who was possessed by burning jealousy.' She sighed. 'And now she's gone and written her own end to the story.'

Postscript

Rosa was never more thankful than when, on the day after Evelyn Henshaw's death, Peter arrived without warning at the Hotel Mimosa and swept her off to the Négresco.

'I feel I could have been here for the rest of the century,' she said to him.

'We'll soon see about that,' he had replied in a determined tone and before the day was out had arranged for Maître Dejean to look after Rosa's interests.

François Dejean was an old friend of his and was more than eager to repay some favour or another. He was voluble, fat and perspiring: and a shrewd lawyer to boot.

Rosa often thought later that but for François she might still be in France. As it was, the police (if with considerable reluctance) allowed her to return home three days after she had undertaken to fly back to France whenever she was needed. François Dejean told her he had struck a good deal and she had nothing to worry about. He had then commended Peter for bringing him such a charming client.

Fran Gifford was kept kicking her heels for a few further days before also being allowed to go.

The morning after she had flown home, Rosa arrived at the office nearer eight thirty than nine to find that Robin, Stephanie and Ben had all got there ahead of her, something that had never happened before. She wondered if they were going to burst into song with 'For she's a jolly good fellow'.

'Welcome back,' Robin said. 'There were times when we feared it would take a cross-channel expedition to rescue you. Thank goodness you survived the carnage. The papers have been having a field day, uninhibited by the English laws of libel which don't stretch to comment on crimes committed in a foreign jurisdiction.

And a *crime passionnel* involving step-daughter and stepmother is something of a novelty. I suppose that part is true'

'Looking back,' Rosa said, 'one must concede that Evelyn Henshaw couldn't have done more to rouse Anthea to a murderous fury than steal her boyfriend. She was obviously determined to get her revenge, however long it took her. Stefan had to be made to pay for his betrayal and Evelyn Henshaw for her even worse act of treachery. After all, if you hate your stepmother with the venom that Anthea did, it's difficult to think of anything more humiliating than have your boyfriend swap your bed for hers.'

'Do you think Evelyn Henshaw did it deliberately to goad her step-daughter?'

'I'm sure of it. The only thing was she miscalculated the reaction.'

'And what about Ralph Henshaw?'

'Everything he did was done to protect his daughter. He may have felt guilty for having brought her into the world. But there was undoubtedly a very strong bond between them. Even when he realised that she'd killed an innocent man, he felt that she'd done it for him. He loved her.'

'Are you going to be able to persuade the CPS to drop the charges against him?'

'The first step will be to get him out on bail. I don't think that should be too difficult. Thereafter, it'll be a question of pounding on various doors of the establishment. I've already drafted an affidavit in support of my application for his release.'

'How's he going to take the news of his wife's death at the hands of his daughter?'

'With outward stoicism and considerable inner relief would be my guess,' Rosa observed sardonically.

'He sounds a really nasty bit of work.'

Rosa was thoughtful for a moment. 'Tough and ruthless, certainly,' she remarked, 'but with a streak of decency. Not many fathers are prepared to go to prison for their daughters' crimes.'

'He obviously reckoned he'd be acquitted at the end of the day. Nevertheless, you'd better watch your step, for he could still be dangerous.'

'Don't worry, Robin, he won't get an opportunity. He'll be glad to slip back into the woodwork.'

That evening Rosa drove down to Bromley to see Mrs Upjohn.

The front door was opened by the half-coloured young man she now knew as William Smith. He gave her an engaging smile.

'Are you here to see mum?'

'If mum is Mrs Upjohn, the answer's yes.'

'Who is it, Willie?' a voice called out.

'Miss Epton. In person,' he added, giving Rosa a broad wink.

Mrs Upjohn appeared in a doorway, looking more distracted than usual.

'You've come to tell me about poor Evie,' she exclaimed. 'I tried so hard to make contact with her, to warn her of the danger she was in. Tell me that she didn't suffer.'

'I'm sure she didn't,' Rosa said.

'Why, oh why didn't she listen to me?' Mrs Upjohn moaned. Then in a complete change of mood she asked, 'Have you seen the will?'

Rosa shook her head. 'Her family solicitor will be attending to that.'

'That doddering old fool, he's been enough trouble as it is.'

'Are you expecting to benefit?' Rosa enquired curiously.

'Not me, Willie.'

'Who I gather is your son?'

'My adopted son.'

Rosa stared at her in silence, too stunned to draw the obvious conclusion.

'You mean Mrs Henshaw was his natural mother?' she said at last. When Mrs Upjohn made no reply, she went on, 'But why did she make out he had been adopted by a French couple and had died as a baby?'

'It was the best way. After all, she had a social position and didn't need a small coffee-coloured infant to remind her of her fall from grace.' She paused. 'Poor Evie, her conscience finally had more than it could take! But as long as she's done the right thing by Willie . . .'

'Does he know she's his mother?'

'He's always been a carefree lad and long may he remain so. Knowledge only brings trouble. Look at Adam and Eve.'

'How did you first come to meet Mrs Henshaw?' Rosa asked.

'My father was the caretaker of the boarding school Evelyn was sent to. We've been friends ever since. She hated it there and we used to cling together. My name was Vera Solly in those days.'

Soon afterwards Rosa left.

It was several weeks later that she and Peter went out for a celebration dinner. The Crown Prosecution Service had agreed to drop the charges against Ralph Henshaw and while she had been steeling herself to go and see him, he had slipped out of the country with Fran.

The last she heard of either of them was a postcard from Fran saying, 'I wish we could have met under other circumstances.' It was postmarked Durban.

It was toward the end of their dinner, which had been a muted occasion, that Peter remarked, 'Thank goodness my clients don't have consciences. They're such a complicating factor in a case.'